THE LADY
WAS A SPY

THE LADY WAS A SPY

TR Garrison

THE LADY WAS A SPY

iUniverse books may be ordered through booksellers or by contacting:

iUniverse
1663 Liberty Drive
Bloomington, IN 47403
www.iuniverse.com
1-800-Authors (1-800-288-4677)

ISBN: 978-1-4917-6619-4 (sc)
ISBN: 978-1-4917-6618-7 (e)

Library of Congress Control Number: 2015906123

Print information available on the last page.

iUniverse rev. date: 05/29/2015

ACKNOWLEDGMENTS

I wish to thank my lovely wife, Cindy, who is a talented writer, for her support and help in completing this unique story. I wish to thank iUniverse for their talented staff and support.

PART ONE

THE WAR

PROLOGUE

On a cold winter night in 1943, a camouflage DC-3 departed England at midnight, heading for the North Sea. On board, an agent of the Office of Strategic Services had been assigned a vital mission by high command.

OSS Capt. Jean Webb had the unique capabilities to accomplish the mission successfully based on her previous assignments during the past year. Once the aircraft leveled off, a tense warrior knew it was time for her to review the mission one more time. She pulled out her instructions and map and put her mind to work.

"First of all, I've got on my long johns," she whispered to herself. "Then, they've got me in native clothes under this winter uniform. Hopefully that'll keep my ass warm. Next, I'm carrying forged papers, and being five foot nine should be a plus, since most Norwegian women are tall. I have also downplayed my looks, appearing to be more of a plain-looking woman. Then I like the plan we developed and coordinated where the pilot drops within three hundred feet of the water when we are a hundred miles from the coast to avoid the enemy's radar. Then fifteen minutes before reaching the coast, we'll be joined by four British bombers, Mosquitoes. Two of them will attack the German batteries at Stavanger on the west coast, and the other two will do the same at Kristiansand on the south coast, creating a diversion and allowing us to climb to 2,500 feet and fly dark between the two targets. Like I said, I like this plan.

"Then the pilot will be on a compass heading to my drop site on the eastern slope at 1,800 feet elevation, and I'll jump at 2,500 feet on a static line for a low-level drop. Because the air temperature will be below freezing, I'll be breathing in an air bag, or my lungs could freeze and cause me to pass out and land in those damn trees nearby, which I'd hate. After I jump, the aircraft will turn west and down the steep western slope north of Stavanger. When it reaches the coast, it will level off at an altitude where the radar will pick them up. The reason being—the Germans are building a plant north of their descending route, and hopefully they'll think it was checking out the construction site, located in a coastal fjord."

Jean took a deep breath and continued talking herself through the plan. "My contact is Leif Larsen, an underground leader. We'll have a two-day march to Oslo—or should I say a skiing adventure. I'm glad I took some skiing lessons and had a chance to strengthen my legs, because I think I'm going to need them to endure this damn cold outing they gave me. Now, to read my final instructions. 'Extract your package, and by no means shall it or you be taken alive.'"

As Jean finished reading, she felt her secret pocket for her little black box and then proceeded to destroy the instructions.

Just then, the crew chief walked over and said, "It's time, Captain."

Jean walked over near the departure point and heard, "Stand by the door, and hook up." The crew chief then checked her gear, put the air-breathing mask on her, and tapped Jean's helmet to signal the okay. Then the green light came on, and Jean heard, "Go!"

CHAPTER 1

Now safely floating down, Jean thought to herself, *It's damn cold, all right*. The cold struck her even though she was dressed for it. A moment later, she spotted the signal in the trees and prepared for her landing, hoping to land in a pile of snow and not those damn trees. Landing safely on the ground with a roll, Jean was covered with wet snow. She quickly stood up, brushed off the snow, and shed her chute as she pulled off her face mask. Looking up, she immediately spotted three men coming from the trees.

"You better be the right ones," she mumbled as she made ready her Thompson submachine gun.

Then she heard, "Welcome to Norway, Captain Webb. I'm Leif Larsen."

Jean relaxed and took a deep breath, recognizing him from a photograph. After shaking her hand, Leif handed her some skis. "Here's your skis, Captain Webb. Are you ready for two days of skiing?"

"Believe me when I say I hope so, but you look big enough to carry me if I can't," Jean said, smiling.

Leif gave her a funny look and said, "No, we'd just drag you in the snow." He flashed a smile, adding, "The first four hours will be on slopes, and the rest of the day will be minor slopes and some cross-country skiing. That's when we'll have to be careful of German patrols, but I do have lookouts along the way to hopefully warn us."

"Where's my package in case we get separated?" Jean asked.

"He's located in a Catholic church on the south end of town near the docks, and it's only twenty minutes to the fishing trawler, *North Star*."

"That's good, Leif. And it's Jean."

Jean followed her guide to the nearest group of trees. "We'll rest here until daylight," Leif said.

Once on the slopes, Jean found it exciting. But then came the cross-country traveling, and her legs were feeling it. She was glad for the breaks her six-foot-two Norwegian guide had planned. When they reached the next lookout, it was almost dusk. That night they enjoyed cold food with some hot tea—thank goodness.

Leif asked, "How are you feeling, Jean?"

"I'm glad you don't have long days, and I'm plumb tuckered out."

Leif smiled and said, "Well, tomorrow we'll be traveling slower because it's mostly cross-country and more German patrols." When it was time to get some shut-eye, Leif said, "Here's a sleeping bag. It's for two, and if you don't mind, we can share it to help keep each other warm."

Jean looked at her not-so-bad-looking Norwegian and asked, "Do we have to keep our clothes on?"

Leif had a surprised look on his face and then smiled, saying, "It is tempting, Jean, but you need all the rest you can get. It'll be at least thirty-six hours before you get another chance for some rest or sleep."

"Oh, shucks. I only get one benefit," she noted, giving Leif a big smile.

Leif laughed and then said, "My men and the lookout will keep watch, and you need a good night's rest."

Before getting in forty winks, Jean was thinking Leif was probably right. It could be thirty-six hours before she got the package safely out of Norway. The second day of their trek did go slower, just as Leif had said. There were times when the group had to move like a bat out of hell to avoid German patrols. They did finally reach the edge of town after dark, and Jean shed her winter uniform down to the native clothing.

Leif informed Jean, "We need to break up into twos, and we do have people along the way to help avoid the Germans, but we need to hurry so we can get there before the nine o'clock curfew."

Jean noticed they made good time because Leif's lookouts were doing a great job guiding them around the Germans, but when they arrived at the church, Leif's lookout showed him two German soldiers standing in an alley, watching the church entrance.

Jean surprised Leif when she said, "Let me handle this, Leif." She headed for the Germans, acting drunk. When she reached them, she spoke German. "Do you brave soldiers want to have some fun?" She then turned and headed into the alley.

Leif couldn't see anything, but he heard a lot of familiar sounds. Then Jean appeared and motioned Leif to follow. Once inside the church, Jean explained what she had done.

"Here's their money and watches. I don't think they'll admit to being rolled by a woman of the night."

Leif was shaking his head. "You're something else, Jean."

Then, looking at her watch, Jean said, "Let's get the professor. We only have thirty minutes before it's lights-out."

In a secret part of the church, Jean met her mission: *get Professor Lucas Lindberg out of Norway before the Germans get their hands on him, and don't let him be taken alive.*

"Professor Lindberg," Jean said, introducing herself, "I'm OSS, and we have a ride to catch, so let's hurry."

Again, Leif's people guided them safely to the docks. When they arrived, it was ten to nine, and as they were boarding the fishing trawler, two German soldiers appeared out of nowhere. Jean's quick action eliminated them with her pistol/silencer, and they became fish bait. Because the trawler captain had a permit to night fish, they headed out for the North Sea as the captain waved to the Germans' patrol boats. Once out of the Skagerrak Strait and in the North Sea, the captain steered for their designated location. Upon reaching it, out came the fishing gear, and the crew began fishing in case the Germans paid them a surprise visit. At midnight, the captain scanned the area with his field glasses and then flashed a light three times. Suddenly, a submarine appeared, and a rowboat was already in the water ready to transport them to the sub.

Jean said, "Thanks, Leif, and don't forget to duck, you big Norwegian." She shook his hand before they parted ways.

The smiling Norwegian said, "Good luck to you too, Jean."

Once on board, Jean was welcomed by Captain Eric Wilson. "It's good to see you, Captain Webb. And you too, Professor Lindberg. The seaman will escort you to the officer's mess for some hot coffee and food."

"Great, Captain, and when will we arrive in England?" Jean questioned.

"If we don't run into any Germans ships, it'll be midmorning tomorrow. Captain Webb, you can use my quarters to get some shut-eye, and Professor Lindberg, you can use my exec's quarters."

"Thanks, Captain Wilson," said a grateful OSS agent and professor.

CHAPTER 2

Some eight months later at an airfield near London, a pilot informed his copilot, "Looks like it's going to be a rough flight over the English Channel because we're going to catch the tail end of that high-intensity storm that passed through earlier tonight."

The copilot replied, "That means high winds and severe turbulence with bad downdrafts. I hope we don't go for a swim, Captain."

Captain Don Owens replied, "Yeah, me too."

Lieutenant Long asked, "Why wouldn't they delay the mission, Captain? That's pretty important cargo we got back there, and I don't think she's going to like the rough ride."

"You're right about that, Lieutenant, but the mission is too important to cancel."

The war-weary DC-3 took off and struggled, flying through rough weather to reach an altitude of ten thousand feet, hoping to get above the high winds and severe turbulence. The important cargo was OSS Capt. Jean Webb, who had been selected for this highly challenging vital mission because of her multitalented capabilities. She had been busy mentally preparing herself. Outfitted in army dungarees, a helmet, a parachute, and a Thompson submachine gun, Jean could pass for a man seen from a distance due to her height. On closer inspection, the delicate cheekbones, generous lips, and wavy auburn hair identified her as a woman. However, the set of her jaw exposed her innermost beliefs and revealed a stubborn determination to successfully complete whatever she set her mind to, regardless of the cost. Capt. Jean Webb would complete her vitally important mission or die trying.

CHAPTER 3

Jean could barely manage to stay in the canvas bucket seat because the plane was being tossed around like a ping-pong ball. The aircraft offered little comfort with those drop-down seats and nothing to grab on to. *I hope we climb through this damn storm soon*, she thought to herself. *Around midnight I am supposed to be dropped over the target, and I just hope and pray that they drop me in the right place.*

Later, the crew chief hollered over the engine noise. "We should be approaching the coast soon. Once we are above this weather, we should have smoother flying."

Jean heard most of what he said and nodded her acknowledgment. She knew this mission could be her most important one yet. Colonel Chase made a point of telling her that he'd recommended her for this particular mission because of her mastery of the French and German languages, her ability to operate under extreme pressure, and her demolition expertise. She'd come a long way from those frustrating days in the army, where her fellow officers gave her a rough time for being a woman. After enduring two years of harassment in the army, the OSS had offered Jean a chance to make a difference and get away from all that. She jumped at the opportunity and had hoped to experience more excitement in her life by joining the OSS—and she did.

Truth be told, her life was an adventure. Jean's first mission came just after finishing OSS training. The Spanish ambassador to the United States informed a US statesman that Adolf Hitler had sent all neutral countries an invitation to a party in Berlin at the chancellery. OSS contacted the ambassador and convinced him to let Jean go with their representative. It required her to fly to Spain and attend a party in Berlin with Assistant Ambassador Antonio Perez. She had pretended to be his niece, Juanita Perez. The party fairly represented the kind of over-the-top hospitality the Germans were known to share with their friends. Elegant foods, expensive wines, and impeccable service had continued throughout the night. During the welcoming line, Jean had met Adolf Hitler. He appeared to be a very gracious host. Later that evening, using very bad German, she spoke to him. He gently corrected her German with a smile. She then said, "It must be exciting being a world leader."

Hitler smiled again and replied, "It is, but it's trying at times."

"Ah, but I think you like a challenge," she suggested.

"Yes, my dear lady. You're absolutely right."

Jean had one more question to ask, and she knew it could be risky. "I am curious. What do you see as your ultimate goal for Germany?"

He started to answer but then hesitated, saying instead, "That's a surprise, young lady." He then excused himself and chatted with other guests.

I'll have some surprises for you, Adolph, and you won't like them! Jean thought to herself as she recalled the meeting.

Jean's most recent mission had required her to gather certain information for the high command on the French coast. Springtime in France can get warm and humid. She frequently wore shorts and a low-cut blouse while biking along the coast. Those Nazi soldiers shouted and whistled their approval of her appearance. She, in turn, listened carefully to their conversations and their tipsy talk in the taverns. They told her things they didn't realize could be important because they didn't know she spoke German. She took pleasure in duping the bastards.

As Jean became aware again of her surroundings, she realized they were getting close to the coast, as the turbulence had decreased quite a bit. A few moments later the turbulence disappeared completely. *Finally, a break!* she thought. *Maybe we can make up for some lost time. I have to accomplish my mission objective before dawn. I prefer being slightly ahead of schedule rather than cutting it close. A little leeway would be welcome. Besides, I want to continue living my life on my terms.*

Boom! Boom! Jean couldn't help but think that the German antiaircraft guns sounded too close for comfort. The crew chief noticed her concern and shouted, "We're flying dark, and the gunners can only guess where we are."

She gave him the *okay* hand signal and thanked God that they hadn't been hit and the engines were still running. *Boom!* The plane shook from the concussion of another near miss. Jean could hear shrapnel hitting the rear of the fuselage and suddenly yelled. "They're guessing too close for my taste!"

The explosive sounds eventually faded into the continuous droning of the DC-3's powerful engines. Without the drama of turbulence and antiaircraft fire, Jean hoped the remaining flight would be smooth sailing. Thirty minutes later she felt the plane turning. She figured they must be just north of Paris, which served as a checkpoint for the pilot. At the mission briefing, they had said that the pilot would be able to see the city lights because Paris never sleeps. *I would like to see Paris at night someday, minus being shot at,* Jean thought. She checked her watch and realized that she had about thirty minutes until the drop. She decided to take advantage of the time to review her mission map.

Next, Jean noticed the aircraft losing altitude. She had just turned off her penlight when the crew chief shouted, "Drop in fifteen minutes!"

"Roger that!" she shouted back.

Time to face your fears, ole girl. When I step out of the plane, I step into God's arms. I just hope he doesn't keep me! Jean started humming the song "Accentuate the Positive," which was a favorite tune with the troops. It helped pass the time.

Then she heard, "Stand by the door and hook up." While standing by the door, the crew chief rechecked Jean's gear and parachute and then silently tapped her on the shoulder and pointed to the red light. Moments later it turned green.

"Go!" the chief shouted.

For a moment, Jean stiffened as she looked out into the inky darkness. She had a lot of lives depending on this mission. She had to jump. She stepped off the plane and hollered, "Oh hell!" as her body plunged into the dark sky.

CHAPTER 4

In a low-level jump at 1,500 feet, Jean anxiously waited for her chute to fully deploy. Once the chute had opened, she allowed herself to relax a bit before flashing her light three times. Next, she received three flashing lights in response.

In appreciation, she saluted the plane. "Thanks, flyboys, for being on target!"

After a textbook landing, Jean went about the business of extricating herself from the chute and hiding it and any other evidence of her arrival. Seeing movement, Jean reached for her Thompson to defend herself if necessary.

A middle-aged man in dark clothing approached her cautiously, saying, "Captain Webb, I'm Andre. Welcome to France!"

Jean relaxed after hearing the name given her at the briefing. Andre's men had already dug a hole for the chute and buried it.

Andre said, "Follow me, Captain Webb."

And he sent out his scouts who knew where the land mines were and moved quietly and quickly through the French countryside, avoiding interactions with people and especially Germans. Occasionally, Andre's men eliminated some German lookouts. They were behind schedule due to increased patrols and had to hurry as much as possible.

Andre expressed concern about circling around the township to reach the target. "Many German soldiers inhabit that area. Eliminating any of them could initiate alarm and lead to capture, death, and a failed mission. We must go quickly, quietly, and intelligently," Andre emphasized.

Jean whispered agreement, and Andre's men fanned out to strategic positions around Jean and Andre. Someone nearby stepped on a dry branch, which caused two nearby German lookouts to become excited. Fortunately, two team members silenced them for good, which was not so good. Seeing the dawn breaking through the night, Jean realized that rigging the explosives in the daylight would be much more dangerous, but it had to be done. With the Metz main railway artery in shambles, the Germans would not be able to get supplies and reinforcements to the coast. She knew that the Allies would be launching an invasion, and that it may have already started in Normandy.

"This is for you, fellas," she said, dedicating the first charge placement.

An hour and a half later, Jean finished the final charge placement. She rechecked her work to make sure everything lined up.

Just then, one of the Frenchmen shouted, "Germans! Germans coming!" A shot rang out, and the Frenchman fell onto the bridge railroad tracks.

Andre came out of nowhere hollering, "Take cover!"

Jean said, "Damn! They must have found the dead lookouts."

Jean then headed for the detonator as fast as she could go. Unfortunately, she needed to get to the same side of the tracks as the Germans. She saw some cover approximately twenty feet from the detonator and made a run for it with bullets hitting all around her. The French underground struggled to make a stand, but the Germans had them outnumbered and outgunned.

Andre came alongside Jean and said, "I'm going for the detonator."

Jean said, "No. Wait, Andre. Let's throw a couple of grenades at them. When they duck, I'll go."

They each grabbed a grenade, pulled the pins, and threw them at the German gunners. As soon as the grenades exploded, Jean took off like a gazelle, headed for the detonator. Andre opened up with his machine gun, keeping the Germans seeking cover. Jean made a diving roll at the detonator just as the Germans started firing again. With bullets bouncing all around her, Jean detonated the explosives. The blast momentarily surprised and disoriented the Germans. Jean ran toward Andre while debris from the explosion was falling all around her.

"Andre! It's time to go!" she called out.

"Yes, my men will hold them off while I get you the hell out of here, as you Americans say." Andre promised, and he did just that.

Soon Jean, Andre, and his men were out of danger and able to relax a little. Members of the French underground provided all of Jean's needs until they reached the designated pickup point. So much had happened during this mission that she didn't have time to think or worry.

On the plane coming back to England, Jean thought about the soldiers who would take part in the invasion of Normandy. She hoped that many of them would live because the railroad transportation had been destroyed, thereby cutting off supplies and reinforcements to the Germans. She knew Jake Blakely would be with his Second Engineers on Omaha Beach. She really hoped Jake could succeed at his mission without endangering himself. As a colleague, best friend, and a lover, she valued Jake immensely.

Besides, Jean thought, *we've planned a romantic getaway soon where I get my tall, brown-haired, blue-eyed Texan all to myself. I can't wait!*

CHAPTER 5

The quaint little cottage nestled on the edge of the forest served as the perfect backdrop for Capt. Jean Webb and Maj. Jake Blakely to have a romantic getaway. They each looked forward to having more time together in the future, but for now, the picturesque cottage fit their needs perfectly, providing home-cooked meals and a comfortable bed—a very comfortable bed. They had spent the better part of the last couple of days in that bed. The lace curtain above the bed billowed softly from the warm breeze as they listened to the birds chirping their morning songs. The scent of roses wafted into the room, and Jean greedily breathed it all in. She couldn't remember ever being so happy and permitted herself to fully enjoy the moment. She shut her eyes and listened to Jake's steady breathing, becoming drowsy herself. Awareness returned quickly when she felt Jake's hand brush her neck and then cup her breast.

Knowing full well what the answer was, she asked, "What are your intentions, Major?"

"I intend to have my way with you again." He rolled her onto her side and kissed her left breast. "And again." He kissed her right breast. "And again. You're gorgeous," he said as he kissed her luscious lips.

An hour later, the two exhausted OSS agents were resting from their exertions on the tangled sheets.

"Wow! That was incredible," Jean exclaimed. "What are you trying to do? Make up for lost time?"

Jake rolled over and kissed Jean and said, "When you're in my arms, sweetheart, I just can't help but get carried away."

Jean then rolled over onto Jake's chest and playfully placed her breasts in his face. "Rest up, my wonderful man," she said softly. "As the Brits say, we'll have another go at it, ole chap."

An unexpected knock on the door cut their banter short. A voice belonging to the hostess of the cottage boarding house, Mrs. Beal, yelled, "There's a call for you on the blower, Major!"

Jake answered. "I'll be right there, Mrs. Beal." He stepped into his clothes lying next to the bed.

Jean couldn't believe how quickly he got dressed—almost as fast as he got undressed, she remembered. As he left, Jean said in her Mae West voice, "Hurry back, handsome; you're not done yet."

He left with a big smile on his face. Shortly, Jake returned to find Jean lying nude on the bed, looking like every man's dream. He wore a sad expression, and Jean felt alarmed.

"I've got to report to Colonel Chase immediately," he said. Seeing the disappointment on her face, he added, "I'm so sorry, dear. Believe me. I wish I didn't have to go."

"I thought you had a week off. What's up?" Jean said, sounding disappointed.

Jake replied, "Don't know, but I guess it's important enough, or Colonel Chase wouldn't have called me back."

He went into the bathroom to bathe, shave, and get dressed. While he was bathing, Jean got some tea, biscuits, and jam, which they enjoyed before he had to leave to report in.

"Bye, dear. I'll call you later. Maybe we can have lunch together," he said optimistically, but they both knew the chances of that were almost zilch.

He didn't call her later, and she lunched alone.

Mrs. Beal made Jean a delicious stew with homemade bread for supper, and Jean wondered where Jake had gone and what he was doing. She felt sure he could take care of himself, but she couldn't shake the bad feeling she had about Jake's important mission.

CHAPTER 6

Jean woke up before dawn all alone in that big bed. Jake had left three days earlier, and she hadn't heard a word from him or the OSS since. Sleeping in the mornings had been a novelty and something Jean thought she could get used to doing. She'd had lots of time to get caught up on her reading and to wonder what was going on with Jake. But the truth was that she was starting to go crazy in this bucolic environment.

Jean stopped what she was doing when she heard a knock at the door.

"Captain Webb, there's a call for you," Mrs. Beal announced.

"I'll be right there, Mrs. Beal," Jean responded while putting on her robe. She picked up the phone and discovered that Colonel Chase needed her for a very special mission. She needed to get to headquarters as soon as possible. "Yes, sir. I'll be there soon," she assured Major John Williams.

"Mrs. Beal, I only have time for tea and biscuits," Jean noted and then added, "I've had a really nice holiday, but it's time to go back to work. I hope we can come back someday."

She immediately bathed in the antique claw-foot tub before dressing, drinking her tea, and wolfing down a couple of biscuits with jam. While Jean finished up her tea, the motorcar arrived to whisk her away to OSS headquarters on the outskirts of London.

"Reporting as ordered, sir," Jean said while saluting the colonel.

"Have a seat, Jean," he said sternly. He paused as if to select his words carefully. "I need to send you in to get Major Blakely out of Eastern France."

Jean felt a little weak in the knees. Having never succumbed to that sort of weakness, Jean forced herself to straighten up before speaking. "May I ask why, Colonel?"

"Earlier this morning I received a communication informing us that there's a double agent in the French underground that Major Blakely is with right now." The colonel walked over to Jean and put his hand on her shoulder. "Jean, I'm asking you to volunteer for this top-secret mission."

"May I ask what Jake's mission was?" Jean felt that she needed to know why he had gone. She wanted to know everything that concerned him, but the Colonel would only tell her what she really needed to know to get Jake out.

The colonel hesitated for a moment and said, "He went behind enemy lines to join up with a French underground unit to discover how many German divisions are still operating west of the Rhine River. I can't tell you more than that."

Looking him in the eye, Jean said, "I'll go, Colonel. When do I leave?"

"Tonight. Major Williams will brief you," he said shaking her hand. "Good luck, Jean."

On the way to Major Williams's office, Jean muttered to herself, "Jake Blakely, you better not have gotten yourself captured or killed! I'll never forgive you if you did!"

After a four-hour briefing, Major Williams took Jean to the DC-3 hanger where the crew chief assisted her into the proper gear, settled her in, and left her to her thoughts. Jean wasn't crazy about flying or jumping out of planes. She had to admit, though, that it gave her a bit of a rush once she took that first step off. In that moment, she decided that on this trip, she'd focus on Jake. He was the only true male friend she had in this man's army. He respected her for her abilities and opinions. He was a wonderful lover and a potential life mate. Jean had so many more questions than answers about Jake's situation, but she would know soon enough. After several hours, she felt the DC-3 losing altitude and turning east. According to the information in the briefing, she figured they were approaching the drop zone.

The crew chief came out of the cockpit and hollered over the engine noise. "Captain Webb, we'll be over the drop site in less than twenty minutes." He must have noticed her troubled expression because he asked, "Are you all right, Captain?"

She yelled back. "Yeah, but a shot of tequila with lime and a beer chaser would be pretty helpful about now."

The chief laughed and said loudly, "You need to place your drink order ahead of time, ma'am. Why do you do it?"

"It's my job!" Jean said. She got a nod of agreement. "Next time I'll place my drink order ahead of time."

"Roger that, Captain." The crew chief spoke loudly and smiled.

CHAPTER 7

"Chief, I just realized that tonight I jump for the eighteenth time! Today's date: August 18. Get it?" Jean asked him.

"A good luck sign," he yelled. "By the way, drop zone in ten minutes."

Jean carefully moved to the door where the chief checked out her gear. She certainly needed some good luck. Jean had never liked free-fall jumps, but it was the safest way for a single jump to be made behind enemy lines. She'd be landing at the north end of the Argonne Forest and north of a river, hopefully without getting hung up in the trees or dropped into the lake. As she prepared to jump, Jean watched the light switch from red to green and then stepped off the plane. While in free fall, she watched her luminous altimeter and waited for the thousand-foot level before pulling the ripcord. When the parachute opened, she felt the usual relief. After flashing her light three times, she saw three answering flashes of light—another reassuring sign. Jean knew she'd found the landing zone as she hit the ground with a roll. By the time she managed to get up, she found herself surrounded by Germans.

Jean's heart jumped into her mouth as she gasped. "What the hell?"

Then she heard a voice call out to her. "Hit the deck, Captain Webb!"

She quickly dropped like a sack of potatoes and covered her head. She heard lots of automatic firing. When she looked up, six dead German soldiers surrounded her. A group of men ran toward her, and she readied her Thompson just in case.

One of the men addressed Jean as he approached. "Captain Webb, I'm Sergeant Sanchez of the US Rangers. Let's get the hell out of here, Captain. My men will take care of your chute."

Jean quickly got to her feet and removed herself from the chute, saying, "I'm right behind you, Sergeant."

After running southeast for a good twenty minutes along the edge of the wet and humid Argonne Forest on their left flank and the Meuse River on their right flank, Sergeant Sanchez finally gave a halt hand signal. All five military personnel struggled to catch their breath after running such a distance while loaded down with equipment. The two men whom had taken care of Jean's chute rejoined the group fifteen minutes later.

The sergeant motioned to everyone. "Gather around, and keep it quiet. Captain, we found three dead Frenchmen at your drop zone, and those Krauts were waiting for you when we got there. What the hell's going on, ma'am?"

Jean decided to tell them what little she knew. "Everybody move in tight and listen up … We believe that there's a double agent among the French underground. Nobody should have known about my arrival and where. Yet someone knew and passed the info to the Germans. Any ideas, Sergeant Sanchez, on how to protect ourselves between here and our destination?"

"Just one, Captain Webb."

"I'm listening, Sergeant," Jean noted, encouraging him to lay it out for her.

In muffled tones, he briefly shared the details of his plan. It sounded both creative and practical, and Jean watched with interest how he went about setting everything up.

"Corporal Banks, take two men and proceed southeast on the other side of the river. We'll see you north of Verdun tomorrow afternoon, here," Sergeant Sanchez noted, pointing to his map.

Jean spoke up. "However, if we don't show up, head for the village of St. Mihiel. The underground maintains a hideout south of the village. Your number one goal is to get Major Blakely out."

"Roger that, Captain." The corporal saluted, immediately chose two men, and left.

"Pathfinder, front and center. Okay, Joe, find us a safe way to Verdun without having to kill any Germans if possible." The sergeant directed the Native American soldier.

"Got it, Sergeant," Pathfinder answered and then disappeared.

"He wasn't wearing combat boots, Sergeant," Jean commented.

"No, ma'am. Moccasins." The sergeant could not hide his admiration for the man. "Joe's half Navajo and half Apache. You'll never hear him coming. He fights like a wild Indian." The sergeant described him proudly.

"Thanks, Sergeant. That makes me feel a whole lot better," Jean noted while rolling her eyes.

CHAPTER 8

Jean continued southeast along the Argonne Forest with the remaining Rangers. She couldn't help but have bad thoughts about the forest's famous World War I battle where the Marine Corp had their bloodiest engagement ever. It was where her Marine lieutenant father was killed in 1918. The beautiful scenery and tragic history of the battle failed to keep her interest. Instead, her mind played out various ways they might entrap the double agent. Outing a double agent could be difficult and dangerous. Just as difficult as their journey to the underground hideout proved to be. Several times on the way the group had to hide from the German patrols. Fortunately, Pathfinder Joe had things under control because they were making good time. The group would be in Verdun on schedule, barring the unforeseen.

Just before dusk, Sergeant Sanchez said, "Captain, let's move into the forest and find a secure place to bed down for the night."

Jean felt exhausted and was very happy to rest awhile. "Great idea, Sergeant," she noted, gratefully agreeing with his suggestion.

Sergeant Sanchez assigned two men to the first watch, himself the second watch, and before anyone could say anything, Jean volunteered to take the third watch.

The sergeant answered, "Yes, ma'am."

After an uneventful night and a bit of rest, the group headed for Verdun again. Just before they reached Verdun, Jean halted the group and had a conversation with Sergeant Sanchez. "Sergeant, I have a plan. We'll need a prisoner, preferably an officer. I think it's likely that we'll have a surprise party waiting for us in Verdun, especially if they have discovered their men at my drop site. Maybe it's time we have a surprise party of our own," she said excitedly.

"Roger that, Captain Webb," he said with a grin.

When the group reached their designated rendezvous by late afternoon, they were greeted by the other detail.

Sergeant Sanchez greeted them, "Good to see you, Corporal Banks. Any problems?"

"None, Sergeant … Joe did all the recon in this area, and the situation … well, two squads of Germans waiting for us," Banks said apologetically.

Jean asked, "Did you see any officers with them?"

"Yes, ma'am—a captain and a lieutenant, and each of them have a machine gun. All we had were three Thompson submachine guns and a Browning automatic rifle."

"Correction, Corporal. Four Thompsons, and I'll trade you my Thompson for your carbine. Now listen up, we have an even better weapon than all of theirs," Jean said boldly.

"What's that, Captain?" Banks looked truly intrigued.

"A surprise, Corporal Banks … A surprise that just might work if we play our cards right."

Sergeant Sanchez spoke up. "You heard the captain. Let's get ready and do what we do best. Right, Banks?"

Banks responded, "Roger that, Sergeant."

"Joe, I've got a special assignment for you," said Sanchez who went on to describe what he wanted Joe to do.

After carefully circling west of the Germans, the group reached a well-covered attack position where the sun would be shining into the Germans' eyes. Sergeant Sanchez placed his men strategically and awaited Jean's call to strike.

Jean watched the Pathfinder do his thing. The Germans appeared relaxed and overly confident. They were not Hitler's best soldiers. It was clear to Jean that they expected her group to show up but didn't consider them much of a threat.

"I wish you were here for this surprise, Adolph!" Jean muttered to herself.

With her field glasses, Jean could see Joe moving silently behind the Germans. He took out a forward observer and kept moving.

"Sanchez? He's good, real good," Jean whispered. Sanchez flashed a smile and a nod. When she found him again with the field glasses, he came up behind the German captain and put a knife to his throat.

"Now, Sergeant!"

Jean gave the call, and Sergeant Sanchez had a rifleman fire a single shot. The Germans jumped up, grabbing for their weapons, thereby exposing themselves to the enemy's field of fire. Sergeant Sanchez and the other Rangers opened fire on the Germans, with the BAR and four Thompson submachine guns. When the shooting stopped, only two German soldiers remained alive. They had thrown down their weapons and raised their hands. Joe had protected the two officers from being accidently shot. Jean and Sergeant Sanchez immediately headed over to them.

"Oh, no you don't," Sanchez yelled at one of the supposedly dead Germans before plugging him with a short burst from his Thompson.

Jean immediately realized that he'd probably saved her life.

"Thanks, Sergeant. Maybe we should make sure the rest of them are really dead," Jean noted.

Sanchez nodded to the other Rangers to spray the rest of the bodies. When Jean reached the Nazi captain, she cocked her pistol and put it in his face. She spoke to him in German. "If you don't want to die, tell me who the double agent is in the French underground." The hardcore Nazi refused to answer, so Jean turned to Sergeant Sanchez. "Line up the lieutenant and the two remaining soldiers." Jean continued, talking in German, "When I give the word, shoot them, Sergeant." This time she aimed her weapon in the direction of the captain's family jewels and spoke again in German. "You Nazi bastard, if you don't tell me what I want to know, I'm going to blow off your balls and leave you to die and then kill your men." This time Jean saw a reaction on the Nazi's face, but he was still trying to hold out. Again in German, she said, "Looks like hard-ass isn't talking, and I'm running out of patience and time … Shoot them!"

Of course, Sergeant Sanchez didn't know any German, but the German officers didn't know that. Suddenly, the Nazi lieutenant started singing like a bird, and the Nazi captain started hollering for him to shut up.

"I've had enough of you," Jean said just before she coldcocked the bastard.

As it turned out, the lieutenant only knew the traitor's code name—*le lion*—and he thought he could recognize the traitor's voice.

"That'll do," Jean noted. "Bring him along, Sergeant Sanchez. Corporal Banks, gather up their weapons. We won't be outgunned now. Right, Corporal?" she asked with a smile.

"What about the others? We can't leave them behind," Sanchez said.

"That's right, Sergeant. I can't let anything jeopardize this mission. Perhaps the Pathfinder could solve this problem," Jean hinted as she handed her pistol and silencer to the sergeant.

Spying is a nasty business, Jean thought to herself.

CHAPTER 9

A short while later Jean noticed that Pathfinder Joe had rejoined the group. When she caught his eye, he nodded slightly, which let her know that the problem had been resolved. Jean felt herself becoming rather obsessed thinking about the double agent. Suddenly, it dawned on her what to do next.

"Sergeant, I would assume that the double agent has a small short-range radio," she noted. "That would mean that the Germans would have to be nearby, right?"

"Yes, ma'am. And if you're thinking what I'm thinking, it's time we split up again," Sergeant Sanchez suggested.

"Roger that, Sergeant," she agreed.

They traveled another ten miles and decided to make camp for the night in a protected area off the beaten path. They took turns taking guard duty and getting some sleep. The next morning Sergeant Sanchez sent Corporal Banks and two men to the right flank, west of the river heading for St. Mihiel, fifteen miles farther. By one o'clock, the group was within three miles of St. Mihiel when the Pathfinder showed up and made his report.

"There's another two squads of Germans on our left flank about a mile away if we stay on this heading. I also saw two Germans hiding about two miles northwest of what looked like the French underground camp. They had a radio," Joe reported.

"Good job, Joe," Jean said, rather amazed by his surprising abilities.

He nodded in acknowledgment of Jean's comment and stepped aside. In that moment, Jean began to understand why the Germans hadn't attacked the French. The traitor had passed on information about what the Allied forces planned to do.

"Sergeant, get on your walkie-talkie and let Corporal Banks know where the radio is located," she strategized.

"Yes, ma'am. Right away." Sergeant Sanchez raised Banks on the walkie-talkie and reported. "Corporal Banks is on it, Captain. He'll take them alive when he hears the shooting."

Jean replied, "Good. Thanks, Sergeant. Now I think it's time for Lobo."

Two confused Rangers looked at each other and then at Jean for more information. She laid it all out for them and could tell they liked it, especially Joe, because he had the most dangerous part to play.

"Sergeant, let's break out the radio," she said dramatically.

"You heard the captain. Front and center, Carter." Sanchez barked the order.

Carter put the radio in front of Jean, keeping the power unit.

She opened it up, and when she was ready, she said, "You ready, Joe?" Joe would translate what she said in Navajo—a language the Germans could not decode. "Start cranking, Carter," she added before beginning her message. "This is JW calling Lobo. This is JW calling Lobo. Over."

Minutes later, the answer came in Navajo. "This is Lobo. Go ahead, JW."

"Special delivery at map coordinates … Can delivery be made in one? Over."

"Hold one, JW … Delivery will be plus fifteen. Over."

"Roger, Lobo. Look for red, south, and fifty. Over and out." Pleased with the communication, Jean said to Joe, "Good job. That ought to confuse the Germans."

"I got most of that, Captain, but not all," Sergeant Sanchez admitted.

Jean explained to the Rangers. "Air support will be here in an hour and fifteen minutes." She paused to look at her watch. "As of two minutes ago. Note the time, Joe."

"I take it you want a red smoke fifty yards north of the Germans," Joe interpreted.

"You got it, Joe, and here's the smoke," Jean said, handing him the canister.

Joe took off like a charging bull.

"Okay, let's pack up and move out," Sergeant Sanchez ordered the remaining men. Forty minutes later, the group came within a hundred yards of a small ridge with cover west of the Germans.

"How about that ridge?" Jean asked the sergeant.

"That's perfect, Captain. Let's go quietly and stay low," he warned everyone. He worried that Carter might have trouble keeping the German lieutenant quiet, but Carter held a knife against the German's back with instructions to cut his throat if he tried to make a sound. The lieutenant made no attempt to be a hero. The midafternoon sun would be blinding to the Germans as they approached the group's position. They were ready. Sergeant Sanchez had the BAR set up.

Jean looked for Joe in the field glasses. "Joe's in position, Sergeant," she noted as she checked her watch. There were just thirteen minutes to go before the fireworks started. She kept watching through the field glasses. "Oh no!" Jean suddenly called out. "Look what's coming from the south, Sergeant."

Now looking through his field glasses, Sanchez said, "It's the French underground, and they are walking right into a trap."

"I know, Sergeant," Jean lamented.

"Captain! Whattaya want to do," asked an excited sergeant.

Jean glanced at her watch. They had eight minutes to go.

Sergeant Sanchez reported, "The Krauts are preparing to ambush the Frenchmen in less than five minutes."

Jean looked for Joe and saw he was on the move. "Hurry up, Joe, and get the hell out of there!" In that moment, Jean knew she had to act immediately. "Open fire on the Germans," she directed the sergeant.

Jean's quick decision accomplished two things: it pinned down the Germans and warned the French. When she checked on Joe again, he had ducked for cover amid some small boulders just as the air support flew over and began firing on the Germans and dropping a small arsenal right on target. When the smoke cleared, only a few Germans were still alive, and they threw down their weapons and raised their hands.

"Cease fire! Cease fire!" Sergeant Sanchez hollered so that the prisoners would not be harmed and could be interrogated.

"Sergeant, check on Joe and secure your prisoners," Jean told him. "I'll take the lieutenant with me to meet with the Frenchmen."

"Roger that, Captain," the Sergeant respectfully answered. Jean kind of like being respected.

CHAPTER 10

Jean was anxious to identify the low-life scum who betrayed his own people and had nearly gotten her killed. Before reaching the Frenchmen, she instructed the German lieutenant in his own language, "If you recognize the traitor's voice, look toward me and blink twice. Don't even think about lying to me, or I'll turn you over to the French."

He replied in German. "Yes, Captain. I understand."

As the three Frenchmen approached, Jean identified herself. "Captain Jean Webb, OSS. I'm here to retrieve Major Blakely."

One of the Frenchmen stepped forward and introduced himself. "I'm Pierre, the leader of this underground unit, and I want to thank you for saving our lives, Captain." As he shook Jean's hand, he added, "We can take your prisoner off your hands."

"Thanks, but he stays with me for now. Where's Major Blakely?" Jean desperately wanted to see that he was okay.

"Follow me," Pierre said. "I'll take you to him." Pierre led the way to a nondescript farmhouse with several hidden rooms where they had taken him when the action started. In one of those rooms, they found Jake lying on a homemade stretcher with a blanket over him. A mildly attractive French woman sat near him, tending to his every need.

"Well, Major Blakely, what happened to you?" Jean questioned, grateful that he was alive. Her fears were finally put to rest.

The French woman raised the blanket, revealing a four-by-four bandage on his right buttock.

"Didn't I warn you about messing around? That someday you'd get your ass shot off, Major?" Jean added.

"Quit with the jokes, Jean. It hurts like hell," Jake complained.

"Really?" she asked, trying to suppress a giggle. "How bad is it, Jake?"

"I can't move without hurting, damn it," he blustered.

The French woman took Jean aside and informed her that a local village doctor had removed the bullet and said that there may be some damage to the pelvic bone. She had changed the dressing every day to prevent infection. Jean thanked her for taking such good care of the major and walked back over to Jake and took his hand. "Sorry, old boy. We're going to get you home, but I have some business to attend to first. Just sit still. I'll be back soon."

When she realized her mistake, it was all she could do not to snicker. Some of the other people in the room tried unsuccessfully to restrain their laughter.

Outside, Sergeant Sanchez and Corporal Banks had arrived with four prisoners, two of which were the radiomen. Jean handed the lieutenant over to them as well. She then caught Pierre's attention and said, "We need to talk privately."

"What about, Captain Webb?"

Pierre appeared to be unaware of the threat to his underground organization.

"Follow me, Pierre," she said, leading him into a vacant room within the underground house. "Pierre, besides you, who else knew that I was coming and where my drop site location would be?"

Fear and disbelief filled Pierre's eyes. "Why?" he asked hesitantly. "Do you think we have a traitor among us?"

"I know that someone has become a double agent," she stated confidently. "Three Frenchmen died at my drop sight, and the Germans were waiting for me."

The anguish on Pierre's face was clear, and he hesitated before saying, "Only two other people: my second-in-command and my best friend, whom I trust with my life. I can't imagine either one of them betraying us."

"We need to settle this matter. Go and bring those two men to where the prisoners are being held. I will meet you there directly."

Jean could once again see the pain on his face as he went after his men. She walked back to the makeshift prison and noticed that Joe had returned from his grisly cleanup job.

"Everything okay, Joe?" He flashed Jean a nice smile and an okay sign. She then looked over to Sergeant Sanchez and said, "After working with you this long, I think I should know your first name."

"Carlos. My name is Carlos, ma'am," he answered.

"Thanks. I'm very glad to know you, Carlos," she responded. "Are we ready? Here comes Pierre and two suspects!"

Carlos knew what to do next. He and Joe got ready to play their part to uncover the truth. Jean positioned the German lieutenant and the two radiomen by her side so that she could see their faces. When Pierre and his men approached, she could see the anguish on Pierre's face.

In spite of what he might have been feeling, Pierre introduced the man he called his second-in-command as Francois. Jean questioned him in French. "How long have you been with the underground, and where are you from?" He surprised her by answering in English, very good English.

Jean glanced over at the lieutenant and the radiomen. They made no sign of recognition. However, Pierre's other French associate appeared to be extremely anxious and looked as though he might run for it.

Carlos, who stood behind the man, stuck his Thompson into the man's back and said, "Going somewhere, monsieur?"

Joe grabbed the man by his shirt and dragged him over to face Pierre and Jean.

A shocked Pierre shouted. "Claude! What's going on? Answer me, damn it!"

"Sorry to interrupt," Jean said. "Is he the one who suggested that you come out to meet us?"

"Yes, Captain. He was our forward lookout, and he nearly got us killed," Pierre agreed.

Claude started pleading for his life. "Please understand, Pierre. They've my family!"

"Do you think that you are the only one who has lost loved ones? Most of us have experienced terrible losses! Our pain has made us stronger and more motivated. Yours has turned into cowardice. I don't know you," Pierre said with finality.

The German witnesses all identified Claude as the double agent.

Jean turned to Pierre and said, "He's all yours, but first I need some answers. We need to know what he has told the Germans. I have someone who can get that information for us."

Pierre looked at Claude and said, "That's okay, Captain. He'll talk willingly if he wants a quick death instead of a long, slow one."

Sergeant Sanchez turned to Joe, saying, "Get it done, Joe."

CHAPTER 11

A flock of birds suddenly launched into the bright, blue sky when a bloodcurdling scream broke the silence. Thirty minutes later, Joe and Deon, a French interpreter, reported their findings.

Joe, still wiping the blood off his hands, reported what had happened. "He wasn't much for pain, so here's what he told us." Joe nodded to Deon.

"He told us that he'd told the Germans what he knew about Captain Webb and Major Blakely and what their mission was," Deon reported.

Joe added, "I don't believe he knew you were a woman, Captain."

"Pierre, is that right? You didn't know I was a woman?" Jean figured Pierre would know that information as well.

Pierre replied, "That's correct. There was no indication that Captain Webb could be female."

Another party jumped into the conversation. "That's right, Jean, because I didn't tell them that you were a woman," Jake said.

Jean turned around and smiled at Jake on his stretcher. She then took Pierre's hand and said, "I am sorry for your pain. Claude is yours to deal with as you see fit." As he walked away, she turned to Joe and said, "Thanks again, Joe."

That night Jean soaked up as much information as she could from Jake regarding his mission. He confirmed what she already knew and left her with a lot to think about. The Germans had ambushed Jake at Nancy, France, not long after he had begun the mission. Claude had let the Germans know about the plot.

Jean could tell Jake needed to rest, but he insisted she answer one more question. "Jean, do you know what the top secret part of the mission is?"

"No, Jake," she said truthfully. "Colonel Chase didn't think I needed to know that. My job was to get your ass out of France, and that's what I'll do."

Later, Jean couldn't get to sleep. *What was so top secret about this mission?* she wondered. Because she had been an intelligence officer before becoming OSS, Jean had a pretty good idea what the top secret part might be. Her best guess was that the intel gathered would be used to decide if Gen. George Patton's tank division could make an end run through southern France to the Rhine River, and by doing so, secure as many bridges as possible for crossing into Germany. This information seemed too important to just leave it a failed mission. Before Jean got in forty winks of sleep, she wrestled with the pros and cons of a decision that would cause some heavy discussions.

"Good morning, everybody," Jean said the next morning, trying to sound cheerful. "I hope everybody got plenty of rest."

Most everyone looked like they really needed some coffee and plenty of it. Jean had her breakfast and a couple of cups of strong coffee and called a meeting with Pierre, Carlos, and Jake. "I did a lot of thinking last night. I weighed all the pros and cons, and I have decided to stay and continue the mission," she informed them, expecting varied responses.

Jake, the first responder, yelled, "What are you thinking? No way, Jean! I want you safe. I want you out of here! It's too dangerous."

She interrupted him. "Jake, due to your injury, I am the ranking officer here. I respectfully ask you to pipe down."

"Excuse me, Captain, but the major is correct. This mission will be very dangerous. I fear for your welfare," Pierre said, agreeing with Jake.

"Your concern for me is touching, but gentlemen, war is dangerous. I find myself in danger most of the time. I believe I am the right person for the job at this particular time. I speak fluent German, Spanish, and French. The Germans have no idea I am a woman—a real advantage, I think. We need the information because thousands of Allied lives could be saved."

Pierre looked at Jean and smiled. "Then we will get the information, Captain."

"Captain," Sergeant Sanchez said as he stepped up. "I'd like to volunteer to stay with you."

Jean felt honored by his offer more than he would ever know, but he was needed elsewhere. "Sergeant," she responded. "I am counting on you to get everyone back to our lines, including the German lieutenant who has agreed to talk to H-2, our intelligence people."

"If not me, how about Joe? He'll have your back, ma'am. Besides, he wants to stay."

Jean thought for a bit and then asked, "Won't you need him to get back to our lines safely?"

"No, ma'am. Corporal Banks will make that happen."

"Okay, Sergeant. Tell Joe he's staying. Now get the hell out of here, Sergeant Sanchez," she said with a smile.

"Yes, ma'am! It's been an honor and a pleasure serving with you, Captain Webb," he said with a smart salute.

She returned the salute "smartly" and said, "Me too, Carlos. You take care!"

Jake butted in again, repeating, "I still think it's too dangerous for you to stay."

Patiently, Jean responded, "What's too dangerous around here is a wounded major who got shot in the ass and needs to be in the hospital."

"I know when I'm beat. You just watch your ass, Jean. I'll see you when you get back. Don't you dare disappoint me!"

Jake looked so vulnerable that he got past Jean's professional demeanor long enough for her to give him a kiss and a hug that would have to last him until she returned. "Of course I'll be careful," she added. "We've got a date. Remember?"

Once the returnees had left, Pierre, Joe, and Jean had a serious conversation. "According to Jake, the other town is Metz. Do you have any ideas, Pierre?" Jean counted on the others to contribute their thoughts and opinions to the operation.

"Yes, I do. We need to get you and Joe some civilian clothing, a priority, I think. Then I'll send out some scouts to check things out before you go in," Pierre noted. "Oh, we'll need papers for you and Joe as well."

Jean pondered what they could use for a cover story. All of a sudden it occurred to her what their cover might be. "Pierre, I just got an idea for our cover story. I'll need to contact headquarters right away and schedule a drop."

Chapter 12

Jean appreciated Pierre taking the initiative and setting up the radio to contact Lobo. Pierre asked, "Are you ready, Captain?"

"Yes, Pierre. Let's do it."

One of the Frenchmen started cranking for power, and Joe began speaking in Navajo. "This is JW calling Lobo. JW calling Lobo. Over."

"This is Lobo. Go ahead, JW."

Joe let them know what all was needed, and Lobo responded in Navajo. "Allow five days for procurement, JW. Lobo will advise when and where drop will be. Lobo over and out."

Jean figured that Lobo would need some time to obtain all the items on the list, and she didn't mind it. There were plenty of details to work out in the meantime. Pierre, Joe, and Jean put their heads together and developed a plan of action. Jean felt confident that the cover story she had brainstormed would help the group achieve their goals. Joe expressed frustration in trying to act passively, but he promised that he would stick to the script unless Jean's life was in danger.

Pierre reported the lowdown on Metz. "And it comes down to this, Captain. Metz is the German command center for Eastern France, and it's heavily fortified." He paused before adding, "Are you sure you want to go there?"

Jean answered the question quickly and definitively. "Yes, we're off to see the Germans in Metz because the information we need is in Metz. I hope we're clear about this. I may be a woman, but I do not change my mind unless I have a very good reason."

Pierre grinned and tried to suppress his amusement. Joe almost smiled but rolled his eyes instead. A couple of days later, Lobo made contact and provided the drop details. The day of the drop, Pierre and Joe went to the drop site to pick up the necessary items. While waiting for the men to return, Jean revisited the events that had led to her being in this place.

As a college freshman, Jean signed up for Reserve Officer's Training Corps (ROTC) for the excellent leadership training courses. Surprisingly, she thrived in that militaristic environment. After graduating with high honors, she accepted an appointment to Officer's Candidate School and successfully completed OCS and received her first assignment to Army Intelligence at Ft. Mead, Maryland. Being the only woman among a bunch of male chauvinistic assholes could have ended Jean's career in the army, but instead, she fought back. She rejected their sexual advances and kicked their asses in the gym with judo. She ignored the cold-shoulder treatment and disrespectful remarks. She endured the abuse until the army began looking for volunteers to learn German. Jean signed up and left right away for language training. She had always learned languages easily, and after eight weeks, she could speak and understand German fluently. Jean was then reassigned to US Army Headquarters in Washington, DC, where she spent all day reading and translating German communications and doing research on high-ranking Nazis. It became obvious to her that war with Germany was inevitable.

A lot of service personnel can't go home for the holidays, so many of them meet their social needs by attending parties. The weekend after Thanksgiving, Jean attended a party at the Officers' Club. The party offered lively music, close dancing, and tasty refreshments, but no tequila. Jean hadn't decided what to do first when this tall, dark, and handsome dream of a man walked up to her.

"Lieutenant Webb, may I have this dance?" he'd asked.

His silky smooth voice gave Jean goose bumps. "Why, yes,"—Jean looked at his nametag—"Captain Blakely."

That night Jake had whirled Jean around the dance floor skillfully. Besides being a great dancer, he excelled at making conversation, displayed above-average intelligence, and behaved like a real gentleman—all that and looks too. Jean stood about six feet tall with heels, and he was a few inches taller, which she thought *perfect*.

The next weekend neither Jean nor Jake had duty, so they decided to spend the weekend in Baltimore. They took in a movie early Friday night and returned to their hotel room. The couple shared a slow, sweet kiss, which built in intensity until they couldn't get their clothes off fast enough. Jean discovered that Jake's talents included the art of lovemaking. The pair spent the rest of the weekend in their room, interrupted only by room service and a sensuous shower Sunday morning. After the shower and brunch at a fancy hotel in downtown Baltimore, they decided to go to the movie *Shepherd of the Hills*, which starred John Wayne. They both liked him and figured he'd become a big movie star someday. Just before the movie ended, the film disappeared from the screen and the theater lights came on.

Then a man came running onto the stage hollering, "The Japanese have bombed Pearl Harbor in Hawaii!"

Jake gasped. "Oh my God! We're finally in the war!" Then he turned to Jean and said, "We better get back to our commands ASAP."

The newly formed couple headed back to DC and said their good-byes before each going separate ways.

Jean arrived at her operations at about sixteen hundred hours. The major announced, "People, it's going to be a long night. Coffee is being made, and we'll eat and sleep in shifts."

The next day Pres. Franklin D. Roosevelt declared war on Japan. Minimum-sleep nights continued for several months due to increased shipments to England—up by 300 percent. Troop movements to the West Coast for training increased. Jake received a temporary assignment to a unit in England for special training. During the months that followed, Jean kept busy but thought about Jake a lot. She'd hoped those English women were not as good looking as rumor had it. Being busy made the next six months pass quickly.

One afternoon Jean heard a voice from behind her. "You must have gotten more beautiful every day I was gone."

Jean immediately whirled around and ran straight into Jake's waiting arms. They kissed each other hard.

Then he asked, "Are you free tonight?"

"Yes, you bet I am."

"I have to run right now, but I'll pick you up later for dinner. Okay?"

Jake kissed Jean again but this time very tenderly. Then he left her to wonder if he had really been there. She looked forward to seeing him later for dinner and finding out about his new uniform.

During dinner, Jake spoke excitedly about the Office of Strategic Services (OSS). He had experienced their special English training, which actually took place in Scotland.

"The British Commandos trained us in hand-to-hand combat, all kinds of weapons, night fighting behind enemy lines, and rock climbing. Our uniforms are designed to reflect the nations that support the OSS. That's why we wear a French beret. And your concern about the beautiful English women—the Army and Air Force guys pretty much have all bragging rights."

"Well, they don't know what they're missing," Jean purred.

Jake suggested they continue their reunion back at the hotel where they got very little sleep. When Jean was with Jake, sleep didn't seem as important to her. Approximately two months after seeing Jake, the major ordered Jean to speak to someone in his office.

"Come in, Lieutenant Webb, and have a seat. I'd like to ask you a few questions."

"Yes, sir," Jean responded.

He asked several questions that sounded more like a job interview than general information. When the interview ended, Jean still didn't know who he was, but she was told that she was now a member of the OSS organization. That week she would begin three months of intense training in espionage, self-defense, using a field radio, demolition, and weaponry.

CHAPTER 13

Jean woke suddenly, realizing she had put herself asleep by reliving her past.

"It's a good thing I was just talking to myself," she chuckled as she splashed cold water on her face and left it to air dry.

A few minutes later, about noon, Joe and Pierre returned with the delivery. Jean looked through the contents and was pleasantly surprised that everything she had asked for had been sent. Later, Jean and Joe dressed up in character for the parts they would be playing.

Joe looked ill-at-ease in his costume, so Jean tried to help him relax. "Welcome to the spy world, Joe."

"Yeah, thanks a lot, Captain. They shoot spies, don't they?"

Jean chuckled to herself. Joe had actually made a joke! She couldn't believe it. "Not today, Joe," she reassured him. "Not today."

Once everyone was ready, Pierre needed to make sure that they safely boarded the Paris train at Verdun station headed east to Metz. If things went badly, Pierre and his men would be available to bail them out of a bad situation.

At the train station, a German captain kept smiling at Jean while he checked over their papers. "Everything looks in order, mademoiselle," he said while holding eye contact.

"Thank you, Captain," she answered in German. Jean smiled back at him. *He didn't check my papers very well at all*, she thought. *I'm a señorita.*

The train ride to Metz took about fifty minutes. Two of Pierre's men kept an eye on them without bringing any attention to themselves. However, a couple of German soldiers stared at them like they had never seen a woman before. Jean knew that she looked nice in the fashionable French red low-cut gown, but that kind of admiration could interfere with the mission. One of the young soldiers came over to speak to her, but Joe instantly stood up and intercepted him.

"This is Jose. He is my manservant and protector," Jean explained to the soldier in German.

Then she noticed Joe give him one of his malicious angry looks, and the German promptly returned to his seat. Jean had to cover her mouth to hide her smile.

When they departed the train in Metz, Jean saw a major waiting at the end of the station platform. She walked up to him and asked in German, "Major, could you tell me where the German headquarters are located?"

The German took his time while looking them over carefully and asked, "Can I see your papers, mademoiselle?" Jean handed him their papers. "Ah, I see you are a Spanish Nationalist. Why are you here, señorita?"

"I was going to explain that to your commanding officer, but since you have asked, I hope you will bear with me, Major."

"Please go on, señorita. I'm listening."

Jean began her explanation. "My uncle, Antonio Perez, is Spain's assistant ambassador to Germany, and several years ago I accompanied him to a special party at the chancellery in Berlin at the invitation of Adolph Hitler, your führer."

"You've met the führer?" The major appeared impressed.

"Oh yes, and I found him to be most charming. Anyway, my uncle has since married, and his wife has a daughter somewhere in this part of France."

"What is her name?" the major asked. "Maybe we can help find her, Señorita Perez."

"Her name is Margarita Felisha Espinoza. I have been spending most of my time on the Riviera during this nasty war where a lot of good men are being killed. My uncle contacted the chancellery, and they sent these papers for me and my manservant, Jose. They allow us to search for his stepdaughter. So you see, that is why I am here, Major." Jean finished her explanation with a big smile just for him.

"Forgive me, señorita," he said sincerely. "Let me properly introduce myself. I am Maj. Heinrich Steinbach of the SS Corp."

Jean sensed Joe stiffening up a bit, so she said, "Jose, it looks like we are in good hands." Joe managed to smile a little in response.

Then the major said, "Please let me give you a ride to headquarters."

"How very kind of you, Major," Jean said sweetly.

The major brought his car around, seated Joe beside the driver, and invited Jean to sit beside him. After a fast trip, they arrived at German headquarters. The place was abuzz with activity. The major guided Joe and Jean through the groups of people all the way to the commanding officer's office. On the way there, they happened to pass by the military information board. Jean rolled her eyes at it so Joe would notice it too. When the trio reached the CO's office, Jean indicated for Joe to wait outside so he could take a better look at the board.

The major knocked on the door. "Come in," an authoritative voice answered.

"Colonel, I'd like to introduce Señorita Perez," the major said with pleasure. The colonel looked up and stared at Jean for a moment.

Then he jumped up and introduced himself. "I'm Colonel Schoenfield. I remember you, but you probably don't remember me," he said as he took Jean's hand and kissed it like a gentleman.

"Why, Colonel Schoenfield, you surprised me. Yes I do, sir."

Chapter 14

"I met you at the führer's chancellery party in 1942. I believe you were with your uncle, if I'm not mistaken," the colonel explained.

Much relieved, Jean's heart began to return to its normal pace. She teased him a bit. "Why, Colonel Schoenfield, I am flattered that you should remember me among so many guests."

The colonel suddenly became more professional, asking, "Señorita Perez, why are you here?"

"Well, as I told the major, I'm looking for my uncle's stepdaughter," she stated plainly.

Turning to the major, he asked, "I assume you have the necessary information to begin a search?"

"Yes, sir," the major replied.

"Then you'll help Señorita Perez find her relative and report to me."

"Yes, sir. Colonel, sir. Heil Hitler!" The major raised his arm in salute, and the colonel automatically returned the salute. The major left immediately to attend to the colonel's directive.

The colonel then focused his attention upon Jean once again. "My dear, do you have lodgings for tonight?"

"No. I had hoped to make arrangements upon arrival for myself and my manservant."

"I will have my aide make arrangements for you and your manservant," the colonel offered and continued by asking, "Would you do me the honor of dining with me tonight?"

"How nice … I'd love to dine with you, Colonel." Jean gushed.

"My driver will pick you up for cocktails at six, followed by dinner at seven," he noted as Jean got up to leave.

"Thanks for your help. I'm really looking forward to this evening," she said, wearing her best killer smile.

Jean left the colonel's office and joined Joe in the hallway. Joe had memorized the war board during the time she had been in the colonel's office. True to his word, the colonel's aide took the pair to a very nice hotel not too far from German headquarters. Once in Jean's room, she and Joe wrote down everything they could remember that was on the war board. As they combined their mutual memories, Jean learned that Joe had a photographic memory in addition to all his other talents.

"I think I will call you the secret weapon from now on," she kidded him.

Once they were done, Jean unpacked and hung up the evening dress she planned to wear that evening—a red satin low-cut evening dress. She wanted to look her best for the colonel, so she took great pains with her hair and makeup. Finally, she put the dress on and asked Joe to come in and fasten the back of it.

After he finished, Jean whirled around and asked, "Well, what do you think?"

At first, Joe was speechless, but he soon found his tongue. "You wearing that dress constitutes a very dangerous weapon," he said, smiling and shaking his head.

The colonel's driver arrived promptly and delivered Jean to a luxurious hotel suite on the top floor. The elegant furnishings and décor convinced her that the colonel enjoyed the best Metz had to offer.

"Welcome to my home, Señorita Perez. Or may I call you Juanita?" He appeared uncomfortable as he asked the question.

"Yes, Colonel, please do," she answered him as she shrugged off her wrap.

His eyes lowered to her breasts, which appeared to be trying to bust out of the dress. Lust and longing had put Jean's plan into action.

"Please come and sit down," he said, inviting Jean in. "What would you like to drink?"

"What are you having, Colonel?"

"Please call me Franz," he suggested, "and I am enjoying a French burgundy, my dear."

Jean could handle her liquor, especially wine. "Excellent choice, Franz. I'd love some."

Franz brought over the drinks and sat down on the sofa beside her. "You are a very beautiful woman, Juanita," he said softly. "I must properly welcome you to Metz."

He leaned toward Jean and kissed her nicely. She enjoyed the kiss. The pair finished the first bottle of wine and had started on the second one when dinner arrived. Franz had ordered roast chicken with potatoes, cooked vegetables, and French bread. Jean enjoyed the meal but knew that the chicken had been taken from a French family—the spoils of war. After dinner, Franz fixed stronger drinks to deliberately try to get Jean drunk and into his bed. After a few bourbon and waters, Franz had lost his ability to stand up.

Assessing the situation, Jean spoke up. "Let me fix us a drink, lover." She put knockout drops in his drink and switched hands when he wasn't looking. When she set down his drink, he cautiously chose the other glass just like she expected he would. After taking a few swallows of his drink, he pushed Jean back on the couch and began to kiss her passionately. His hands roamed over her body, ultimately releasing her breasts from the restraining cloth. He worshipped them with his hands and lips until the knockout drops kicked in. Jean quickly pushed him off, stood up, and put the girls away. Then she started going through the papers on his desk. Minutes later, she found the Germans' plan for withdrawal and quickly took the necessary pictures of it with her microfilm camera. Next, Jean walked over to Franz's unconscious form.

"What a shame," she said. "We could have become an item if it weren't for this darn war. Good-bye, Franz. Maybe I'll see you again in Berlin."

Next, Jean gathered up all her things and left the suite, being careful not to appear suspicious. The colonel's driver snapped into action when she stepped outside. Without saying a word, he returned her to the hotel. When Jean arrived back to her room, Joe wanted to know how the evening went. She grabbed a change of clothes and went into the bathroom to change. Through the door, she described the highlights of the evening, which culminated with finding the German withdrawal plans.

"Joe, we have found everything we came for and then some. Colonel Schoenfield probably won't remember much about tonight except that he almost had the woman of his dreams and got too drunk to make her his own." Jean nervously giggled. "Seriously, though, we need to get out of here as soon as we can!"

"I'm with you, Captain." Joe agreed. "We need to get these documents to the folks who can use them to end this war."

Jean walked out of the bathroom nearly ready to leave when someone knocked on the room door.

Getting back into character, Juanita Perez, Jean asked, "Who's there?"

"Major Steinbach here." He paused briefly and asked, "May I come in?"

"Just a minute please. I am getting dressed." Jean answered him while taking the opportunity to arm herself. Joe hid in the bathroom out of sight.

When Jean opened the door, Major Steinbach stood out there all alone. He glanced at her derringer and spoke in perfect English. "Protection, I see."

"Yes, Major. A woman never knows when it might be needed." Jean hesitated, confused by his perfect English and the unexpected visit.

"That's true, Captain Webb of the OSS," he said, responding to her comment.

Jean quickly pointed the derringer in his face. About the same time, Joe came crashing out of the bathroom with his weapon trained on the major.

"Hold it! Hold it!" The major put his hands up and nervously stated, "I'm with British Intelligence, and I report to Colonel Chase, same as you do, Jean. If you have everything you came for, it's time to get the bloody hell out of here."

Because his information checked out as far as they could verify, Jean and Joe decided to go with him, but very cautiously.

CHAPTER 15

"You first, Major Steinbach, if you don't mind," Jean said, her derringer pressed against his back.

Outside the hotel, the trio passed a dead German, whom Steinbach identified as the driver of the military staff car he had arrived in.

Steinbach said, "Get in. I'm driving. Let's get the bloody hell out of here. We have one roadblock to get through. The machine guns in the backseat floorboard might come in handy."

Jean was beginning to feel more comfortable with Major Steinbach, or whoever the hell he might be. They had not gone very far when the major started slowing down.

"Roadblock is just around the next curve." He warned them. "Get ready."

Steinbach returned to his previous speed toward the roadblock. Just as he was about to stop the vehicle, he gunned it, and Joe and Jean opened fire, taking out the first two guards. Then two more guards showed up, and Joe picked them off. A few miles down, Steinbach pulled off the road just short of the bridge. All three passengers got out and pushed the vehicle into the river. Then, they quickly crossed the bridge and headed north.

The supposedly British spy said, "We'll meet up with the French underground south of Verdun."

"I know where," Joe said confidently and took the lead.

Jean's curiosity could not be restrained any longer, so she asked the man in the German major's uniform. "Just who in the hell are you?"

"Let me introduce myself. Captain Kurt Rutger of the Dutch Army assigned to British Intelligence. I arrived just three days before you did, Captain."

"Is there a Major Steinbach?" Jean asked the question, knowing what his answer would be.

"Yes, but I'm afraid the poor chap is dead." He paused then added, "By the way, I thought your cover story was excellent."

"Thanks," Jean responded to his compliment. "Well, it worked. I got what I came for. Mission accomplished."

Joe performed admirably, leading Jean and Kurt through the countryside while avoiding the German patrols. Before long, they were south of Verdun. From there, Joe led them northwest. Approximately thirty minutes later, they arrived at the French camp.

"Captain Webb, it's good to see you again," Pierre said excitedly. "Come and have something to drink before we head for the landing site."

The group enjoyed a little wine and a lot of camaraderie before leaving for the landing area. Pierre had his men spread out around the area to stop any uninvited Germans from messing up their plans. Minutes later, the group heard aircraft engines getting closer. Pierre flashed his light three times, and more lights came on, forming a landing strip.

"Captain, please follow me," Pierre said as he led Jean, Joe and Kurt toward the center of the field. "When the airplane stops, you must quickly board it, and as you Americans say, get the hell out of here."

When the plane landed, Jean noticed it had German markings.

Captain Rutger commented, "Germans don't shoot at their own planes."

"Yeah, but our guys do," Jean pointed out.

"Not when they know who we are," Kurt reassured her with a friendly smile.

Jean gave Pierre a big bear hug before boarding the aircraft. "Thanks, Pierre, for everything," she said sincerely.

"*Au revoir, mademoiselle*," Pierre said.

Jean, Joe, and Kurt then boarded the plane as quickly as possible. Jean felt privileged to have an actual seat on this ex-German plane, although comfort was obviously not an important consideration. Once everyone had boarded, the aircraft immediately took off for friendlier skies.

The pilot announced, "We'll reach London in just about two hours."

When the plane entered Paris air space, it picked up an escort. Jean felt relieved seeing those two P-51 Mustangs and knowing they weren't shooting at their plane. They landed at a military airbase outside of London. Jean's commanding officer, Colonel Chase, and Major Williams greeted the three on the tarmac.

"Welcome back, Captain Webb," said the colonel.

Jean saluted and handed the colonel her microfilm camera and then said dramatically, "Here are the German withdrawal plans and their current war board, as of two days ago."

Both officers looked at each other, and the colonel shook Jean's hand. "There's probably a decoration in this for you, Jean," he said solemnly.

"Don't forget my partners. I couldn't have done this without them," she emphasized.

The officers went over to Joe and Captain Kurt Rutger and congratulated them as well. A few hours later, Jean felt free to visit Jake. The debriefing took much longer than she had expected.

Jean caught Jake off guard, sitting on a toilet chair playing cards with other patients.

"How's your ass, Major?" Giving him a hard time tickled Jean, but something in his face stopped any further mischief.

"Don't say anything smart, Jean," Jake pleaded.

She walked over and gave him a big hug and many kisses. Words weren't necessary, really.

CHAPTER 16

After enjoying two days of rest, Jean reported in at London OSS Headquarters.

"Captain Webb reporting as ordered, sir." Her accompanying salute received an acknowledgment from Colonel Chase.

"Have a seat, Jean. According to the doctor, Major Blakely may not be fully recovered for another six weeks. Apparently, the severe bone damage will require more time to heal than previously thought. Would you be willing to encourage Major Blakely to make healing his number-one concern?" The colonel paused for effect, slightly grinning, and continued on. "Of course, you would both be on leave until Jake has recovered. I would like you to stay in touch in case I need you. That's all, Captain."

"Yes, sir, and thank you, Colonel," Jean said cheerfully and saluted once more.

As the war continued, Jean tried to fill her time with working out at the gym, swimming in the indoor pool, and spending time with Jake at the hospital. She tried to practice contentment and gratitude concerning her so-called vacation time, but she missed the excitement that work provided. Jean recognized that the restlessness she felt now had first appeared during her college years.

She really loved Missouri University with its green lawns, majestic oak trees, and flowering dogwoods and hawthorns in the spring. The fall colors and winter snows brought seasonal interest to the campus.

Although she took a heavy course load each semester, she needed to fill her spare time with additional studies and activities. During her first year at MU, she met some really nice people. Her roommate, Kim, lived in China and had come to MU for an American education. Jean had offered to help her with her English and other studies, and she offered to teach Jean judo in return. She knew judo extremely well, and Jean wanted to be as good as she was.

Jean joined the ROTC her freshman year. Her workload increased along with her stress level, but she loved learning so many new things. The next three years flew by, and graduation day neared and finally arrived. Jean's mother and grandfather, Senator Howl, attended the ceremony and watched her receive high honors and an appointment to the US Army's Officer's Candidate School, OCS. She took in their compliments on her achievements, as well as the occasional encouragement to do better.

Jean thought her mom looked fantastic as usual and at least ten years younger. Her salt-and-pepper hair framed her face with loose curls. Gramps looked much older than he had just a few months earlier. Jean learned that his health had worsened, so she decided to spend the summer after graduation with her mom and grandfather. They decided to take a trip to Arizona, and the trio couldn't believe how diverse Arizona proved to be. They found deserts, lakes, mountains, valleys, canyons, washes, and creeks. The pines in the mountains replaced the Saguaro cactuses in the lower elevations. Jean enjoyed the scenery, which changed continuously as they traveled around the state. They soon learned that the lower the elevation, the higher the temperature. The day they arrived in Phoenix, the temperature jumped to 109 degrees Fahrenheit.

During the trip, Jean's mother noticed that Gramps seemed to have trouble coping with the heat. Jean suggested that they take him back home to Springfield, Missouri, so they left the next morning after breakfast and arrived home three days later. For the rest of that summer, Jean visited with Gramps and her mom as much as possible. She had reason to believe that she would not have many opportunities to visit with them once she entered the army.

When that day finally arrived, Jean's mother said, "Your grandfather wants to retire in Arizona."

"What about your career?" Jean asked her. She couldn't see her mother leaving the life she had built in Springfield.

"I'm ready for a fresh start," she said. "I have been recommended for a few opportunities in the Arizona state government."

"I hope you both enjoy your new home," Jean said tearfully. "I'll miss you!" She grabbed both of them and enjoyed a three-way hug. That memory kept the home fires burning in Jean's heart for many years to come.

CHAPTER 17

Jean could see Jake's impatience increase regarding his slowly healing ass. He wanted to get back to work, and Jean shared his sentiment. She hated waiting. She looked at Jake sleeping in bed and thought how he looked more boyish than the rugged Texas cowboy she'd come to know so well. His dark hair was damp with sweat from the overly warm room. Jean had spent many hours with Jake at the hospital, often even staying for meals.

She knew his healing had progressed when he started walking again, although he still needed his pillow whenever he sat down. One evening, Jean snuck some French bread, cheese, and wine into the hospital. The couple found a quiet area for a picnic, where no one would disturb them. While enjoying the food and wine, they talked about how thankful they were to still be alive. They reminisced about some of the close calls each of them had experienced and shared how wonderful it had been knowing each other the past three years.

"Hopefully, next year we'll celebrate our fourth anniversary at Thanksgiving stateside," Jake said.

"I hope so, Jake."

After six weeks of waiting and healing, the doctor came in and said, "Major, I want to see you back here in one week for a final follow-up exam before I release you for active duty."

Jake's face brightened at this news. "Thanks, doc. I'll see you in one week," he said excitedly. The doctor left, and Jake grabbed Jean and said, "Let's get out of here. I'm hungry for more good French food and wine, sweetheart." With that, he patted her behind firmly.

"What was that for?" Jean asked. He had clearly recovered his playfulness.

"I remember a certain captain who gave me a hard time about my wounded ass two and a half months ago," Jake teased with a laugh.

She responded, "Yes, and I enjoyed it too."

"That's why the pat on the ass, sweetheart," he said as he pulled her close and hugged her tightly.

The couple spent the following week touring London at night, going to nightclubs and officers' clubs and then going to bed to get caught up. During the day, they toured the English countryside and frequently returned to the bedroom for more catching up, of course. One day while on a tour bus enjoying the English countryside, Jean commented, "I wonder what our next mission will be."

"Whatever it is," Jake answered, "it sounds like we will be together."

"Remember, Major Blakely—on a mission, it's strictly business."

"Right, Captain Webb," he murmured as he put his arm around her waist. "Serious business."

Jake's final exam went flawlessly. Immediately following his official medical release, Jean and Jake reported in to Colonel Chase.

"Major Blakely and Captain Webb reporting as ordered, sir," Jake announced.

"Have a seat, you two," Colonel Chase said cordially. "Your mission will include joining up with the Italian Partisans in Northwest Italy to help plan their attacks when the big push begins early next spring." He paused before revealing the more exciting part of the mission.

"You might be included in the manhunt for Mussolini, and we want him taken alive."

"Why are we supposed to deliver Mussolini alive, Colonel?" Jake really didn't understand why a murderer like Mussolini deserved any kindness.

"The free world wants Mussolini, Hitler, and other war criminals to stand trial for their crimes. They want to see them humiliated. They want to know that justice has been served by executing these criminals," the colonel said solemnly.

Jake and Jean looked at each other, but neither said anything.

"Now, Jean, I have something else to tell you." The colonel's countenance brightened. "In two months, you and Jake will fly to Paris where you will be awarded a medal by Gen. Charles de Gaulle for your action in destroying the Nazi supply trains outside of Metz in June of '44 and your recent action in eastern France. Congratulations, Jean." The colonel offered his hand and one of his rare big smiles.

Not to be left out, Jake turned to Jean and said, "Yes indeed. Congratulations, Captain Webb."

"I almost forgot to tell you that after Paris both of you will head for Italy," Colonel Chase added.

"Excuse me, sir, but what will we be doing the next two months?" Jean hoped that some kind of adventure might come their way.

The colonel answered, "More training and learning to speak Italian. You report to Major Williams in the morning. You're dismissed."

Jean and Jake saluted their CO and left.

The next morning, Jake met Jean for breakfast, and they hurried a bit to not make Major Williams wait. They waited outside his office for him to arrive.

"Welcome, Major Blakely and Captain Webb," Major Williams said warmly. "Come on in and have a seat." He handed each of them a paper. "As you can see, your training schedule includes learning to speak Italian, using the upgraded field radios, advancing your judo skills, fighting hand-to-hand with a knife, using a pistol with a silencer, and using the new explosive types."

He smiled in response to the expression on their faces—incredulity. Jake and Jean looked at each other and both spoke at the same time. "No time to get bored!" They started laughing, and Major Williams joined them in their frivolity.

CHAPTER 18

The next morning, October 30, 1944, Jean and Jake made their way through the thick London fog to the training center.

"Halloween would be spooky here," Jean noted.

After making a few introductory remarks, Major Williams introduced the pair to their new instructor, Sgt. Mark Halloran, who informed them of their weekly activities.

"This first week you'll be learning a new language and new skills. Four hours of Italian and four hours learning the operation and repair of the new field radio with the long-lasting battery." With that, the sergeant sent the pair off to their first class.

Jean really enjoyed learning Italian, and having a good-looking Italian instructor didn't hurt either. For Jake, learning to speak Italian was a little bit of a struggle due to his Texas drawl. Now and then, Jean would mimic him, and he'd give her that I'll-get-you-back-later look.

The new radio would be a real asset over the ones they had been using. Both Jake and Jean breezed through that class without any trouble. The following week, they continued their study of the Italian language and began working on their judo skills. Jean got to go first and showed the instructor what she could do.

After a couple of days, he asked Jean very kindly, "Captain Webb, I'd like it very much if you would just sit down and rest. I can't teach you anything that you don't know, and my butt can't take anymore hard landings."

Jean watched while the others, including Jake, worked on improving their judo skills and rubbed their sore butts.

During the third week, the pair continued the Italian and added the pistol range with a revolver and silencer. Within three days, Jean managed to group six rounds in a three-inch circle on a target twenty-five yards away. That earned her the nickname of a modern-day Annie Oakley. Jake spent the whole week getting his first target from a twelve-inch circle to a six-inch circle.

For the remaining five weeks at the training center, only Italian could be spoken. All public speaking had to be in Italian anywhere in the training center. Jean had no problem due to her aptitude for learning languages. Jake, on the other hand, still struggled with the language.

"You know, Jake," Jean teased, "you'll need to know more than just how to ask a pretty girl out on a date." He didn't say anything, but Jean could hear him grumbling under his breath.

The final week brought them the opportunity to learn more about C-4 explosives and hand-to-hand training with a knife. Jean surprised herself with how well she did. She repeatedly hit the target from fifteen feet away. She felt a little bad that she seemed to keep upstaging Jake, who came in about average or slightly better, but Jean soon got over that.

On December 21, Sergeant Halloran called Jean and Jake into his office and said, "You two have done very well, and we wish you luck." He smiled as he shook their hands and then added, "Colonel Chase requests that you report in to him."

Jean and Jake gathered their gear and returned to command. Upon arrival, they went directly to Colonel Chase's office.

"Reporting as ordered, sir," Jake said as they both saluted.

"Close the door and have a seat," he said in a very serious tone. "There has been a change of plans. You can forget about Mussolini because the Partisan's movement has stated that Mussolini isn't going to leave Italy alive. Instead, you two will assist OSS Agent Allen Dulles in getting Air Marshall Hermann Göring out of Nazi Germany. Of course, we are assuming the current talks with Mr. Göring will be persuasive and successful." Colonel Chase paused for a moment and then continued brightly. "You both are scheduled to leave for Paris on January 3. Enjoy the holidays! Good luck!"

Jean and Jake stood and saluted before leaving and saying, "Yes, sir!"

The couple had no problem obeying that last order. They spent all Christmas and New Year's together, feasting on Christmas goose and spicy plum pudding as well as several American favorites, including candied yams and pumpkin pie, just to name a couple. They ate so much for Christmas that they switched to wine, bread, and cheese for New Year's Eve. The next day their hangovers convinced them that they consumed a little too much wine. By January 2, they were feeling normal again.

CHAPTER 19

On January 3, Jake and Jean boarded a DC-3 for Paris.

"Relax, Jean," Jake said, trying to reassure her. "This flight will be short and sweet."

"I can't help it," she replied. "I admit it. I hate flying."

Jake suggested, "Think about something besides flying, honey."

Jean leaned back in her canvas seat and tried to relax while letting her thoughts drift. How ironic it seemed that she had earned a prestigious medal for carrying out her mission successfully. The past two years had been as enjoyable as they had been dangerous as hell. And yet, her first twenty-four months in the army had been miserable thanks to the male chauvinistic officers who tried to keep her in her place. Thank goodness for the OSS, or she wouldn't be on her way to receive a medal. Suddenly, Jean's thoughts were interrupted as she felt the aircraft pitch forward and stiffen up.

Jake took her hand and said, "It's okay, Jean. We're landing."

A textbook-perfect landing brought the pair to the airport on time. A lieutenant met them on the ground and drove them to a nearby military occupied hotel.

Before the lieutenant left, he said, "I'll pick you up at nine o'clock and take you to the ceremony."

Jean and Jake checked in to the hotel and proceeded to their separate rooms.

"Let's meet in the lobby in half an hour for some refreshments and later, lunch," Jean suggested.

Jean's room proved to be a luxurious suite. Antique French furnishings and exquisite décor made her feel like royalty. She enjoyed the view of Paris from the balcony before going out with Jake. Jean thought it would have been nice to put on something pretty, but her uniform would have to do, as it was still wartime. Jake appeared to be asleep as Jean approached him waiting in the lobby. He woke up and smiled at her.

"You ready to go?" Jake asked.

"Yes, I'm thirsty and starving, Major."

"Well, we need to feed the troops, Captain."

"Sounds great to me," Jean answered.

The couple found a quaint little sidewalk café not far from the hotel.

After ordering a couple of glasses of wine and an early lunch, Jake asked, "Are you nervous about tomorrow, Jean?"

"Maybe just a little. I've never received a medal before."

Jake responded, "There's always a first time. Everything will be all right. I'm so proud of you, sweetheart!" He tenderly kissed her before continuing. "I'd like to show you how much."

"What do you have in mind, Major?" Jean knew what his intentions were, and she thought about making love with her handsome cowboy the rest of the day. When night finally came, the anticipation led to the couple's most memorable lovemaking encounter ever.

The next morning, they enjoyed an early continental breakfast of coffee, croissants, pastries, and fruits. The young lieutenant arrived exactly at nine o'clock and drove Jean and Jake to the French government building and parade grounds. General Kenneth Rogers, commander of the Paris garrison, received Jean as one of the honored recipients.

"Congratulations, Captain Webb, job well done," he said. "We're very proud of you." He shook Jean's hand and saluted her.

"Thank you, sir," Jean said, returning his salute. She chatted briefly with the general before excusing herself when she recognized some familiar faces in the crowd.

"What are you guys doing here?" she asked.

Captain Rutger explained, "Pathfinder Joe and I were invited to be recognized along with you for helping you complete your mission and protecting your behind." He smiled broadly after making that remark.

"Especially you're behind, ma'am," Joe added with a big grin on his face.

Jean hugged both of them, ignoring military protocol.

"Oh, Captain Rutger, I want you to meet Major Blakely. Jake, you remember Joe?"

"Yes I do. How are you doing, Joe … It's nice to meet you, Captain Rutger," Jake said politely.

Conversation helped pass the time, and once again, Jean recognized two more familiar faces.

"Excuse me. Pierre and Andre! It's so good to see you!" Jean hugged each one in turn, feeling so happy to be sharing the day with her friends.

At ten o'clock, a French captain approached the microphone and asked, "Recipients, please take your places. The ceremony will begin soon."

After his announcement, the band started playing, and Gen. Charles de Gaulle walked onto the stage. Jean and the other recipients were lined up in front of the general. Standing from his right to left were a French woman, Andre, Pierre, Captain Rutger, Joe Toritino, and Jean. She was happy to see Jake in the front row as she looked out into the crowd. His obvious support made her feel even more confident in their relationship.

General de Gaulle stood in front of the recipients and began presenting the awards. As the French captain called out the names, General de Gaulle saluted and presented medals to Alexis Petit ... Andre Girard ... Pierre Le Noir ... Capt. Kurt Rutger ... Joe Toritino. When the general presented Joe his medal, Jean's hands were sweating a little. Then the general stood in front of her. He smiled and saluted while waiting for the announcement. Just before the captain spoke, a man sitting across the aisle from Jake jumped up and headed for the stage.

Jake saw that the man had a pistol and quickly jumped up, hollering, "Man with pistol!"

Joe quickly grabbed Jean and pushed her to the stage, covering her with his body. At the same time, Pierre did the same thing to General de Gaulle. Using his long legs, Jake made a flying tackle before the potential assassin could reach the stage and quickly disarmed the would-be killer. When Jake forced the assassin to his feet, a gun went off, and Jake caught one in the shoulder.

"Damn, not again!" Jake's words preceded him falling to the ground.

Captain Rutger spotted the shooter and fired his weapon before the second assassin could fire again. The French MPs immediately took charge by securing the assassin Jake had tackled. After Jake went down, Joe and Jean rushed to his side. Joe ripped Jake's shirt open to locate the gunshot wound.

"Looks like it went clear through, Major," he reported.

Jean felt relieved to see that the American medics and MPs had arrived on the scene. She remained at Jake's side while the medics worked on him.

General de Gaulle came up to Jake and shook his hand, saying, "*Merci beaucoup, monsieur.*" Then he turned to his staff members. "Get this man to the hospital immediately!" And they did.

A few days later, Jake saw General de Gaulle standing in his hospital room doorway.

A French captain asked, "May we come in? The general would like to make some presentations."

"Yes, please do," Jake answered.

Jean stood up and saluted the general, who stepped up and returned her salute. General de Gaulle turned to the French captain, who handed him a medal.

Jean addressed the general. "*Je parle français,* general." He seemed pleased that she spoke French and smiled.

In French, he said, "Captain Webb, it gives me great pleasure and honor to award this medal for bravery and valor for saving thousands of lives because of your successful missions behind enemy lines."

He expertly pinned the French medal, *Croix de guerre* (Cross of war) to Jean's uniform, kissed her on both cheeks, and saluted again. Then the general walked over to Jake's bed and saluted him. He instructed the French captain to interpret to Jake what he had to say.

De Gaulle began. "Major Blakely, it gives me great pleasure to award you the *Medaille Miliaire,* for bravery and being wounded saving lives by stopping an assassin during the ceremony. *Merci beaucoup, monsieur.*"

The general gave Jake a hearty handshake and left after saying, in broken English, "God bless both of you."

The next day Jake seemed depressed. Jean asked, "Why so down, my friend?"

"I'm sorry that our mission will have to be given to someone else or scratched altogether. I know you were looking forward to it," he said gloomily.

"What makes you think that? I'll do the mission by myself if necessary," she said matter-of-factly.

"No, you cannot go solo. It isn't safe. I refuse to lose you to an act of supreme stupidity," Jake protested.

Jean could tell he was really angry because his ears were bright red. "Calm down, Jake. I'm a big girl, and I can take care of myself," she asserted and then sweetly whispered, "I love you too."

Three days later, Jean escorted her wounded major onto a DC-3. She looked for an empty seat and found one next to Kurt Rutger.

"Hi, Kurt. Look after the major for me?" she asked. He gave her the okay sign in response.

Jake seemed disagreeable as he sat down and buckled up. "You didn't hear a thing I said," he declared. Then his features softened, and he looked at her with tears in his eyes. "Be careful, sweetheart. I want to see you again!"

"Have a nice flight, Jake. I will see you as soon as I get back. You get well, because we have some catching up to do."

CHAPTER 20

The following day, Jean received orders to report to the US Army Headquarters in Paris by a sergeant who drove her to headquarters and escorted her to a conference room door. When Jean entered the large conference room, she was surprised to find Colonel Chase and Major Williams waiting for her.

"Come in and have a seat, Captain Webb. You're probably wondering why I'm here. I'm here to discuss the status of the mission in northern Italy," Colonel Chase said.

As Jean sat down in the chair, her CO continued, "Agent Dulles failed to convince Göring to leave Germany. With Jake injured again, I had to find someone qualified to go with you."

"Colonel, I can handle it by myself," Jean said convincingly.

"No, Jean, this mission is too important to let you go alone. You need backup in case something happens—God forbid."

Jean knew the colonel well enough to realize that once he decided something, it was law, so she accepted the inevitable. She just hoped her backup crew was made up of seasoned veterans.

"So who's going with me?" she asked.

"It seems that you have a fan club that volunteered. Come in, gentlemen." The colonel directed the men to enter the conference room through a side door.

Sgt. Carlos Sanchez, Corp. Joe Toritino, Corp. Howard Banks, and PFC John Carter had come back into Jean's life. Surprised and pleased, she looked at Colonel Chase. "What's this?" she asked.

"It seems that your fan club was concerned about your backside being protected while you're on this mission," Colonel Chase said with a smile. "And, by the way, Captain Rutgers volunteered first, but I had another assignment for him. Briefing starts in one hour."

Jean took the little time they had to catch up with her support team. "What have you guys been up to since the last time we were together?" she asked.

Sergeant Sanchez replied, "Colonel Chase has kept us busy supporting other agents where we could."

"My guess is that you rangers can do just about anything," Jean declared.

In response, she got a simultaneous, big "hoorah!" from the men.

The newly formed crew entered the conference room a bit early and sat together for a few minutes while waiting for Major Williams to enter. As usual, he appeared on time and prepared for the meeting.

"Good morning, everyone. Let's get started." The major looked at Jean and the rest of the team and said, "In three days, on January 11, you will bail out near Biella, Italy, which is on the southern side of the Alps."

As he talked, he pointed to the location on the wall-mounted map and continued. "Your mission is to help the Partisan unit become combat ready by the time the Allied forces attack, which may occur in April. Additionally, you will help coordinate the Allies' attack with the Partisan unit. Are there any questions?"

Jean raised her hand.

"Go ahead, Jean."

"Sir, are there intelligence reports available?" she asked.

"Yes. And you'll receive that information, along with maps, the Italian Partisan leaders' names, passwords, and countersigns upon your departure. Are there any other questions?"

Sergeant Sanchez asked, "What's their strength, and how many are trained, Major Williams?"

Major Williams thoughtfully answered, "I understand that they are about three hundred strong. We do not know at this time how well they are trained. That will be part of your job, Sergeant." He paused and then continued. "Any other questions? No? Thanks for your attention, and good luck on your assignment!" He then left the conference room.

Jean and her team decided to enjoy some relaxation prior to the mission. The group got together that evening and went out on the town in Paris. They ventured into a number of military hangouts before walking into a civilian nightclub. The nightclub lived up to its reputation for providing great food and drink.

Jean raised her glass and said to her comrades, "Tonight we howl, tomorrow we sober up, and the next day we bail out of a damned aircraft. Down the hatch, gentlemen." Jean then tossed back a shot of tequila. She was enjoying the evening until an airborne lieutenant came over to the table and made a very derogatory remark directed at her. It totally ticked Jean off.

In response, she jumped up and grabbed the lieutenant by his military blouse, "Apologize before I kick the crap out of you, Lieutenant," she said, tightening her hold on him.

He hadn't anticipated this reaction and sobered up a bit when he recognized that Jean was an OSS officer surrounded by Army rangers.

He answered her, saying, "I'm very sorry for what I said."

"Thank you, Lieutenant," Jean said before spinning him around, pointing him toward the exit, and shoving him so hard that he almost fell down.

Finally, Carlos said, "And we're supposed to protect *her* behind?" Everybody laughed and gave three cheers in Jean's honor.

CHAPTER 21

At an airfield outside of Paris, four Army Rangers stood beside a camouflaged DC-3 anxiously waiting for their captain's arrival. "Here she comes," Corporal Banks said.

The jeep Jean was riding in with Major Williams stopped beside the aircraft.

"Here are your orders, intel reports, and maps, Jean," said Major Williams as he handed her a brown envelope.

"Thanks, Major." Jean climbed out the jeep and grabbed her gear. "I'll see you when I get back."

Major Williams reached out and took Jean's hand, wishing good luck to her and the whole team before leaving the area.

Speaking to her team, "Good morning, gentlemen. Are we ready to go?"

In unison, they answered, "Yes, ma'am!"

"Well, let's get this party started, you bad asses! Our chariot awaits us!"

They responded with their signature phrase: "Hoorah!"

After a bumpy takeoff, the flight became routine, and Jean opened the envelope and handed out the maps, a list of Italian Partisans, names, passwords, and countersigns. She kept the intel report to study it and see what they were up against with the Germans. It also gave her something to think about besides her fear of flying. Jean studied the map and located the Germans' positions and identified their strongholds. The German and Italian forces now occupied Milan with General Albert Kesselring's army unit located east of Milan at Brescia, seventy miles away and Verona another sixty miles east. Jean wondered if General Kesselring would reinforce Milan if it started to fall. She realized they needed to be prepared for that possibility. Their flyboys could take care of that problem and also General Friedrick Emelsen's army located about fifty miles east of Verona. Their strength was reported to be about 60 percent, which was to their advantage. Looking further, Jean noticed that General Heinrich von Vietinghoff's army was positioned about seventy-five miles north of Verona. His purpose seemed to be keeping the back door open to Germany.

His army strength was reported to be about 80 percent. Jean hoped that the Allies had strong and effective plans to overpower the Germans. According to the plans, the French Expeditionary Corp would cross into the Acosta area in northern Italy and help take Milan. Then they would push east toward Verona, and at the same time, General Clark, in southern Italy, would push north toward Verona with all seven divisions of his army. The Partisan group located about fifty miles northwest of Verona and also east of Verona would push toward Verona, causing the Germans to be compressed to a small area and easily surrounded. The demand to surrender would be offered, and if the bastards refused, the Allies would bomb the hell out of them. Then they'd see how long it took for them to surrender.

Moving on to the intel reports, Jean discovered that Mario Caruso and Lazzaro Mato were the unit's leaders and that her group's call sign would be Red and the Partisan's call sign would be Red, White, and Blue. Jean felt as if she were forgetting something, but she couldn't imagine what it could be. Suddenly, she remembered Colonel Chase handing her the gold leaves, which would raise her rank to major.

He had said, "You will impress the Partisans much more as a major, although it will not be a permanent promotion."

Jean reached into her pocket and pulled out the gold-leaf pins. After removing her captain's bars, she attached the gold leaves. The four rangers noticed her new rank immediately, but before they could say anything, she interjected. "From here on, there will be a little more respect for majors."

"Yes, ma'am, Major Webb!" Big smiles accompanied their response to her statement.

Shortly thereafter, the crew chief approached Jean and said, "Two P-51 Mustangs serving as escorts will go treetop high to check out the drop zone before we arrive there."

"Roger, Chief," she said sincerely.

Left to her own thoughts, her fear of flying and especially jumping out of an airplane began to rise up. She could feel the tension building up inside.

Pathfinder Joe, who occupied the seat next to her, noticed Jean's discomfort. Joe said, "Captain … I mean, Major, do you mind if I ask you something?"

"Not at all, Joe," she said. "Ask away."

"When we were in France and we captured the Nazi captain, what did you say to him when you aimed your pistol between his legs?"

Jean smiled and answered, "I told the son of a bitch that if he didn't tell me what I wanted to know, I would blow his balls off."

"That's what I thought you might have said," Joe said while trying to suppress his laughter.

The crew chief announced, "Twenty minutes to the drop zone. The Mustangs will be going in shortly."

"Let's get ready to party, boys," Jean said.

Everyone stood up and made their final preparations.

Minutes later, the chief ordered, "Hook up and check your gear!"

Checking their own gear and the gear of the person behind them, they each made themselves ready for the jump. When the crew chief removed the exit door and instructed them to move up, Jean noticed that it was damn cold outside. She let that thought go as her eyes, along with everyone else's, focused on the red light at the exit. When the light turned green, Pathfinder Joe jumped first, followed by Banks, Carter, and Sanchez.

The chief hollered, "Go!"

Jean stepped off the plane and into her next adventure. The group jumped just before dusk, so she could see four parachutes below her. Snow covered the ground like a fluffy white blanket. The others began to land, so she braced herself. She hit the ground a little hard, but doing a little somersault in about six inches of snow spared her from injury.

"No German welcoming committee this time, thank goodness," Jean said to herself.

After burying their parachutes in the snow, the group gathered together.

"Joe, we need to find cover," Jean said.

Joe's sharp eyes spotted a copse of trees and bushes a short distance away, so they scurried over to it.

Then Jean said, "Banks, see if you can make contact with the Partisans on the walkie-talkie."

Corporal Banks immediately began trying to make contact. "This is Red, White, and Blue calling Red, over."

The rest of them kept moving around to hold off the cold.

"I'm glad we wore our long johns. Damn it's cold," Jean said, shivering.

Finally, they heard a response over the radio. "This is Red calling Red, White, and Blue. Over."

Banks repeated. "Roger, Red. Go ahead."

"Proceed south two hundred yards. We'll be waiting. Over."

"Roger Red, Over and out," Banks said, signing off.

As usual, Pathfinder Joe took the lead, and the rest of the group followed about twenty yards behind him. Joe used his heightened senses and innate abilities to safely get them to their meeting place.

CHAPTER 22

Unaffected by the snow, Pathfinder Joe led the group south toward their contacts. Soon, dusk enveloped them, which was followed by the shadowy darkness of moonlight. With his extra-sharp vision, Joe scanned the area for movement. Approximately thirty minutes later, he observed a subtle clue that they were not alone.

"Red, white, and blue!" a voice shouted out from the shadows.

Joe answered, "Red!" Then he flashed his light four short times, and the others returned with two short and two long light flashes.

He muttered, "Right countersign," and then walked toward them with his weapon ready. As he neared their location, one of them stepped forward and identified himself.

"I am Mario Caruso," the portly little Italian said, "and this is Lazzaro Mato," he added, indicating the taller and thinner man behind him.

"I am Corporal Joe Toritino, the Pathfinder," Joe said matter-of-factly, thus concluding the recognition ritual. Joe gave the all clear, and the group joined him to become acquainted with their new friends. Mario informed them that they would have to hike about three hours to reach the first campsite and another four hours the next day to the main camp forty miles west of Milan.

Jean asked, "Mario, what is your unit's strength?"

"We are three hundred strong," he proudly answered.

The group arrived at the main camp ahead of schedule without any incidents. Mario called a general assembly of his troops and introduced the Americans.

"Listen up! These Americans are here to help us run the Nazis out of Italy," he proclaimed. The troops excitedly clapped and shouted their desire to kick the Germans out. Mario added, "These Americans are our guests, and we will treat them as such."

Jean caught his eye and said, "Thanks for the introduction, Mario. Would you let your troops know we will be around checking on their weapons and gathering information regarding how we can help improve your firepower and battle readiness?"

While he interpreted the message, Jean looked out at the troops. No doubt, there were at least three hundred. Jean was pleasantly surprised that some of them were women. That afternoon while in briefing with Mario regarding the conditions at Milan, Jean's team toured the camp to gather the information they needed to fulfill their purpose there. Sgt. Carlos Sanchez overheard a conversation between a big sergeant and his troops in the mess hall area.

The big sergeant said, "No Nazi prisoners will be taken alive. Only Italian soldiers will be taken alive, so long as they decide to come over to our side."

The interpreter with Carlos relayed the conversation to him.

Carlos felt troubled by this inhumane remark and asked, "What's that sergeant's name?"

At the command tent, Jean said, "Mario, we need to know where the tanks, artillery, and Nazi troops are located. Also, have your observers watch for tank or vehicle movement." Then she wishfully added, "Hopefully, they're out of fuel."

"Yes, Major," Mario responded. "Lazzaro! Orientate your men accordingly."

"Right away, sir." Lazaro agreed and left hurriedly to inform his men.

A little later, Carlos approached Jean looking very troubled. "Major, can I have a word?"

"Excuse me, Mario," Jean said politely and led Carlos outside of the tent. "What is it, Carlos?"

Carlos repeated what he had heard the Italian sergeant say about how the prisoners would be treated. Jean felt her blood pressure begin to skyrocket. *Such cruelty must not be allowed!* she thought to herself.

"Carlos, I want to tell Mario what you just told me," she said while entering the tent again with Carlos. "Mario, we need to talk," she said, trying not to sound as angry as she felt.

"You seem upset," Mario noted.

"Damn right I am! I just heard that one of your sergeants has instructed his troops to kill Nazi prisoners. That's not acceptable, Mario!"

Mario responded, "I agree, Major. This sergeant, was he a big man?"

"Yes," Carlos answered. "I believe he's called Sergeant Basso."

Now clearly seeing the situation, Mario said. "Yes, Vito Basso. He has been warned for not following orders before."

Wanting to know how big a problem they were facing, Jean asked, "How many of your people have killed prisoners?"

"Major, we fight as a hit-and-run unit and have not taken prisoners before," he said defensively.

"Mario, call a general assembly. I have an announcement to make," she said boldly.

Mario left the tent to do as she had asked. Carlos looked at Jean quizzically.

"What do you have in mind, Major?"

Jean looked him straight in the eyes and said, "Call me Jean, Carlos, and just watch my back."

"You got it, Jean."

At the general assembly, she said in Italian, "The upcoming battle will be fought under the Geneva Convention. Prisoners will be treated accordingly. There will be no killing of prisoners. I repeat—no killing of prisoners!"

As Jean expected, the big Italian sergeant stepped forward, clutching his weapon and said defiantly, "Nobody is going to tell me not to kill Nazi prisoners."

Chapter 23

Sergeant Basso blatantly refused Jean's direct order and posed a threat to her military command. In mere seconds, Sergeant Sanchez appeared on Basso's left side and Pathfinder Joe on his right, with their Thompson submachine guns pointed at him.

Jean spoke to him in Italian. "Drop your weapon or die, Vito."

Realizing his situation, Basso dropped his weapon. Joe patted him down and removed his knife.

Jean walked around the big Italian with her back to him and said in Italian, "If I see or hear of anyone killing a prisoner, I'll make sure they meet the same fate!" She turned around and faced Vito. "You big dumb ass. Try to kill me."

Jean's taunting enraged Vito even more. He charged at her, and she braced herself for his attack. Just before he reached her, Jean moved swiftly toward him and used the clumsy oaf's weight against him. He hit the ground hard. As he struggled to stand up, Jean quickly walked up to him and buried her knuckles in his throat, shoving his Adam's apple temporarily to the back of his throat. He started choking and gasping for air. Jean grabbed one of his arms, twisted it behind his back, and knocked him off his feet. He collapsed heavily to the ground.

Jean straddled him, sitting on his chest, and asked, "Do you want to live Vito?" She paused for effect. "Or should I push your big Italian nose bone into your brain?"

Jean then placed the palm of her hand on his nose to let him know that she would follow through if necessary. Sweating profusely, Vito shook his head up and down to indicate that he wanted to live.

"Good. Maybe you're not as dumb as I thought," she said to him.

Using both of her hands, Jean hit him on both sides of his throat, returning his Adam's apple to its correct position. Vito started breathing normally again. Jean got up and offered Vito her hand. Vito's attitude appeared to be much improved.

He said in Italian, "I'm sorry, Major."

The troops clapped and cheered in recognition of the positive resolution of a dangerous situation.

A week later, Jean received a map that indicated the most current info on the positions of the enemy's tanks, artillery, and troops. She received a list of weapons, ammo, and supplies required by the Italian Partisans in order to function fully for the big push. She planned for weapons and combat training of the Partisans once the weapons arrived.

"Banks, contact HQ in Paris and order a light pickup ASAP," she directed.

The corporal went immediately to the wireless and returned a few minutes later.

"Major, the pickup will be at ten hundred hours at these map coordinates," he said, handing Jean the paper he had written the information upon.

"Thanks, Corporal," she said while checking the location against the map. "Banks, inform Sergeant Sanchez to organize a patrol and to be ready to leave at 0500 hours."

"Yes, ma'am. Right away," Banks said and went out to find Sergeant Sanchez.

The next morning, Jean joined Sergeant Sanchez, PFC Carter, and four Italians. One of the Italians was Sergeant Basso.

Jean asked Carlos, "How did he get on this detail?"

"He volunteered, Jean," Carlos answered.

One of the Italians who spoke English heard their comments and clarified the situation. "Vito wanted to make sure you would be safe, Major."

"It's nice to know so many men are watching my ass," she said.

Carlos, Carter, and the English-speaking Italian were grinning. After a couple of hours of walking to the rendezvous site, Jean spoke to Carlos, who was near her.

"Where's home, Carlos?"

He answered, "Santa Fe, New Mexico."

"I've heard it's a nice place to visit."

"Yes, ma'am. It's a great place to live too. Lots of history," Carlos said. "I miss my family and friends." Jean could hear the longing in his voice.

"I think that I would like to visit there someday," she said.

The two walked quietly for a few minutes until Jean decided to ask a more personal question. "If it's not too personal, I am curious to know what nationality you are."

Carlos looked over at her and answered. "It's not too personal. I'm part Apache, Mexican, and a little Aztec, and proud of it."

"Wow! Sounds dangerous, Carlos," she said.

The two laughed as quietly as they could. "Well, you're pretty dangerous yourself, Jean, and you're part what?"

"Irish and a little Cherokee and good ole US of A," she told him.

The remainder of the journey required silence. The group reached the makeshift landing strip at 0930 hours.

"Let's find some cover and wait," Jean directed.

As luck would have it, one of the Italian scouts spotted a German patrol heading their way.

Sergeant Basso suggested, "I have a plan to lead them away from here." He briefly shared his strategy.

"Excellent idea, Sergeant. Just be careful. Make sure I'll see you back at camp. Okay?"

Jean received a salute and a smile from the big Italian, which she returned willingly.

The aircraft missed the appointed time o f 10 hundred hours. "We'll give him another twenty minutes," Jean noted.

Those twenty minutes seemed to take forever. Carlos and Jean kept checking the sky with their field glasses.

"I think I hear something," Carlos said.

"I do too," Jean said. "It sounds like a small aircraft engine."

Flying low, an aircraft appeared out of a cloud. The US Army L-5 observation plane circled and landed on the temporary airstrip. When Jean ran up to the pilot and handed him the package, he apologized.

"Sorry I'm late," he said. "Rough wind flying over these mountains, you know."

Jean stepped back, and he took off again and returned to flying low back to headquarters. A few days later, HQ notified her as to when and where the drops would be made and when the main attack would be.

After Banks decoded the message, he said, "It will take place on April 9."

The next two months kept everyone busy. A number of drops brought machine guns, rifles, mortars, grenades, bazookas, medical supplies, food, and two jeeps to be used by the Partisan army. Jean and her team spent many hours training the three hundred Partisans for combat readiness. Also during this time, Jean had Mario conduct raids on the German installations, so the Germans would believe that they were fighting a small enemy.

Everyone rejoiced when the news came about what happened at Bastogne and the Battle of the Bulge counterattack. Everyone cheered for the 101st Airborne Division and General McAuliffe who said, "Nuts," to the Germans' request to surrender.

Chapter 24

On April 7, 1945, Jean received a message from OSS headquarters in London. After the message was decoded, it read:

> Major Webb. Gen. Mark Clark's staff agree with your evaluation of the situation in northern Italy and what could happen during the April 9 attack. Your contact will be General Clark's chief of staff, General Benjamin. The French Expeditionary Corp contact will be Colonel Leferve, operations officer. Your code name will be Applejack, and your countersign will be Lioness. Good luck, Applejack.

Jean called a briefing with Mario's observers and her team. Based on previous recon, they decided that there were three ideal attack positions on the west side leading to the center of Milan.

"Sergeant Sanchez will be assigned to the north attack group. I'll be with the center attack group along with Corporal Banks," Jean revealed. "Pathfinder Joe and PFC Carter will be with the south attack group. The French Expeditionary Corp under the command of the fifth army will arrive tomorrow. Once they've been briefed, we'll call for the air strikes."

After the briefing, Mario asked, "Can I talk to you in private, Major?"

"Certainly, Mario," Jean answered. "What's on your mind?"

"It's Sergeant Basso. He insists on being assigned to your attack group," he said with obvious frustration. "When I asked him why, he said something about protecting your beautiful—"

"Yeah, I know … my ass," Jean interrupted. Mario looked a little shocked, so she added, "I hear that a lot. Tell Basso he's welcome to be on my team."

The next day, April 8, Colonel Rene Leferve arrived and found Jean. He said, "Major, I'm looking for Applejack."

"Yes, Colonel Leferve. I'm the Lioness, Major Jean Webb. Let me give you a cup of joe and bring you up to date."

Now, two days later, with the French forces in place, the first wave of air strikes took place with Liberator bombers by the 779th and 459th squadrons with an escort of Lightning P-38 fighters. P-51 Mustangs carried out the second wave of destruction by coming in at treetop level and striking their targets. The pilots chose their targets the second time around. During the air attacks, the French forces were preparing their field artillery batteries for action and were dividing their tanks into three groups. In the midst of the entire hubbub, Mario caught up with Jean with important info.

"Major, our observers will report on what damages the Germans have encountered from the air strikes."

"Terrific, Mario. We'll call a briefing at 1800 hours tomorrow with everybody's staff."

The next day at 1700 hours, Mario's observers arrived, and Jean noticed one of them had a bandage on his leg.

Mario asked, "How bad is it?"

"It's just a surface wound, Mario," the wounded man assured him.

After hearing a brief report from his men, Mario told Jean, "I believe we are ready, Major."

She nodded a silent yes and then said in Italian, "Mario, I'm proud of your men." Next, she spoke directly to the brave men. "Thanks, men, for a job well done."

They responded by saluting her. In return, Jean stood at attention and gave them a smart salute back.

The first observer, Deon, reported, "Most of the Tiger tanks have been destroyed or damaged. Only a dozen remain operational, and they are being used to protect their western defenses."

The French tank commander asked, "Is it possible for you to penetrate their defenses and use bazookas to blow off their tank treads?"

Deon answered, "Yes, sir. We could try. If we are successful, they would be sitting ducks for your Cobra King tanks."

Pathfinder Joe said, "Those Cobra King tanks impress me. I look forward to sabotaging some German tin cans, so I'll take that walk in the park. Maybe I will have a chance to see the inside of one of those cobra tanks later on."

The second observer, Maurice, reported that the Germans' field artillery had been severely damaged. He added, "About 90 percent of their artillery is out of action with the majority of their operational placements on the east side."

Pleased with that information, Jean said, "That's very good news. Next, we have a report regarding the German troop activity."

Renaud, who had compiled the troop information, stepped to the front and began his report. "The German troops have been greatly weakened by the air strikes on the western front. I saw troops that had been in the eastern front moving west."

Mario thanked his men for their contribution, and several individuals came up to thank them and shake hands. Because the attention was on the observers, Jean thought it would be the perfect time to meet with Mario and Colonel Leferve. She grabbed Mario's elbow and approached Colonel Leferve.

"Colonel, we'd like to share with you an alternative plan," she said.

"I'm listening, Major Webb," he responded.

CHAPTER 25

Jean shared the details of their plan with Colonel Leferve, who listened very attentively.

"If General Kesselring is foolish enough to send troops to Milan from Brescia, we'll know about it because Mario maintains close contact with the Partisans north of Brescia. Once the German troops begin to move, we'll call for an air strike," Jean said confidently. "Meanwhile, we need to request an airborne unit to join the Partisans northeast of Milan and attack the eastern German defenses, which are much weaker."

Colonel Leferve thoughtfully stroked his chin and said, "I like it. I'll inform my command right away, Major."

Mario walked with Jean back to the tents. "Major Webb, it has been an honor working with you," he said.

"And with you, Mario," she responded sincerely. "You're a good man. Good luck tomorrow."

"You too, Major," he said as he headed for his tent.

The next morning, April 11, Jean positioned her group behind a Cobra King tank for a 0600 hour jump-off. Sergeant Basso and Corporal Banks covered her rear as promised. Jean checked her watch and realized that only five minutes remained. Suddenly, the French artillery opened up on all three designated routes, and the tanks moved out with cannons and machine guns blazing. Using the tank for cover, Jean's group moved forward, quickly reaching a company of French Raiders. They soon realized that they had walked right into an active battle with deadly bullets flying all over the place. Jean jumped when a bullet ricocheted off the tank's metal skin inches from her. She felt just a little out of her element, as she had never experienced the battle up close before.

Jean found herself thinking, *Somebody could get killed around here.*

From her vantage point, Jean could observe the French Raiders routing out the hidden Nazis. Once they discovered a Nazi bunker, they used tanks, bazookas, and grenades prior to charging the Nazi positions. Most of the Nazis threw down their weapons and raised their hands in surrender. It appeared that they'd had enough of Hitler's war. By nightfall, Jean's group had advanced to a position about two miles from the town plaza.

A familiar voice out of the darkness startled Jean momentarily. "I see that you managed to dodge all the bullets so far," Pathfinder Joe said in greeting.

"I'm glad to see that you didn't get your ass shot off either," she said with a smile.

"We knocked out most of their Tiger tanks along the German front. Many of the German soldiers have pulled back," Joe reported. "Tomorrow should be easier going."

"God, I hope you're right," Jean said sadly. "We lost some good men and women today."

Sensing her mood, Joe attempted to distract her. "When did you last eat?" Joe didn't wait for an answer. "Let's find some chow. You'll feel much better with a little food in you," he insisted.

Sergeant Basso, who was standing nearby, recognized the word *chow* and motioned for the others to follow him. He led them to an outdoor cooking and dining area. Appetizing aromas permeated the air.

"Damn! That smells awfully good," Jean said as she turned to Vito and patted him on the shoulder in gratitude.

Vito Basso bestowed upon Jean a rare gift—a smile. When they returned to the command center, Corporal Banks delivered a message from the Partisans. Once Mario joined them, Banks read the message.

"It appears that the Germans intend to leave for Milan as soon as this evening," Banks reported. "The airborne unit has joined up with us, and we plan to march on Milan."

"I am concerned that the Partisans could get caught between the German forces," Mario said thoughtfully.

"You're right, Mario," Jean agreed. She paused to think for a minute before continuing. "Banks, get on the radio, and get me an L-5 observation aircraft here at dawn. Let command know I'll want some directed air strikes ready for bombing the area between Breisca and Milan. Also, have them send along some P-51 Mustangs to strafe the area before the bombing run."

Jean did the math and realized that a forced march could put them halfway to Milan in twelve hours. The timing would be critical. The next morning, an L-5 landed, and Jean hurriedly climbed into the backseat and put on the headset.

"Head north of the woods between Brescia and Milan," she instructed the pilot. Thirty minutes later, she saw the combined forces heading for the Germans' eastern defenses at Milan.

Using her walkie-talkie, Jean called them. "This is Lioness calling attack force three from watchdog up above. Over."

"Roger, Lioness. We read you loud and clear. Over."

"Hold your position. The woods on the left are full of Germans. An air strike has been ordered with strafing from P-51 Mustangs preceding the bombers. Once the strike concludes, return to orders."

It was crucial that they understood the message, so Jean repeated the instructions in English and Italian.

"Wilco." That small word assured Jean that her message was understood. She breathed a quick sigh of relief and turned her attention to the part she would play in this battle.

Jean instructed the pilot. "We'll start from Brescia and head west so the sun will be to our advantage. We can see them, but when they look back into the sun, they won't be able to see us coming."

"Excellent strategy, Major." The pilot agreed.

The pilot stayed north of the woods, and before he reached Brescia, he turned south, dropped down to the treetops, and then turned west. With her field glasses, Jean could see the Germans moving toward Milan without drawing any fire from their forces.

"I don't think the Germans want to advertise their presence in the woods, Captain," Jean noted. "Let's call in an air strike for both sides of the road and chase them out of the forest, starting from the smoke and going east to Brescia."

After Jean dropped the smoke canister, they headed north of the woods, climbed to a safe altitude, and circled the air space until the air strike ended. The Mustangs arrived with extreme ferocity. Each of them fired all five of their rockets and used their six .50-caliber machine guns, which effectively pinned down the Germans. After two passes, they were done. The Liberators came in at about ten thousand feet and dropped their arsenals on both sides of the road. Thirty minutes later, the woods were ablaze. Using her field glasses, Jean saw fewer Germans retreating back to Brescia. Satisfied by what they had accomplished in this sector, Jean wanted to take a look elsewhere.

"Captain, let's take a look at the German defenses east of Milan."

The pilot took the plane up to a higher altitude and headed west. As they approached the east side of Milan, Jean began studying the

German installations with her field glasses. Peculiar black puffs of smoke started appearing.

The pilot yelled, "Antiaircraft guns!"

He instinctively took the plane into a turning dive. On the way down, one of the antiaircraft shells exploded just under the right wing. One-third of the wing had disappeared causing the L-5 to go into a downward spiral.

The pilot hollered, "I've been hit!"

Jean knew that bailing out wasn't an option, so she braced herself for the inevitable crash. "Wouldn't you know this would happen just as I have almost gotten over my fear of flying?" she muttered.

Then the pilot said the words no one ever wants to hear. "Hang on real tight. We're going to crash."

CHAPTER 26

This is it! Jean had good reason to be afraid of flying after all. *If only—* Jean's thoughts were abruptly interrupted by the pilot hollering at her.

"Get on the controls with me, Major!"

The L-5 had dual flight controls, and Jean recognized that they were in a clockwise spiral. The pilot acted appropriately by kicking in the left rubber hard and moved the stick to the left. His wounds made this task extremely difficult, but with Jean's help, her stick went all the way to the left, and the aircraft stopped spiraling. The pilot started pulling back on the stick, so Jean did too.

Out of fear, Jean said out loud, "Damn! The ground is coming up awfully fast!"

The aircraft began to level off, but it was too late. The pilot made a last-ditch effort to land the plane, but the engine stalled, and they came down hard on the nose. Jean came to a few minutes later. She felt grateful to be alive and wanted to thank the pilot for saving her life. However, she felt intense pain in her leg. The pilot had been pitched forward and had suffered a number of severe injuries. When Jean checked for vital signs, she discovered that he had died upon impact. Jean took a moment to thank God for this man whose expertise had let her live.

Jean peeked out of the airplane to see if the crash had caught any attention. Germans were firing at her from about two hundred yards away, and bullets were hitting all around her position. She spotted a shallow trench about twenty yards away but doubted she could reach it. While she considered her chances, the aircraft started to flame up. It was time to go. Just as she got out of the plane, a tank shell exploded very close.

"Here goes nothing," she said.

Jean hobbled about ten yards, keeping the aircraft between her and the Germans. The ditch appeared to be another fifteen yards away with a few patches of tall grass. She was just about to make a mad dash for the ditch when gunfire erupted from the woods. To her surprise, two airborne soldiers came straight to her, grabbed her arms, and helped her to the ditch. As luck would have it, Jean took a hit to the right thigh just as they reached the ditch.

"Oh! Damn, that hurts like hell!" she hissed.

Jean had a number of stronger expletives ready to express, but she never got the chance to say them. They were forced to take cover due to the plane exploding. The shallow trench was deep enough to protect the group from small arms fire but not from German tanks. As Jean evaluated the situation, she didn't like their chances of surviving.

The corporal hollered, "Incoming!"

Kaboom!

The sergeant shielded Jean from the explosion and flying debris.

"Damn, that was close," the corporal added.

The sergeant began the task of tending to Jean's bullet wound. He used the morphine needle in the first-aid pack, cleaned and dressed it with bandages.

"We may need to move if they get any closer, Sarge," the corporal suggested.

"I hear you, Corporal," the sergeant said and then commented to Jean, "Ma'am, twelve inches higher, and you would have been shot in the—"

"Ass. Yeah, I know," she said, finishing his sentence.

"That would have been a damn shame, ma'am, 'cause it's a good-looking ass."

Jean didn't feel up to further discussion, so she gave him a little smile and hoped the topic wouldn't come up again. A few minutes later, another shell landed even closer, causing a deafening sound accompanied by flying debris raining down on them.

The alarmed corporal said, "I think they have our range, Sarge. It's time to go."

With that, the three of them prepared to make a mad dash for the woods. A familiar sound of a P-51 Mustang tank killer offered the trio a much better option. The tank killer fired a rocket at the Tiger tank that had been firing at them.

The corporal narrated the attack, "Kaboom! That was a thing of beauty!"

More P-51 Mustangs appeared, taking aim on the German defenses and knocking out their remaining tanks and artillery. The corporal continued his commentary while using his field glasses until a jeep with a stretcher pulled up next to the ditch. The two airborne soldiers helped Jean onto the stretcher and then climbed into the jeep themselves. Although she had received appropriate care on the battlefield, Jean needed more intensive medical care and a break from being a damn target.

CHAPTER 27

"Thanks, guys, for saving my ass," Jean said as a smiling sergeant and corporal waved good-bye.

Then someone else appeared. "Hi, Major. I'm the corpsman. I'm going to take a look at your wound." The corpsman carefully unwrapped the bandages and took a good look. "Good. The bullet passed through. I'll rebandage your wound after I apply some medicine to help prevent any infection." A little later, the corpsman said, "Now let's take a look at your other leg."

After moving it around, Jean groaned in pain. "Oh! Damn, that hurts."

The corpsman finally said, "It looks like a badly sprained ankle, a severely bruised kneecap, and probably some pulled leg muscles and ligaments. You're going to be bedridden for a while, Major."

"Thanks for the good news, Corporal. I need to speak to your commanding officer right away. I'm an OSS officer, the Lioness."

"Yes, Major. Right away."

A short time later, a major walked in and said, "I'm Major Howard. Are you the Lioness?"

"Yes, I am. My code name is Applejack, and I'm Major Webb."

Major Howard said, "I'm the one you talked to earlier. Thanks for the warning. I'm glad you survived the crash and my men got to you in time. Now, what do you need, Major?"

Jean said, "Thanks for saving my behind, Major, and I need your radioman."

Major Howard turned and said, "Front and center, Corporal James … Here's your radio, and if you don't need me anymore, I've got a battle to win." He saluted as he left.

Jean instructed Corporal James to contact a Corporal Burns. "Call name is Applejack Burns, and calling is the Lioness."

Once Burns was on the radio, Jean was handed the mike. "What's been happening? Over."

"We are moving forward. Another air strike is on its way, and Colonel Leferve thinks one more air strike and the Germans just might start surrendering tonight or tomorrow. Over."

"That's great, Burns. Make sure Leferve notifies General Benjamin, chief of staff at General Clark's headquarters, about Milan."

"Roger, Major, and are you all right? We heard your plane went down."

"Yes, I'm all right, Corporal. Over and out. Thanks, Corporal James."

He said, "Yes, ma'am."

Later, Jean got the word that a group of Cobra King tanks had broken through the German lines and joined up with the airborne/Partisans unit and had the Germans surrounded by nightfall. She also heard the Germans were already surrendering as well.

"Thank God. No more killing."

The next morning, April 13, the word was out that President Roosevelt had died the day before, and Jean hoped he had heard what had happened in northern Italy and knew the war in Europe was about over. "Thanks, FDR," she whispered.

A few days later, at an established MASH unit in Milan, Jean was taking a nap, and when she woke up, there were guests waiting.

"Hello, Major Sleeping Beauty," said Pathfinder Joe.

Sergeant Sanchez said, "It's good to see you, Jean. You're looking rested and fit." And the rest of the fan club agreed.

Looking around, Jean commented, "It's good to see all of you in one piece."

Then Joe asked a peculiar question. "Where did you get hit?" Everyone leaned in closer to hear her answer.

Jean looked at all of them and answered with a smile. "Not my ass."

Joe responded, along with the others, "Thank goodness." They all smiled in return.

About that time, Colonel Leferve showed up, "At ease, men. I see, Major Webb, your fan club is here. Good afternoon, gentlemen."

"Yes, sir, Colonel," said Sergeant Sanchez as he stood up. "Have a seat, Colonel."

"Thanks, Sergeant Sanchez."

Jean asked, "How are we doing, Colonel?"

"Well, we'll have Brescia surrounded by next week. The Fifth Army should be here, and then it's a matter of time before the remaining Germans surrender."

Following his announcement, there were a lot of hoorahs and clapping.

"I also have some other good news," he added. "Major, your team will be awarded a special braid and the Soldiers Medal for heroism for your successful mission on making the Partisans an effective fighting force." Then he looked over at Joe and said, "Corporal Toritino, you're being awarded the Bronze Star for your little walk in the park while knocking out six Tiger tanks and killing two dozen Germans behind enemy lines." He then looked back Jean. "Major Webb, for your action in taking an initiative that helped save many lives and for your heroic action, you're being awarded the Army's Distinguished Service Cross, DSC, and one will also be awarded to your pilot, Captain Thomas Hornsby, posthumously."

There were more hoorahs. The colonel got up and said, "I salute you all." After his salute and before leaving, he added, "I'll see you later, Major."

CHAPTER 28

Once Jean received her crutches, she was up, moving around, and learning to use them when she received word that Colonel Leferve wanted to see her when she was mobile. So, she had Sergeant Sanchez acquire a jeep and drive her to the French Expeditionary Corp headquarters.

"Come in and have a seat, Major Webb," Colonel Leferve said.

"Thank you, Colonel."

"Major, may I call you Jean?"

"Yes, Colonel. I prefer Jean."

"Jean, I've some more news for you. Gen. Mark Clark will be here on May 2, four days from now, to make some presentations and possibly start some talks with General Kesselring about a German surrender of their remaining forces in Italy."

Jean commented, "That's great news, Colonel."

Colonel Leferve continued. "Apparently, the general has heard about you and would like to meet you." Colonel Leferve congratulated her again for receiving the DSC and said, "It's been a pleasure and an honor to have served with you, Jean."

"Thanks, Colonel. The same goes for me, sir." Jean firmly shook his hand before she turned to leave.

"Oh," the colonel noted, "they found Mussolini and his mistress, and they'll be here tomorrow at the town square under arrest."

Jean acknowledged the info and waved good-bye.

Sergeant Sanchez was waiting, and Jean said, "Let's go, Carlos."

Back at the MASH unit, Corporal Burns was waiting. "We got orders, Major," he said as he handed Jean a copy.

She first read it to herself and then aloud so everyone could hear.

> To Applejack Team, Congratulations, Jean. After your presentation on May 2, you and your team will fly out for London and report to me upon your arrival. Colonel Chase.

Jean looked at her team, who were all smiling, and said, "I guess we better enjoy Milan while we still can." That got a little chuckle from her fan club.

Then PFC Carter spoke up, "Hey, I heard Mussolini has been captured and will be here tomorrow at the town square."

Jean responded, "Yeah, I heard the same thing earlier today."

The next day, April 29, Jean and her team headed for the town square. As they drove through the bombed-out city, which had very few buildings left standing, Jean commented, "It's a shame, because this was such a beautiful village. I'll bet it was a nice place to live too."

When they arrived at the square, the team got the shock of their lives. Even the hardened combat vets couldn't believe what they were looking at—five dead humans were hanging by their feet from a beam.

In shock, Jean said, "It looks like Mussolini and his mistress and three other fascists. It also looks like they've been badly chopped up … I've seen enough. Let's get the hell out of here."

On May 2, Gen. Mark Clark presented twelve medals. As he presented each medal, he said, "Congratulations on a job well done," and then added, "Thanks."

After the ceremony, Jean and her team spent thirty minutes visiting with the general. Just as he was about to leave, General Clark said, "Jean, if you're ever looking for a job, you have one on my staff as an intelligence officer."

"Thanks, General Clark, but I believe I'll pass for now," Jean responded.

"No, Jean, thank you." And yet another handshake took place.

The next morning everyone piled into a DC-3 headed for London.

Six hours later, Jean and her crew checked in with Colonel Chase. "Reporting as ordered, sir," she said.

After returning a salute, Colonel Chase got up and shook everybody's hand, congratulating each of them.

After visiting a little while longer, Colonel Chase said, "Gentlemen, please report to Major Williams for your next assignment. You might want to say good-bye to Jean, as you'll be flying out later tonight."

Jean managed to stand up without her crutches and said, "Each of you has permission to hug an officer." All four men promptly stood up and got in line. She told them, "Take care of yourselves and don't forget to duck."

Colonel Chase watched with admiration as a smile crept across his face.

When Jean and the colonel were finally alone, he said, "Jean, please report tomorrow morning with Major Blakely, who's back on active duty. Now, get out of here and get some rest."

"Yes, sir, Colonel."

That night, Jean and Jake celebrated her safe return by having dinner and drinks and enjoying each other's company.

Jake finally got around to asking a curious question, "So, where did you get hit?"

She told him, "Well, only twelve inches higher, and we might have had matching scars."

Because Jean was still using crutches, dancing was out of the question. Just drinking and conversation was all she could enjoy, and still no tequila, her favorite poison.

The following morning, "Reporting as ordered, sir," said Major Blakely as Jean hobbled in behind him.

The colonel said, "Have a seat, Majors."

Jean did a double take and looked at a smiling colonel.

"Yes, your promotion came through, Major Webb."

Colonel Chase and Jake shook Jean's hand and both said, "Congratulations."

"You earned it, Jean," Colonel Chase added.

"Thanks, Colonel." Jean had to look away a little, because she was about to cry but didn't.

When everybody was seated, Colonel Chase informed the majors, "You both are going stateside and will be assigned to a new organization called Interim Research and Intelligence Service, IRIS, at US Army Headquarters in DC. It's one of the new groups OSS is being split into, as the OSS is being deactivated next month. It's been a pleasure serving with both of you. Good luck." When he was done speaking, Colonel Chase shook each of their hands instead of saluting. He even got a hug.

A month later in Southampton, England, the two majors boarded a ship leaving for the States. Jean was finally walking normally and was looking forward to getting home.

PART TWO

CENTRAL INTELLIGENCE GROUP

CHAPTER 29

In the early morning hours of June 18, 1945, the USS *Alexander*, carrying three thousand soldiers, entered New York Harbor. The harbor was full of tugboats and other types of vessels, which were making all kinds of noise to celebrate the troops' homecoming. An excited Maj. Jean Webb, dressed in officer's Ike jacket, skirt, and tie, was taking two steps at a time up the narrow stairs to the forward castle deck. She didn't want to miss seeing a longing sight. When she stepped through a water-tight hatch onto the deck, she heard all kinds of horns, whistles, and sirens celebrating. She turned left, facing the ship's bow, and hurried forward. There she saw Maj. Jake Blakely standing at the port gunwale, looking up at Lady Liberty.

Jean rushed to his side, wrapped her arms around his waist, and called out over all the noise. "It's a great morning, Jake."

"Yes, it is," Jake said. "Welcome home, Jean." He put his hand on her shoulder and looked back at a passing sight. "She's a beautiful sight, isn't she? The Statue of Liberty."

"That she is, and welcome home, GI," Jean said, putting her hand on his as he held onto the handrail. "Damn! It's good to be home again. You, good-ole US of A, you." With that, Jean kissed her wonderful man.

Once the ship was moored in place at the dock and the gangplank was in position for the passengers' departure, the hollering and shouting continued as warriors hurried down the gangplank to plant their feet

119

on home ground once again. Some of the fortunate warriors had family and friends there to welcome them home.

Once Jean and Jake cleared the crowded docks, they headed to downtown Big Apple and found Broadway and Times Square. As they moved through the streets, they had to dodge people, mostly GIs and women, who were busy celebrating. The couple finally found the nice hotel they had talked about while still onboard. Their room was on the fifth floor, and they could hear the celebrating in the streets below. They ordered room service, turned on the radio, and found some soft music before hitting the couch for some serious necking.

"I've waited ten days for this," Jake said. He continued kissing Jean all over her face and neck and back to her luscious lips again.

Finally, room service showed up. Jake accepted the order while Jean was in the bathroom taking off the rest of her clothes. Then Jake stripped down to nothing, and they hit the couch again. This time, there was some serious drinking going on and a little necking at the same time. Later, it was time to soak in the tub, which was a deep, claw-foot type.

"It's your turn to wash by back, darling," Jake noted.

"Okay. Quit staring at the girls and turn around ... Down, boy," Jean joked, looking down at his manhood.

"What do you expect? It's been ten days on the high seas with three thousand GIs."

Once out of the tub, they both dried off in a hurry. Then a horny male chased a gorgeous female to the bed, hollering, "I'm on top!"

"If you insist, handsome," Jean said.

The two horny warriors didn't even bother to remove the bed covers. Jean wrapped her arms around her wonderful lover, and the adult games began. Later, after resting up, cleaning up, and putting on pajamas and a robe, it was time for more room service. The couple was enjoying their big, juicy steaks with all the trimmings and champagne to celebrate surviving the war and being back home again.

"Oh, Jake, this is wonderful."

"The sex or the food?" Jake asked.

"Both, and I'll have some more champagne, you big wonderful hunk of man," she answered, smiling.

When the champagne was gone, it was bedtime, and Jake got to say good night to the girls—and Jean, of course. The next morning Jean got a wake-up call when she felt lips kissing one breast and a hand cupping the other one.

She reached down and felt Jake's manhood. "Still trying to get caught up, I see," said a thankful female as she guided it toward her entrance. When she felt it entering her, she began moaning with pleasure.

Later, two exhausted lovers managed to make it to a hot bath. When they were finished bathing, it was time to order room service. This time, it was a champagne breakfast with steak and eggs and delicious pancakes. With their bellies full and their bodies dressed, it was time to see the New York sights. Jean dragged Jake all over downtown, still dodging people while seeing the sights. When they could get in, they took in several movies and Broadway shows and dined at some of the finest restaurants. After spending six busy days and nights in the city, they agreed to spend their last night having a nice quiet evening in their room, complete with room service, to talk about what lay ahead for them and what the next day may bring.

Jean asked, "Jake, what did the colonel say to you about the IRIS while onboard?"

"He knew all about it," Jake answered. "He told me that the president was responsible for breaking up the OSS. He also said the president and General Donovan already got into it over the disbanding.

Then he said the OSS operations are being transferred into a state department agency called Central Intelligence Group, or CIG for short. He commented that's most likely where we're headed, being ex-OSS operatives."

"That doesn't sound too bad," Jean commented. "Maybe we'll still get to work as spies."

"Oh no! I thought we were getting married and going to Texas so we could raise kids and cattle," Jake said, sounding serious.

"Oh no! I'm not ready for that. No way, buster!" Jean quickly said.

"Oh shucks, darling ... I just thought I'd test the waters," Jake replied with a big smile.

Then he had to duck because the pillows started coming his way.

CHAPTER 30

The next day, the two ex-OSS spies flew to Washington, DC, and reported in. They were quickly reminded about an old army saying: hurry up and wait.

Two hours later a man approached them and stated, "I'm Chester Thurston, your supervisor. Please follow me."

Following her new boss, Jean was thinking her tall supervisor might have a British background, detecting a little English heritage in his speech. He looked like a typical narrow-faced Englishman, with a prominent English nose. She hoped he wasn't hardheaded like some Englishmen could be. Walking through the office area, Jean noticed it seem like helter-skelter; some people were busy, and some were not.

Chester entered the small conference room first. "Please come in and have a seat, Majors. We have a few things to discuss." Chester closed the door before walking over and sitting down where two files were already on the table in front of him. Putting his hand on them, he addressed Jean and Jake. "I've already reviewed your files, and they are quite impressive, especially yours, Jean."

"Thank you, sir," Jean responded.

"I have different jobs for each of you ... Jake, we are reestablishing the embassy in Rome, and with your ability to speak Italian I'm assigning you to be stationed there. We need to carefully watch the new Italian government. We have some indications that the

Communist Party wants Italy in its backyard, along with the other countries they already have acquired."

"Sounds good, Mr. Thurston," Jake replied.

"It's Chester, Jake."

Next, he looked at Jean. "Miss Webb, I need an assistant supervisor to help me run this operation. With all the new changes, I need someone with your experiences as an OSS operative, and your education in administration would help whip this organization into shape. You would be a great help to me in accomplishing that."

Jean thought, *You sure do need somebody, but it's not me.* Sounding a little disappointed, she said, "I was hoping for a field assignment, sir."

"That doesn't surprise me about you, Jean. However, the need is for you to stay until I can find someone to replace you, but that doesn't mean I still won't have to send you on a field assignment from time to time."

Chester gave them each a firm stare before saying, "Are we good, Majors?"

Jake looked over at Jean and said, "Yes, sir."

Jean hesitated, remembering what she'd seen earlier, before saying, "I guess you got yourself an assistant supervisor, Mr. Thurston."

Chester immediately stood and said, "Welcome aboard." He then smiled and shook both their hands.

CHAPTER 31

A week later, Jean got to say good-bye to Jake before he left for Italy, which was a hell of a night. Jean knew he wasn't going to have any trouble sleeping on the plane. And besides, she didn't want him looking at all those good-looking Italian women right away.

Jean had jumped into her new position with both feet and without a parachute. After a month of pulling long hours, she was beginning to wonder where the life preserver was. Working with all kinds of different walks of life wasn't always that easy. Chester proved to be very productive, and together, they eventually managed to have an organized operation.

Jean and Chester had modified some of the operating procedures, made a list of required qualifications for future experienced recruits, and specified maximum requirements that would require intense training for raw recruits. Jean knew that would make her a part-time instructor, especially in judo, where she would get to have fun kicking some male asses.

Being busy made the time fly by, which Jean had experienced during the war when Jake left for England and special training. It had been four months since Jake had left, and Chester let Jean know that he was starting to see the light at the end of the tunnel. He then thanked her for her help. There was some excitement in August when the Japanese surrendered, ending the war in the Pacific. One day in mid-October Chester even bought lunch and had it brought in. Well, it was better than nothing. After lunch, there was a staff meeting at two o'clock, and Chester was chairing the meeting.

"Come, everybody, and have a seat," Chester began. "I think everybody knows one another, so we'll get started. Our friends in Russia are still pushing Communism on to some of the free governments, and our Foreign Affairs department wants to beef up our coverage in those countries, whether we have an embassy there or not. So some of you will be sending agents to these countries fairly soon. Another issue is the continual search for escaped Nazis. Right now the FBI is heading up that operation but might need some help later. Finally, the conflict in China between the free Chinese and the Communist Party continues, and it looks like the Party is gaining ground. That's all people … Jean, please stay."

After everybody left, Jean spoke up. "And we fought a war so the world would a better place to live in. I guess our friends in Russia didn't understand that."

Chester smiled. "I think you're right, Jean. Unfortunately, Stalin has turned out to be another Hitler who wants to control the world with Communism."

Chester pulled a file from his briefcase and put it in front of Jean. "Here's that field assignment I promised you." Jean's eyes lit up as Chester continued speaking. "Yesterday, Jake sent a communication, and apparently the Communist Party in northern Italy is getting stronger. Some of the local citizens are not happy, and Jake received a message from the assistant ambassador. So Jake paid a visit to a Mario Caruso in Milan. Apparently, he asked about you."

"Yes, I know him. He was my counterpart in the northern Italy campaign during the war. He's a good man."

"Well, Jean, he's asked to talk to you only."

Jean's mouth dropped open as she looked at Chester. Chester was smiling as he asked, "Have you ever been to Venice, Italy?"

He surprised her again, and she barely got out a, "No, I have not."

Chester proceeded to tell Jean about the assignment. It looked like she might be meeting Mario to discuss what was going on in Milan.

"Jean, I'll hold a briefing with you tomorrow morning, and you'll leave the following day," Chester concluded.

Two days later, on October 17, Jean boarded her flight to Venice with intermediate stops in Gander, Newfoundland, and Shannon, Ireland. The next day, Jean had a short flight to London, and then it was on to Venice, Italy. Once airborne on a seventeen-hour flight, Jean thought, *Thank goodness I don't have to bail out of this damn aircraft, even once.* Once she settled in, Jean unlocked her briefcase and pulled out the file and started viewing the instructions again. Her meet was in two days, and she had an idea why Mario wanted to meet. At least, she hoped she did. Shortly, the TWA stewardess came by and asked Jean if she'd like something to drink.

Jean looked up and asked her, "What kind of liquor do you have?"

The stewardess replied with a list of options.

"No tequila?" Jean asked, disappointed.

"No, ma'am. Sorry."

Jean came back with, "I'll have bourbon with a splash of water, on the rocks."

When her drink arrived, Jean sat back and relaxed, enjoying her drink as she thought about Jake and wondered how he was doing in Rome. In that moment, she realized how much she missed him. Then she hoped he was working his ass off so some good-looking Italian broad didn't have her hooks in him.

To get that off her mind, Jean got up and went to the restroom, checking people out on her way. When she returned to her seat, she estimated the flight was about 80 percent full. After finishing her drink, Jean checked the time. There was another hour and a half of flight time, so she decided to take a nap.

It was eleven o'clock local time in Gander, Newfoundland, when they finally arrived. The passengers deplaned while the aircraft was being refueled. Jean found the restroom and then a small café for some lunch. She sat at the counter and ordered fish and chips with some spicy sauce and a beer.

CHAPTER 32

In Milan, Italy, a secret meeting was being held among concerned residents about what had been happening in their community. The meeting was called to order by the leader of the group.

Mario informed the attendees, "I'm leaving in two days. I have been spreading it around that I'm going to Venice to see my sister, whom I haven't seen since before the war. I didn't know she was still alive until two weeks ago. She has been living in Paris. My fellow comrades, you need to spread this information around to the right people here."

Then one of the attendee spoke up. "What do you expect to do in Venice?"

Mario said, "Get help, so our lives will be as they were before the war."

Another attendee spoke up. "I don't see how we can change anything. One person had spoken out about what was happening and about the lies we've been told. They found him dead three days later, and he had been beaten to death."

"I don't have the answers, but if we don't try, do you want to live this way for the rest of your lives?" Mario asked.

He heard quiet voices, and then he heard some soft-spoken nos.

With that, he adjourned the meeting and told everybody, "Don't forget my story about my trip to Venice."

Mario thought maybe that would satisfy the bastards, and he wouldn't have company on his trip.

Two days later, Mario boarded a train for Venice. Just as he stepped on the platform, he saw his shadows and said, "You bastards don't quit. Do you?"

CHAPTER 33

The next day, Jean's flight arrived at a remote airport west of Venice at little after three o'clock local time. After making her way through customs, Jean boarded a bus to Venice. Being able to speak Italian, she found out that she needed to go to the San Marco area and get a ride in a gondola to her hotel. The Canal Grande Hotel was right on the Grand Canal, and so was her meeting place, which looked like it would be a nice evening stroll along the canal. Jean did enjoy the gondola ride. She noticed that the good-looking young man doing the rowing was smiling at her every time she looked at him and his cute ass.

After checking in to the hotel using her alias, Jean asked the clerk for the nearest café on the canal that had good food. She found out it was only ten minutes away. A short time later, Jean entered the quaint café, Trattoria Marciana, and was escorted to the patio overlooking the canal. On the way to her table, Jean smelled the food coming from the kitchen. It reminded her of Sergeant Basso, who had led her and Joe to that same smell, and the food had been delicious.

The waiter showed up with a bottle of wine in each hand, and Jean ordered a glass of red wine. He set the bottle on the table and took her order. She ordered the house specialty, meatballs and pasta. While waiting, Jean was enjoying the view and wishing a certain tall Texan was with her. Then she thought about the meeting the following night. She figured it would be a lonely place and decided she might want to check it out before the meeting.

Suddenly, Jean couldn't believe her eyes when she saw who was seated across from her. *What's he doing here?* she wondered to herself. She knew better than to recognize him. Instead, she ignored him.

Jean continued to enjoy the view and finished her tasteful meal and wine. She paid her check and casually walked out of the café and headed back to her hotel. Just before reaching the hotel, she ducked into an alley and anxiously waited. When he appeared, Jean grabbed him, shoved his ass up against a wall, and kissed him.

When they were breathing again, she asked, "What the hell are you doing here, Jake?"

"Well, darling. I'm your backup."

"What! Who sent you?" Jean questioned.

"Well, it seems your supervisor wanted to be sure you didn't get your ass in a sling, and that's why I'm here, darling," Jake answered.

"Well … I guess I'm glad you're here, handsome. Tomorrow night could be a little risky."

Jake asked, "What room are you in? Just in case I need to find you."

"Room 224. And yours is?"

"I'm in room 320."

"I'm headed for the bar," Jean noted. "See you later, handsome."

The small bar was a busy place, and Jean stood at the entrance making a quick survey. She saw a table for two next to the back wall and slowly began walking toward the table while glancing at the patrons. She finally reached the table, not recognizing anybody.

As soon as Jean sat down, a waiter was right there. He asked in Italian, "What would you care to drink, ma'am?"

"I'll have a glass of red wine," she said, answering in Italian.

As soon as the waiter left, Jean recognized the next person who entered the bar and watched him look around until his eyes were fixed on her. Mario slowly walked toward Jean and sat at a table next to her.

After the waiter left his table, Mario whispered, "I have shadows, and they just entered the bar."

Jean quickly looked and saw a big man and a medium-sized man. She could tell they looked Russian.

Then Jean heard, "Go see the priest tomorrow morning, and I'll see you tomorrow night."

She leaned back and enjoyed her wine. Shortly, Mario left, and Jean's shadow showed up. *Perfect*, she thought. Jean finished her wine and put enough money on the table to cover the tab. She then left and knew Jake was watching her.

Jean walked up just as the big Russian was getting ready to leave. "Do you have a match?" she asked, putting a cigarette between her lips.

The big Russian started searching for a match when the bartender spoke up. "I have some, ma'am." He then handed them to the Russian.

When the Russian turned around to hand Jean the matches, she got a good look at him and thanked him. When she reached the table where her shadow was, she stopped, lit her cigarette, and dropped the match in his ashtray. "My room in one hour," she said quietly.

Jean was soon out on her balcony enjoying the view of a beautiful city and thinking, *Now I know why Mario wants me involved*. Moments later, there was a knock on the room door.

Jean approached it with weapon in hand. "Who is it?" she asked.

"It's me, darling," Jake responded.

Jean opened the door, and Jake walked in. A happy embrace took place.

After some serious kissing, Jean said, "Let's talk … Did you see the two Russians at the bar?"

"Yes, I did," Jake confirmed.

"They're my contact's shadows and are probably Russian Communists. You think you can take care of that little problem, if need be, handsome?"

Jake smiled. "If need be."

"Now, I think we better come up with a reason why you shouldn't leave right way. Remember—this is Venice, the city of love."

Jean saw a big smile on Jake's face as he started getting undressed … in a hurry.

Chapter 34

After a good night's rest after having her fill of sex, Jean got up and went to her balcony. She stood in a cool breeze, enjoying the sunrise. Looking down at the canal, she knew her meeting place was nearby. *I'll act like it's part of my sightseeing*, she thought to herself. *But after I've a good breakfast. I'm always hungry after a lot of sex.*

Jean climbed into a gondola and gave the operator directions on where to go. Twenty minutes later, they reached the destination. Jean paid the gondola operator and headed for the entrance to the Saint Benedetto church. She could tell it was an old church, and small too. Once inside, Jean noticed that it had possibly been rebuilt over its original structure; the artwork was outstanding. She went to the front, sat in the first row next to the center aisle, and just looked at what was behind the altar. The paintings were so beautiful that she felt something inside; it was a good feeling. Then a priest showed up and startled her a little.

He asked, "Are enjoying being here, my child?"

"Yes, very much, Father," she said, answering him in Italian.

"You speak good Italian, but I think you're a tourist."

"You're right, Father, and I'm enjoying being here," Jean said.

"Please, let me explain what you are looking at," the priest said. "First of all, the local Italians know this church as *San Beneto*. It was founded in the eleventh century and rebuilt in 1685."

135

Because she's been a little bit of a history buff in college, the priest had Jean's attention.

He continued, "Over the doors on either side of the high altar, you have Sebastian and Mazzoni's *Saint Benedict with John the Baptist and the Virtues.*"

Jean continued to look at the beautiful artwork with admiration. "It's hard to realize that someone in the eleventh century could do such great work. The color and texture almost make it seem like it's real."

"You're right, Miss—"

"Carmelina Caruso, Father."

"I'm Father Sergio Carmelina, and I'm sorry. I should have introduced myself earlier."

Jean smiled. "Apology accepted, Father Sergio ... Could we please continue? This is fascinating to me."

The priest continued, "If you look to the right on the south wall, that's Bernardo Strozzi's *Saint Sebastian Tended by the Holy Women.*"

Again, Jean stared at the marvelous artwork and heard, "On the north wall, we have Giambattista Tiepolo's *San Francesco di Paola.*" While standing in the center of the aisle, turning 360 degrees, she heard, "Carmelina, are you planning on coming to our nine o'clock service tonight?"

"Yes I am, Father," she answered.

The priest said, "You should sit in the first row on the right side because the foxes come out at midnight."

Jean froze and looked at the priest who was two inches shorter than her. His facial features reminded her of someone else. Then she gave the countersign. "Hunters come out early too."

Father Sergio immediately said, "Agent Webb, please come with me, and I'll tell what will happen tonight."

Jean followed the priest to the back of the church and to a small room where he began to tell her what to do during the service.

CHAPTER 35

After an informational meeting, Jean regretted leaving the San Beneto church, because it was so beautiful and being there felt good. She waved down a gondola and headed for the San Marco's piazza. Once she arrived, she toured the San Marco tower and the unique shops along the canal. There was a glass shop in the piazza area, and she got to see some beautiful pieces of glassware. Some were like looking at great pieces of art. Jean was enjoying herself so much that she didn't realize what time of day it was, but her stomach did. She remembered seeing a restaurant earlier, so that's where she headed.

It was a very nice restaurant with a ton of selections. In Europe, all restaurants have a special of the day, so she ordered the seafood with pasta—of course, with a glass of white wine. When her meal came, it had clams, mussels, shrimp, and small pieces of Italian sausage over a bed of pasta and a light cream sauce. *If I eat all this, I better not swim back to my hotel, 'cause I'd sink to the bottom,* Jean thought to herself. But she did eat all of it, and it was fabulous. When she was done, Jean paid her bill, thanked the waiter, and told him to give the chef her compliments for a wonderful meal.

Next, Jean rode a gondola to the canal side where her hotel was located and then enjoyed a long walk back to the hotel. That's when she realized she had a shadow, and it wasn't Jake. Upon entering the hotel lobby, Jean found a chair and sat down and waited. When the shadow entered the hotel, she recognized the medium-sized Russian from the bar the previous night. Then it dawned on her that the specious bastard was checking out who she was because she'd sat next to Mario the night before.

Once Jean made it back to her room, she still felt full of food that she decided she needed a workout. She stripped down to her undergarments and got busy working off some of those wonderful calories. An hour later, she jumped in the tub to soak, and later, she set the alarm for six o'clock before taking a nap. Suddenly, she heard a ringing noise, and she immediately sat up and quickly turned off the alarm. Still half asleep, she stumbled to the lavatory and splashed water on her face. Once fully awake, she dialed Jake's room.

Jean heard, "Hello, this is Antonio."

"It's me," she responded. "My room in thirty minutes."

Jake's undercover name was Antonio Bonelli, and if he were in trouble, he would've answered as Tony. If Jean was in trouble, she was to answer as Carmelina instead of Miss Caruso.

Jake was on time, and the couple ordered room service. Jean filled Jake in on what the plan was for that night at the church and let him know she'd had a shadow earlier in the day. Jean and Jake decided to save the wine for later and only had coffee. Then Jean let Jake know she was going to walk to the church so he would have a chance to eliminate her Russian shadow.

Jake left first and headed for the lobby to check things out. Jean left thirty minutes later wearing slacks and a blouse, with a light jacket to hide her weapon. On the way to the meet, Jean took her time stopping and looking at the moon every so often. Then she'd casually stop and window shop at some of the stores that were still open. She did sense she was being followed, and when she stopped at one of the shops, she'd look around to see if she could spot him. Jake's instructions were to eliminate her shadow. Jean had always said that spying was a nasty business.

Jean arrived at the church at twenty minutes before nine and sat in the front row. She sat next to the exterior wall, so she could turn and see who was sitting behind her. Then she saw Mario. A short time later, his shadow showed up, and the Russian sat several rows behind him. *Perfect*, Jean thought. Next, she saw Jake enter. There was no shadow following him. Jake sat in the front row next to the center aisle. Jean thought to herself, *Now the set is ready. Here's when the director would say, "Action."*

The music began, and Father Sergio appeared. The service continued, and forty-minutes later, Father Sergio finished his sermon and made an announcement to the congregation.

In Italian, he said, "Ladies and gentlemen, tonight we have a surprise for you and for one of our visitors. Will Carmelina Caruso please come forward?"

When Jean stood up and looked at the Russian, she noticed he moved forward in his seat. She acted surprised and made her way to the altar.

Father Sergio continued. "Now, will the other person come forward … These two are brother and sister and haven't seen each other since before the war."

Action, Jean thought. Jean immediately ran up to Mario and hugged him and kissed him on the cheek, and he kissed her back. The two continued to hug each other, as they heard clapping. When it stopped, Father Sergio ended the service. When the exit music started playing, everybody got up to leave. That was Jean and Mario's cue to leave quickly through a door and exit the church.

Jake's job was to prevent the big Russian from following by playing a football guard and blocking his way.

Outside was a horse and carriage waiting for the pair. They quickly climbed aboard and hurried away. The horseman dropped Jean and Mario off at another church where they went inside and headed to a private room.

"Oh, Jean, it is so good to see you again," Mario said. "I'm so glad you came. Please come and have a seat."

Jean sat down across the table from Mario. "Mario, tell me what's going on in Milan."

"It's Communism in the worst way," he answered in a disgusted tone of voice. Mario proceeded to explain what was happening in northern Italy and told her about the promises not being kept. "They rule us with an iron hand," he added. "We are not free."

"This is not unusual for them," Jean noted. "We're finding out that wherever there is Communism, this is the way it is for the people. The iron hand rules."

Then Mario told Jean what had happened to Lazzaro Mato. "He spoke out against them and was beaten to death."

"I'm sorry, Mario … Do you know who did it?"

"No, Jean, but I intend on finding out."

A short time later, Jake showed up with Father Sergio, and that's when Jean found out he was Mario's brother. Then she asked Jake, "How did it go with the Russian?"

Jake smiled. "He's never played football before."

Then Jean asked, "Mario, how can we help you?"

Jake listened and then informed Mario, "The United States and the new Italian government will do what it takes to run the Russian Communists out of Italy."

Jean saw a big smile on Mario's face. More hugging took place, and Mario was scheduled for a train ride back to Milan in the morning. Before they all parted ways, Jake let him know he'd be in touch soon.

Then Jake and Jean returned to her room to finish off a bottle of wine and whatever else came up, hopefully.

CHAPTER 36

The morning sun was shining on the balcony when Jean finally woke up the following morning. Jake was sleeping soundly when she got up and headed for the tub. The hot water felt good on her wine-tasting headache. Jean figured that was what happened when you finished off a large bottle of Italian wine. While drying off, she realized there was something on her mind, which is why she had woken up. She put on a robe and ordered some coffee and rolls. Then she went out onto the balcony and felt the cool breeze as she stood in the sunlight and thought about how she'd felt while in the San Beneto church. It was a different feeling, yet a wonderful feeling that had made her feel good inside. And she felt it happening while admiring the beautiful artwork, which had seemed so real, because the artists were that good and, apparently, because she appreciated great art.

Room service arrived, and Jean sat down in a comfortable chair to sip her wonderful coffee and enjoy a sweet roll. She began to think about how she should see the rest of Venice before leaving. The smell of coffee woke up Jake, and he headed for the tub. Then he showed up for his coffee and roll.

The couple both had more coffee and knew they needed to eat something. They got dressed and headed off to the quaint little café, Trattoria Marciana, for a fabulous Italian breakfast and a relaxing day. After breakfast, they toured the San Marino area by riding in a gondola, walking, and visiting the beautiful old churches, as well as a few museums and art galleries. Later that afternoon, they decided to head back to the hotel and make out their report together over a bottle of wine with cheese and crackers.

Jean and Jake sat next to the balcony and left the French doors open as they worked. Jean didn't think they could be in a better place, making out a report with a terrific view and a cool breeze while sipping wonderful wine and eating cheese and crackers.

Suddenly the room door flew open, and in came a big Russian hollering at them. Jean and Jake both jumped up and quickly got ready to take him on. Jake got to him first. The Russian was a quick learner, because he put a body block on Jake, sending him across the room. Then he turned toward Jean, who rushed him. She stopped just before reaching him and fell to her knees just as he took a swing. Then Jean planned a karate blow with her knuckles right into his crotch, crushing his balls. The Russian reacted with a loud holler.

By this time, Jake was back on his feet. Jean nodded toward the balcony, and they each grabbed an arm and raced toward the railing, shoving him over it and into the canal. Fortunately for him, he cleared the canal wall—barely. Jean then called the front desk and reported that a man had broken into her room. She asked that they please call the police and send up a maintenance man to fix the door. Then Jake and Jean when back to enjoying their afternoon and evening.

The next day, Jake and Jean were on their way to the hotel restaurant for breakfast when Jake stopped to check for messages. When he showed up at the table, he had a message. "According to the clerk, they never caught the intruder," Jake reported, "but they're watching the hotel just in case he shows up again."

After they ordered, Jake read the message and then handed it to Jean. They were both instructed to return to Rome for a meeting with the new Italian government in two days. After lunch, it was nap time. Then they would enjoy a bottle of wine, and hopefully something would later, remembering venice is the city of love.

CHAPTER 37

At the US Embassy in Rome, Jake and Jean were in a meeting with Ambassador Glen Gordon and his assistant, Todd Simpson. The duo informed the ambassador about the meeting that had taken place in Venice.

After hearing everything, Gordon said, "I think we are prepared for tomorrow's meeting. Do either of you have any ideas how to proceed from here?"

Jean spoke up. "We need to know the key party members and all the Russians who are in northern Italy. Once we have that information, arrests can be made. I know Milan and the people. The Party believes I'm Mario's sister, so my suggestion is I pay Mario a visit indicating I want to live there instead of Paris. That way, maybe I can get info we need with Mario's help."

Jake objected to Jean's suggestion. "It'll be too dangerous. There may be people still there that would recognize her from the war."

The ambassador said, "Sorry, Jake. It makes sense and sounds feasible to me if you can make sure no one can recognize her. We'll present it in tomorrow's meeting. Thanks, Jean."

Two days later at the US Embassy, Ambassador Gordon said, "The Italians like our idea. It looks like you're going to Milan, Jean."

Then Jake explained what was going to happen next. "I need to contact Mario first, because a lot of people in Milan may remember

Jean, which means, JW, you're going to have to gain weight and not be so pretty. In other words, become a disguised person. Meanwhile, the Italians will be sending in their men one at a time, not to make the party suspicious, located around Milan."

Ambassador Gordon said, "Very good, Jake. Well, Jean, it looks like you're going to get to see some of Rome."

Jean then reminded Jake that the big Russian had seen her at the church as Carmelina Caruso.

Jake said, "I'll take care of that little problem."

Two days later, Jake left for Milan, and Jean met with Simpson so they could create her disguise. Then he'd acquire what was needed for her to become an overweight woman ten years older.

Jean stayed at Jake's apartment and used his motor scooter to get around. She found maps in the apartment and sat down to plan out her next four days. "I'm going to see some of Rome and enjoy myself," she said as she got to work.

The next day, Jean decided her first sightseeing tour would be the Vatican. She jumped on the scooter and headed northwest for an hour-long ride in traffic. When she reached St. Peter's Basilica, Jean wanted to see two items she had seen pictures of in college. When she saw the first one, *Pietà*, she just stared at the fabulous sculpture of Jesus in mother Mary's lap after the crucifixion. Jean saw details that were unbelievable and was in awe of how Michelangelo was able to achieve a classic beauty with naturalism. After admiring it for thirty minutes, Jean decided to go to Michelangelo's next work of art. The ceiling of the Sistine Chapel. She had read about how difficult it was and the frustration he went through finishing the project. Again, Jean just stared up at the magnificently beautiful ceiling in awe, thinking about what a great talent he'd had.

Then she returned to St. Peter's Basilica and walked around, admiring the great workmanship in the structure. Later, Jean climbed the

Borgia tower to get a better look at Vatican City. When she looked out at all the buildings and the grounds covered with beautiful gardens spread out over 110 acres, she said, "This view was definitely worth seeing." She continued to scan the nearby structures, gardens, and other outstanding sculptures and statues. It was a full morning at Vatican City, and now it was approaching lunchtime. The next fabulous sight she wanted to see was the Colosseum.

On the way, Jean stopped at a café for lunch and was enjoying an Italian sandwich with a beer as she watched the busy traffic go by. When she reached the Colosseum, Jean found out she needed a guide to take her through it so she wouldn't get lost. Jean remembered reading about the Colosseum. It had taken ten years to build and was finished AD 80. The architectural planning and engineering was unbelievable for that time period. Touring the complex showed how advanced the Romans had been. It was a three-level, above-ground structure, and a person could easily get lost while walking through the lower level. It was hard for Jean to believe so many human beings had been killed in the arena. And yet, Hitler made it seem like nothing compared to what he had done in seven years.

By the end of the tour, Jean was feeling tried and headed back to the apartment. Jake did have some food in an icebox and some wine to drink, but it looked like she needed to find a food store.

CHAPTER 38

In Milan, Mario had to call for a secret meeting with his trusted friends. His reason for the meeting was to introduce Jake to the group.

Jake addressed those in the meeting. "We need to start eliminating the Communists' iron hand rule over you. We need a list of the hard-core Communist members and any known Russians in the area. But the important list is the people still living there who you are uncertain could be trusted once a movement was started."

Jake talked about getting some weapons in the weeks to come and explained that there were some men gathering around Milan to help if a bad situation occurred. Hours later, he had the lists in hand. The first list was easy, and the second list had at least eight questionable people on it, including Vito Basso.

"If these eight are not confirmed as friendlies, then they may have to be kidnapped and returned after this movement is over," Jake explained.

Mario adjourned the meeting and picked two other members to go with him and Jake to see the eight people on the list. Jake was staying with Mario and his family, and Mario let it be known around town that he was a cousin visiting him from Rome. That was the story if Communist Party members asked, or even a Russian.

CHAPTER 39

Jean decided to stay in and relax. She grabbed an Italian newspaper to read as a way to brush up on her Italian. Later, she took an inventory of provisions. "Yeah, I better find a food store."

Jean had seen a sidewalk food store not too far from the apartment, so she jumped on the scooter and headed out in search of it. Four blocks away Jean found it and noticed a young boy standing near the store entrance. Suddenly he grabbed two red apples and turned to run away. He made a wrong turn and ran into Jean, who grabbed him. Jean could tell he was a street kid and figured he was probably hungry.

She reached into her pocket and pulled out some lire. She handed the boy the coins and said in Italian, "Don't steal if you can help it. But don't starve to death either."

Now both parties were shopping. When the boy was at the checkout stand, Jean was nearby. She looked over at him and noticed he looked nervous. Jean made a loud noise with her throat and gave the boy a firm look. A few seconds later, the boy reached in his pocket, pulled out some candy, and put it on the counter. When the boy left, Jean waved at him, and he stopped to turn around and waved back.

When Jean looked at the store owner, he was smiling. As she was checking out, he spoke to her. "One of these bottles of wine is on me, ma'am."

Jean thanked him and then asked, "Sir, if you have some work around here, why don't you ask the boy to help you. If you do, he won't have a reason to steal anymore." She then left and put the sack of food and wine in a basket behind her and headed back to the apartment to fix herself her version of an Italian dinner.

Meanwhile, in Milan, Jake and Mario had been busy. They had already talked to five of the eight people on their list. All five were acceptable for their plan. Vito Basso was the next one to see, and Mario warned Jake about his temper.

Vito answered the knock on his door, and Mario asked him, "Vito, we would like to talk to you about something very important. Would you mind stepping outside?"

The big Italian did and asked, "Who's this you have with you?"

Jake decided to take a chance and answered, "A friend of Mario's and of Jean Webb's, Vito."

Vito stared at Jake and then he asked, "How is Major Webb?"

"She's fine, Vito … And she said to tell you hi and hoped you were doing well."

Vito led them away from his house and said, "Mario, I know why you are here."

"How, Vito?" Mario questioned.

"Because you have a spy among your group, Mario."

Mario immediately asked, "Vito! Who?"

CHAPTER 40

Because of the wonderful dinner Jean had fixed herself, she hit the sack early. She finally woke up after a very long, restful night. Jake always had a comfortable bed. Jean got up and headed for the tub to soak and finish waking up. After her bath and drying off, she just wrapped a towel around herself. She fixed herself a nice breakfast, and while enjoying her second home-cooked meal, she heard something at the front door and grabbed her weapon.

Jean tightened up the towel around her and casually approached the door. "Who's there?" she asked.

She heard a young voice say in Italian, "I am Gino, the boy at the food store yesterday, and I have your newspaper."

Jean slowly opened the door partway and said, "Thanks, Gino." She struck her hand out for the paper.

Gino then thanked her for yesterday and surprised her when he said, "You are a beautiful woman, and if I was older, I think I would marry you." Then he ran away.

Italian male's hormones kick in early here, Jean thought to herself. Jean decided she better get dressed in case his older brother showed up.

Jean had plans for the day to see the other wonderful sights in Rome. The following day, she would head to Naples. When she was ready to take on the day, she jumped on the scooter and headed for the world-famous Trevi Fountain.

As Jean stood in front of the fountain, she was definitely amazed at the size and again the beautiful sculptures and artwork carved out in stone. She read the information on the backdrop for the fountain. It was 86 feet high and 145 feet wide. Jean spent an hour examining each of the statues and the rockwork, as they called it. Then she saw that it had been built in 1762 and designed by an architect named Nicola Salvi. Next, she toured Rome's central city, looking at gardens and buildings. People often say France is the country for great art, but Jean would put Italy up against France for having great art, plus great sculptures.

It was lunchtime, and Jean decided to go back to the apartment and fix a good Italian meal and then rest up for her trip to Naples. Once lunch was over, she took a glass of wine and decided to read the local newspaper and brush up on her Italian some more.

Chapter 41

Jean was up at sunrise, fixed a good breakfast, and was on the road to Naples in an hour. She was looking at a three-hour ride at forty-five miles per hour. In October, the temperature was a nice, cool low sixty, and the road to Naples was hilly as she traveled through the mountainous terrain. But the countryside was very picturesque with some terrific views.

About an hour from Naples, Jean found a high point overlooking the sea. She pulled over to take in the view. Naples, in the distance, was quite a sight. Jean just stood there and thought about what a beautiful country Italy was.

Naples had been bombed during the war, but the outer townships were untouched. Driving down the narrow streets was fun as she looked at all the different shops and even saw a pizza parlor. Of course, pizza was invented in Naples, so Jean instantly knew what she was having for lunch. Next, she drove down near the harbor and along the seaside road where she saw some swimmers on the beach. Jean guessed it was probably in the low seventies. But she hadn't brought a suit; besides, she wouldn't want to shake up the male population with her big boobs. Although, maybe that wouldn't be the case; she had seen quite a few Italian women with big boobs.

After the beach, Jean headed for the largest public plaza in Italy, which was in the center part of the city. She noticed some reconstruction had started, which was good because Naples was such a beautiful city. She stopped for some petrol and filled the scooter's tank. While she was at the station, she asked where the best pizza was in town, and that's where she headed next. Later, with her belly full of fabulous pizza, Jean was back on the road to Rome.

She arrived back at the apartment at four thirty and poured a glass of wine, although food wasn't on her mind. She listened to the radio and some music and was starting to fall asleep when there was a knock at the apartment door.

Jean armed herself and stood by the door and said, "Who is it?"

"It's Gino from the store with a delivery for you." Then a lower voice said, "There are two men watching your apartment, and I need to come in so we can talk."

Jean opened the door and took the delivery and invited the boy in. He closed the door and locked it.

"So, Gino, how long have they been there, and where are they now?" Jean asked.

"They parked there about two hours ago and are one block to the left of your front door," Gino noted.

"Why are you concerned about them, Gino? And it's Jean."

"Okay, Jean. Because they asked a friend of mine where does the American live. When I saw them, I noticed they're not Italian. So I got my brother, and he told me they look like Russians he saw up north where he was working. I think they are trouble for you. So I have my gang and brother ready if you need us to chase them away."

"No, Gino. I need to find out who they are, so don't do anything and let me handle it," Jean said. "Now go, and thanks for the warning."

After Gino left, Jean called the Italian G-man (or government man, some would say) who was her contact and let him know what was going on. He was going to send some men to check it out.

"No, I'll lead them away from this neighborhood on my scooter," Jean told him. "Where do you want me to go so you can take them? … Yeah, I know where that is. I'll be there in twenty minutes."

On the way to the designated location, Jean's two new friends followed her. She watched them closely in case they tried to run her over. When she reached the fountain, Jean parked the scooter and armed herself. Suddenly, they came on fast, and when they reached her location, three cars appeared and surrounded the men's vehicle. They were directed to get out of their vehicle. It was clear they were reluctantly complying with the instructions as they put their hands in the air.

Jean, along with three G-men, approached the men. "Show me some ID," Jean said.

One of the G-men took the ID and looked it over. "They're Russians," he said, confirming Jean's suspicions.

"Search them," Jean said. Two G-men patted them down, removed their weapons, and told them they were under arrest. But before they were taken away, Jean said, "All right, comrades. What were your orders? If you don't want me to shoot you in the leg, you better tell me." She then cocked her weapon and stuck it in their faces. They were silent, so she shot the bigger one in the leg. The smaller one started talking.

"We were told to eliminate any American spies," he said.

"Who told you?" Jean demanded.

"It was our leader in Milan."

The big Russian, Jean thought. She then turned to the G-man in charge and said, "Jail them and throw away the key until you are told otherwise. And the big one needs some first aid for his flesh wound."

Riding back to the apartment, Jean figured it out. When Jake met Mario in Milan, they followed him to his apartment. That's how they found her. *That's one smart SOB in Milan,* Jean thought to herself.

CHAPTER 42

Back in Milan, Vito didn't know who the informant was, and he wasn't willing to get involved until he was found out and eliminated. Vito was now married and didn't want to endanger his wife in any way.

Mario thanked Vito and said, "We'll get back to you when we find the SOB."

On the way back home, Mario was going over the list of loyal friends in his head and said to Jake, "I've no idea who it could be."

"Mario, we need to set a trap," Jake suggested.

Mario and Jake stayed up half the night coming up with an idea for a trap. The following morning, Mario noticed he was being watched, and he knew why. It was obviously thanks to the informant. Jake made a tour of downtown Milan, saying hi to everybody and acting like a tourist. He realized he had a shadow and wanted them to see he was a friendly, talking kind of guy. This was the beginning of Mario's plan to catch the SOB. Mario was doing the same thing as Jake. The idea was to indicate everything was just fine. Then Mario would meet with two of the group members and pass on some important info. Then he and Jake would stakeout their homes, hoping the informant would have a meeting with his contact. This would continue until they planted the information with the right guy.

On the third night, they got lucky and discovered who the informant was. Mario called a group meeting the following night and informed everybody where the weapons would be delivered; of course, the real location was at the other end of town. Two nights later, the weapons were being unloaded into a warehouse with a secret cellar.

Mario walked up to a young man and said, "Enzo, you look nervous. Are you okay?"

"I'm not feeling good, Mario," he answered. "It must be my dinner."

Jake's job was to make sure Enzo didn't leave suddenly. If that had happened, Mario wouldn't have had his little talk with his informant. Once the weapons were stored safely, everybody began to leave and say good night. Enzo started walking toward his home.

Mario and Jake stopped him, and Mario said, "I'm worried about you, Enzo. Do you need a ride home?"

Enzo quickly replied, "No, Mario. I'll be fine."

"Not if you're Communist friends are waiting for you, because you gave them the wrong information," Mario said, surprising the informant.

Enzo started to run, but Jake was right there and grabbed him.

Mario walked up and got in Enzo's scared face and said with an angry voice, "Enzo Fiore! What the hell is going on?"

Mario could see Enzo go limp in Jake's hold. He started crying and saying, "I'm sorry, Mario … They got to me when they threatened to stop my mother's medal aid. Without it, she would die. Then they said if I cooperate with them, she would be taken care of."

Mario looked away and said, "The damn bastards … Enzo, look. You and your mother are going to take a trip with Jake to Rome where you'll be safe. Now, I want to know what you have told them."

"They already knew about you, Mario. I told them you made us wear hoods so we wouldn't know who was there, and they believed me."

"Okay, Enzo, thanks for that," Mario said. "Do you know if they have gotten to anybody else?"

"No, Mario, I'm the only one, and they'll be waiting for me."

Jake looked at Mario and said, "We may have to do some Communist ass-kicking tonight."

CHAPTER 43

Jake had acquired help from one of his Italian agents nearby, and some Communists did get their asses kicked and arrested. After it was over, Jake was on his way back to Rome with four passengers instead of two. Enzo and his mother would be guests of the Italian government. The two party members would be guests also, but in a jail cell. After completing his six-hour drive to Rome, checking the Fiore family in at a hotel, and delivering the two party members to their iron cage, Jake headed for home. At six o'clock, the dawn hadn't broken through the night yet.

Carefully and quietly, Jake unlocked the door and entered his apartment. He didn't have to look, because Jean was snoring loud and clear, lying on the couch. Jake was tired but hungry and went to the refrigerator to grab some wine, cheese, meat, and bread. He fixed himself a sandwich and sat down, watching and listening to the love of his life.

When Jean finally woke up, it was eight o'clock. She looked over at the big easy chair and saw her big, wonderful lover fast asleep. She didn't know when he had arrived, so she carefully headed to the bathroom to bathe before fixing some breakfast for two. Later, while cooking eggs and bacon, Jean didn't know which woke Jake up first, the smell of cooking breakfast, the coffee, or the noise.

"Good morning, handsome. What time did you get in last night? Or was it this morning?" she asked.

"It was this morning about six," Jake answered.

"Are you awake enough to eat? I'm cooking breakfast for two. That is, if you're interested?"

"Yes, I could eat something and sleep later."

During breakfast, Jake told Jean what had been happening in Milan and about the previous night and his trip back. Then Jean told Jake what happened in Rome the night before.

"Those SOBs," Jake said. "Just wait until I get my hands on that big Russian. I'll teach him how to play hard ball instead of football."

Jean asked, "What's next?"

"On my way back, I thought about your disguise and think you need to become fat and ugly."

"What! You're kidding, right?"

Jake quickly replied, "I think too many people in Milan would recognize you unless your disguise is a radical change. And we're setting it up so you are an active member of the Communist Bloc in Paris."

Jean looked at Jake and said, "You're going to enjoy this, aren't you? ... All right, we need to check with Paris and see if we have an undercover agent in the party I can use for a reference. And we need to remember that the big Russian saw me in Venice."

Jake replied, "He may meet with a serious accident if necessary."

After breakfast, Jake said, "I'll see you later, darling, and wake me up in time for lunch."

Jean mumbled, "You can fix your own damn lunch."

Jake asked, "Did you say something?"

"No! Go to sleep." *Turkey!*

CHAPTER 44

The next day at the CIG's secured office, Jake got busy contacting the Paris office, while Jean was in a special room becoming reborn.

Toward the end of the day, Jean looked into a mirror and said, "What I do for God and country." She now looked like an overweight, ugly woman.

The next day, Jake did a test and took Jean to the embassy and introduced her to Mr. Simpson as Mario Caruso's sister. The test was successful, because Simpson didn't recognize her. The rest of the day was spent at the CIG's office, where Jake was receiving information from Paris, preparing Jean's papers, and booking a flight to Paris and then a train ride to Milan. Jean went to work practicing playing the role of her new identity and memorizing a description of one Yves Le Noir, her Paris contact.

The following morning Jake took Jean to the airport and said, "I'll see you in three days."

On the flight to Paris, Jean was reviewing her mission details. She needed to acquire names of the key party members, including the Russians who were involved, and meet Vito Basso. Then she would attend a party meeting, letting them know she wasn't with Mario's ideas. She was a true Communist.

When she was done going over everything, Jean had a glass of wine and enjoyed the rest of the flight. She took a taxi to the train station and made sure she wasn't being followed. At the train station, she gave her luggage to a porter and headed for the coffee shop. Jean took a seat at the back of the café and waited. Shortly, a man entered the café. Jean recognized him. It was Yves Le Noir. After getting his coffee, he sat at a table next to Jean, facing the opposite direction.

"Welcome to Paris, Miss Webb … Don't talk. I'm going to give you the names of the key members here in Paris."

Jean removed a pad and pencil from her carryall and acted like she was writing something down, pausing and looking up from time to time. After receiving the names and phone numbers, Jean continued to write.

Then her contact finished his coffee and left, saying, "Good luck."

CHAPTER 45

Jean was trying to get comfortable in her seat on a passenger railway car headed for Lyons, France. When she did look out at the countryside, she saw rolling hills and a few trees, finding out central France had beautiful scenery. Finally, Jean was able to get comfortable even with her extra disguise baggage she had on.

Jean muttered to herself, "I sure hope I can get the information we need in a hurry, or this disguise is going to kill me. I'm just glad it's not summer, or somebody might think I was wetting my pants, because I'd be sweating a ton of water." Then she got out her pad and started practicing saying the names in Paris. "Boris Orloff, the man from Russia; Leon Petit, the party leader; and bad guy Severin Deveau, the party enforcer."

Jean's train did stop in Lyons for departing passengers, as well as new boarding passengers. Then it was on to Turin, Italy, a border town just south of the Alps with a large lake on the northwest edge of the city. Jean knew about some of the history, especially the fact that the Communist leader for Italy was born there. Antonio Griamisci became party leader in 1937. However, Turin did have an interesting history, and there were lots of beautiful churches, cathedrals, and art galleries containing some noted outstanding art. Then it was on to Milan.

At the train station in Milan, Mario was waiting for his sister. He was hoping her disguise would be good enough so nobody would recognize her. His other concern was the Russian who followed him to Venice had seen her. Thank goodness he was gone, but if he did return, then that would become a serious problem. When the train pulled into the station, Mario positioned himself where he could see all the passenger cars. He did have a brief description of Jean's disguise. He kept looking and did see an older-looking, fat, ugly lady depart a railway car and muttered, "That can't be her."

Mario stepped forward, still looking for his sister when he noticed the fat lady was headed his way, and then he looked away. Next he heard, "Aren't you going to welcome your sister?" A startled Mario turned toward the fat lady who said, "It's me, Mario, and I won't bite."

A shocked Mario carefully walked over and gave his sister a slight hug. Once Mario had her bags, they were off to his home. When they arrived at Mario's home, he went in first and prepared his family for the surprise that was coming, because his wife had known Jean during the war.

After the introductions, Mario showed Jean her room.

"Thank you, Mario. I'll be out in a minute," she said. Jean shed part of the fat lady disguise but kept on the face disguise and returned to the kitchen. "I'm glad to get off all that fat," Jean said. Then she walked over and gave Marie a big hug. "I'm glad you married Mario. He needed someone like you."

Next, Marie brought over some food and wine, and the three adults ate and talked.

Mario explained what was happening to his kids and said, "Not a word to anybody, or I'll tan your hides."

Mario showed Jean the partial list they had of the party members and some of the Russians.

Jean asked Mario, "When's the next party meeting, and do we need to see Vito before that?"

Mario answered, "It's late afternoon tomorrow, and yes, it would be a good idea. I'd hate for Vito to go into a shock at a meeting."

"Yeah, I might even scare the big lug," Jean said. That got some grins.

CHAPTER 46

Earlier, Mario had sent his son to see Vito and inform him about the meeting at ten o'clock that night. Mario left early in case he was being watched, so Jean could head straight for the meeting place. Jean was keeping a close lookout, and finally, Mario showed up.

"I was being watched, but I was able to ditch them before coming here," Mario said.

Vito arrived soon after, and when he saw Jean, he couldn't believe it was her. Jean walked over and gave Vito a big hug and said, "It's good to see you, Vito."

Vito was at a loss for words and finally said, "What have they done to you?"

Jean quickly answered, "It's a disguise, and the name is Carmelina Caruso, Mario's sister from Paris."

Vito said, "They did a good job, because I wouldn't have recognized you, Major ... I mean Carmelina."

"Good, Vito. Now let's talk. First question—are you happy with the Communist Party?"

Vito didn't hesitate. "No! I'm not happy, but because I'm married now, I don't dare say anything against the party because of her and her safety."

Jean said, "I understand. Now for question number two. Are you willing to help now that Mario and my partner have eliminated the informant, along with his commie contacts."

Vito smiled. "So that's what happened to the two party members and my answer is yes. I'll help."

Mario asked, "Vito, do you know what happened to the big Russian?"

"Yes, he went back to Moscow, but should be back any day now," Vito said.

"If he shows up, that could be trouble. He saw me in Venice as Mario's sister at the church, and I wasn't in a disguise."

"If he shows up, I'll be glad to take care of him, because I never liked the SOB. And he did make a pass at my wife at one of our meetings," Vito said, sounding eager to make that happen. Then Vito asked, "Are you still as good looking as you were during the war?"

Jean smiled and answered, "Yes, I think so. I still get those looks and whistled at. But, Vito, you big lug. You're married now."

Vito smiled and started shaking his head.

CHAPTER 47

Vito Basso escorted Miss Carmelina Caruso to the party meeting at a rebuilt structure on the west edge of town. Jean remembered the area, because it was her jump-off point during the attack on Milan with the French forces.

As they were entering the facilities, Jean saw the warehouse next to their meeting place and asked, "What warehouse is next door?"

Vito answered, "It's the Volpe storage."

Jean knew it had a secret cellar that few people knew about—just the owner and Mario. Vito introduced her to his section leader, Gustavo Copello. When Gustavo found out she was Mario's sister, he apparently had a strange look on his face.

Carmelina said, "I know what you are thinking since I'm Mario's sister, but I'm a party member in Paris. My section leader is Yves Le Noir, and I'm a true Communist." Then she threw out the other names Yves had given her in Paris and added, "We've a good section with very little problems. Most of the people are happy with the support they receive. And I don't want to be held responsible for my brother's beliefs or actions. However, I do plan on talking to him about those things." She sounded serious.

"That would be great and welcome, Miss Caruso, and Vito, would you please introduce Carmelina around to everybody?" Gustavo said.

"I'd be glad to, Gustavo," Vito said.

Jean didn't see the big Russian, so she relaxed a little. While walking around, she did recognize some people she knew during the war. Then the meeting got started, and Gustavo introduced Miss Carmelina Caruso to the attendees.

Carmelina stood up and said, "I'm glad to be here, my fellow comrades."

When the meeting was over and adjourned, Gustavo came over and asked, "How did you like the meeting, Carmelina?"

"Well, I noticed you didn't talk enough about what the party can do for the people. And walking around the room, I sense there are some concerns coming from the people. I hope you are not running this section with an iron fist. That happened in Paris, and it didn't work. Members left. You know, Gustavo, maybe I can help you with some of those ideas. If you keep up the iron-fist approach, my brother will continue to win."

Gustavo hesitated for quite a while, looking at Carmelina. He then said, "Yes, I'm willing to learn. How about lunch tomorrow?"

"Yes, I'd love to." As Jean was leaving, she muttered, "Perfect. Now I'm in."

Chapter 48

The next day, Carmelina entered the Communist Party's large facilities at the invitation of Gustavo. As Jean walked through the assembly area, she estimated about 350 people had attended the meeting the day before, and that was only 25 percent of its capacity. She thought, with that minimum attendance, her plan should work. She reached Gustavo's office and watched him jump up from behind his desk to greet her.

"Welcome, Carmelina," he said. "Please follow me." Gustavo led her to a small conference room where lunch was already laid out. "I hope you are hungry?"

Carmelina smiled at Gustavo and said, "I'm always hungry. Can't you tell?" She patted her stomach, and Gustavo smiled.

During lunch, Gustavo asked, "Why did you leave Milan, and when?"

Jean was expecting this and was ready to convince Gustavo with a hell of a tale, "Mario and I never liked each other, and being his older sister, I did boss him around a lot. His friend Lazzaro I never liked either. So, I decided to leave. I was educated in administration and always wanted to go to Paris. I left in 1936 and was able to acquire a good job and have really enjoyed being there."

"Yes, and I don't blame you. I have been to Paris on a visit. It's definitely worth the trip," Gustavo volunteered.

"Being back, I now realize how much Mario enjoys being a farmer and loves his apple orchard," Carmelina said.

"He should. It's the largest orchard in northern Italy … So tell me, how were you able to control the people in Paris?"

"Well, it was like this," she began. "The Communist Party came roaring into Paris two months after the Germans surrendered. Some members were still around from the twenties when the party was formed and my boss, Andre, was a member. I joined the party right after I started to work for him. Later, he was my underground leader during the war. When the war was over, he had reopened his previous business, a merchandise store, and I went back to work for him."

"You fought the Nazis during the war? Where?" Gustavo asked.

"Yes, near Metz, France. Andre was even awarded a medal by General de Gaulle for helping an OSS agent destroy the railway at Metz on June 6. And we barely escaped the Nazis. We did continue to sabotage the supply lines from Germany for the next two months. Then we were recalled to Paris and disbanded, because the American Rangers took over for us."

Gustavo now showed his admiration for her action during the war. "It's indeed an honor to know you, Carmelina. Now, tell me. How did you change the party in Paris?"

"Oh, yes. Well, things were going great until the Russians showed up at our meetings and began making strong statements on how the Communists would take over the governments. That didn't go over so well with Andre. So he went to see General de Gaulle. For the next two months, the Russians stirred up all kinds of trouble, and the people were having second thoughts about remaining in the party. Finally, General de Gaulle convinced the government to run the Russian Communists back to Moscow. Once they were gone, we saw a change for the better right away. Mario told me you have a big Russian here from time to time. Is that why you are doing these iron-fist tactics?"

Gustavo lowered his head and admitted it to be true. "His name is Gorya Kocyk, and I understand he is known as the Myesnik, the butcher. He is due back day after tomorrow."

"Is he the one who killed Lazzaro?" Jean asked.

Gustavo again lowered his head and said, "Yes, he did. And he did it on his own. Nobody asked him to do it."

"There lies your problem, Gustavo. Did you know Lazzaro was a war hero, and it has caused a lot of resentment among the people? You need to do what we did in Paris. Run his Russian ass out of Italy and establish support for your people."

Jean could tell she was getting Gustavo's attention and continued. "I understand from Mario the support was there before the war, and Palmiro Toglitti was your party leader since 1938, who differently supported that kind of philosophy. My guess is the Russians probably control him as well. And you know how the elections turned out in June. The Communist Party was third out of three, and I think the new Italian government would support you in running the Russian Communists out of Italy. They know Russia wants total control of Italy, just like they did in France."

Gustavo was speechless, and Jean could see he was concentrating intently. Then he looked at Jean and said, "I'd like it to be like it was before the war. But what can I do to change it?"

Jean stood up and asked, "Are you serious about that, Gustavo, and do you really care about your people?"

Gustavo stood up, squared his shoulders, and said, "Yes, I do."

Then Jean started shedding her disguise. Gustavo stepped back and had a startled look on his face. He sat down and watched. Once the disguise was gone, Gustavo was now looking at a good-looking woman with a shapely figure.

Jean said, "Then, I'm here to help you, and so is your government and mine—the United States of America. I'm Maj. Jean Webb, a former agent of the OSS, and I was here in April of 1945."

CHAPTER 49

Now Gustavo's eyes were wide open, and his month dropped slightly open before he spoke. "I know who you are because the people still talk about you."

"Then follow me, Gustavo." Jean led him to the front door, opened it, and stepped outside where Mario and Vito were waiting. "Come in, gentlemen. We are ready to talk."

With everybody in the conference room, Jean pointed out that Gustavo was ready to return to the way it was before the war and get rid of the Russian influence.

"Is this true, Gustavo?" Mario asked.

"Yes, it is true, Mario, and I'm sorry I let the Russians come in and take over."

"Good, Gustavo, but you're not the only one. Other areas have done the same," Mario said.

Gustavo asked, "Then how do we change it?"

"We listen to Jean," Mario pointed out.

"Mario, the Russian killed Lazzaro. The party had nothing to do with it," Jean said.

"That son of a bitch. I'll handle him when he gets back," Vito said, clenching his fists.

"Don't kill him, Vito. It's better if he stands trial in public and is executed if found guilty," Jean explained. "Now let's get down to business. The new Italian government definitely wants the Russians out of Italy, and the United States supports that. Tomorrow, my partner, Jake Blakely, will be here with a group of armed men from the government to support your efforts in getting rid of these nasty bastards. Now, Gustavo, we need your help in naming all the Russians you know about and contacting the other areas to complete a list, so the Italian government can arrest them and send them back to Moscow with a message—never return. And also it will let Russia know that if any more Russian enforcers show up, they will be imprisoned."

Gustavo said, "It will probably take some traveling to collect all the names, starting with Turin, Italy."

Mario spoke up. "Vito and I can visit the surrounding areas, because a lot of our soldiers still live in those areas. And we'll get those names."

"All right, gentlemen, it looks like we have a plan," Jean said. "Now, for the last piece of business. Gustavo, you need to call an emergency meeting for tomorrow afternoon and tell the people what's going on. And, Mario, you need to be there also. Then you need to let the ones who support the Russians know they will be arrested also and sent to prison."

Vito said, "I already know who they are from all the meetings I have attended, and I will make a list too."

"Congratulations, everybody. And now, I'm thirsty. Meetings always make me thirsty. Right, Vito?" Jean said, slapping him on the back and making him smile.

CHAPTER 50

The following day there was a late-afternoon meeting at the Communist Party's facilities. The meeting was being conducted by Gustavo, who had just presented the recommended changes to the meeting body. When he was done, he opened the meeting for discussion. The panel members included an Italian official, Jake Blakely, Mario Caruso, and Gustavo Copello. There were many questions about future protection and what kind of support there would be. Mario was asked if he would now be a part of the party and what kind of support there would be from the new Italian government. Jean and Vito sat on the sidelines watching, and Vito was pointing out the Russian sympathizers and waiting for their unwelcome guest. Also, some of the government men were placed around the room with concealed weapons. Gustavo was answering the questions, and so were the other members of the panel.

Suddenly, Jake received a message on his walkie-talkie. "It's time," he said.

Then there was a lot of movement going on.

*   *   *

On the edge of town, thirty minutes from the meeting, the big Russian, Gorya Kocyk, was with twenty men armed with automatic weapons as they marched toward their destination. With Gorya was Gustavo's assistant, the informant, Giamo.

Gorya said loud and clear, "I want Mario, Gustavo, and the Americans dead!" As they approached the facilities, Gorya barked orders. "You ten men enter through the back door, and the rest of you follow me."

When Gorya and his men reached the general assembly area, it was empty except for a barricade in the front and one on the side.

*   *   *

Suddenly, Gorya heard, "Everybody freeze." The words came first in Russian and then in Italian. Gorya and his men were facing fifteen automatic weapons appearing over the top of the barricades and five weapons behind them in the hallway. Next, Gorya heard, "Gorya, you're under arrest for the murder of Lazzaro Mato. The rest of you men, drop your weapons and get down on the floor or die." Then there was the sound of weapons hitting the floor.

Gorya shouted, "You're not going to take me alive." He immediately began shooting at the barricades.

Jean popped up from the side and shot the Russian's weapon out of his hand. Then Vito jumped the barricade and charged at the Russian. When Vito reached Gorya, he swung at Vito, who ducked and laid a mean uppercut to the Russian's chin, sending him across the floor. Gorya quickly got on his feet and charged at Vito. And again, Vito sent the Russian enforcer to the floor. Vito turned around and said to Jean, "He's all yours now."

Then someone tossed a pistol to Gorya. Before he could use it, Mario quickly fired and called out, "This is for Lazzaro."

It was over. There was one dead Russian on the floor, and twenty men were arrested, of which two were Russians and the others were Communist Italians, including Giamo.

Gustavo walked up to his assistant, Giamo, and said, "I hope you enjoy being in prison."

Before being taken away, Giamo said, "How did you know?"

Gustavo replied, "You asked too many questions about the meeting before I announced it. And Agent Webb asked me if anyone had. Then she figured you were the informant … Oh, by the way, you will stand trial for accessory to murder, so you will be in prison for a very long time. Bye."

Jean and Jake were talking to Mario and Vito. "Mario, I'm glad you remembered about the tunnel connecting to the other warehouse," Jean said.

Vito commented, "Isn't it funny. Italians can move fast when they think they're going to be shot."

"It's a good thing it was a large tunnel, or we wouldn't have been able to move seven hundred people in twenty-five minutes," Jake said.

The next day, Gustavo organized a feast for the people of Milan, and thousands came. Mario and Vito were busy, because a lot of them were war veterans.

Jake walked up to Jean and said, "We have orders to return to Rome, and then you need to head to the States."

CHAPTER 51

On the flight to the States, Jean thought about how things turned out for Mario and the people of Milan. She was just thankful to Yves Le Noir for the information he'd given Jake on how he helped run the Russians out of France. The tale she'd told Gustavo was true except for her part, and it worked—thank goodness.

"Ma'am, what can I get you to drink?" the flight attendant asked.

"How about three fingers of bourbon and a splash of water on the rocks."

Once she had her drink, Jean leaned back and enjoyed her cocktail and the flight. She thought about what an interesting life she'd had. It had been adventurous and extremely dangerous, even rewarding at times, as well as a nasty business at times. Some people would say that at twenty-eight years old, she'd had quite a life.

Two days later, Jean reported in after seventeen hours of flying and a day to rest up and get her apartment livable again.

"Good morning, Chester," Jean said upon arriving at her meeting.

"Hey, Jean. Welcome back." Chester stood up and went to shake Jean's hand before continuing. "Please come in and have a seat. It's so good to see you. Congratulations on your successful assignment."

"Thank you, Chester. It's good to be back. So what's up?" she asked.

"Well, first of all, the boys upstairs, including the president, want to thank you for a job well done. And if you want some time off, you've got it."

"You know, Chester, I could stand a few days off. I should give my mother a call and see my grandfather, Senator Howl, if he's in town."

Chester answered, "I believe he is, Jean … So take five days, and report back to me for your next assignment."

"Thanks, Chester, and the boys upstairs."

Later that night, at about nine, Jean called her mom, knowing she would be home after a day at the state capital. It was six o'clock her time. On the third ring, Jean heard, "Hello. Mildred Webb speaking."

"Hi, Mom," she said. "It's me, your wonderful daughter."

"Oh, Jean, it's good to hear you voice. Where are you?"

"I'm in DC. I just got back from a long assignment in Europe. Guess what? I'm going to see Grandpa tomorrow for lunch."

"That's wonderful, Jean. I know he'll be glad to see you. And when might I see you, dear?"

"I don't know. It looks like I'm going to be busy again. But first chance I get, I'll try to make it."

"All right, dear," her mom said. "Give dad a hug for me. Love ya, Jean. Bye."

After Jean hung up, she thought her mom sounded good, and it would be nice to visit her, but not in August.

The next day it was downright chilly, which is often the case during December in DC. Jean bundled up and took a taxi to her grandpa's favorite restaurant a few blocks from Pennsylvania Avenue. On the way, she was thinking about her grandfather who was a country lawyer from Springfield, Missouri, and was fortunate enough to have met Harry S. Truman. Her mom also knew Truman's sister, whom she'd met in the Eastern Star organization. At the time, his sister was the Worthy Matron of Missouri. She recalled her mom telling her why she'd joined. The Order of Eastern Star was an organization of men and women who worked together in performing charitable, education, fraternal, and scientific events. Their main goal was to promote moral values and personal goodness, and they were associated with the Freemasons, of which grandfather was a member. So, when Harry S. Truman became vice president, he supported grandfather in his quest to becoming a senator.

At the restaurant, Jean saw her grandfather sitting at his favorite table. The maître d' asked, "Jean?"

"Yes, I'm Jean."

And he said, "The senator said, 'When a good-looking woman shows up, send her to my table, and I hope her name is Jean.'"

Jean just shook her head. "Hi, you sexy old man," she said as she approached the table.

Grandfather said, "Have a seat, Granddaughter."

But instead, she went around the table and hugged her wonderful grandpa.

As Jean sat down, she noticed the senator was staring at her. Finally he said, "Jean, my dear, you look so much like your grandmother. It always pleases me to see and hear about your latest accomplishments, and this time I heard it from Harry S."

"Oh, how is the president doing?" Jean asked.

"You know Harry. He's holding his own. Then I told him I was having lunch with you today, and he said to tell our little girl from

Missouri thanks. And as much as he would like to, he hasn't told anybody about you being my granddaughter, because he knows that's the way you wanted it."

"Do me a favor, Grandpa. The next time you see him, tell him thanks from me for being a great president."

The pair had an enjoyable visit and lunch. They always did, ever since Jean could remember sitting on his knee. He had taken her father's place, and she didn't think she could have done any better. He encouraged her to do what she wanted even in a man's world. It was unfortunate that a war had helped her do just that.

Jean asked, "I thought you were going to retire."

"Not yet, dear, but soon," said a tire sounding senator.

Then he asked, "Are you in town for a while?"

"Afraid not, Grandpa. Duty calls."

And then, just as he always reminded her, he said, "Don't forget to duck."

CHAPTER 52

"Good morning, Chester. I'm ready to go to work," Jean said.

"Hey, you do look rested, Jean," he responded. "Come in and have a seat ... Your next assignment is to help the FBI catch escaped Nazis, and you're to report to the deputy director tomorrow morning at nine. And good luck, Jean."

The next morning, Jean was up early. She fixed herself a nice breakfast and then soaked in a very hot tub of water. While soaking, she thought about how chasing after Nazis would probably mean Mexico and/or South America, which was good, because it meant she would get away from this damn cold weather.

Jean bundled up and took a cab to FBI headquarters. At the reception desk, she presented her credentials and was directed to the top floor, conference room number three. When she entered the large conference room, three men were waiting. A tall, nice-looking, well-dressed man got up and came over to introduce himself as Deputy Director Arthur Collins. He shook her hand. At the table, the other two men stood up, and Collins introduced Supervising Senior Agent Williams and Senior Agent Franklin. Both shook her hand.

Then Collins said, "Please have a seat, Agent Webb ... All three of us have read your personnel file, and I might add it's quite impressive. It is indeed an honor to have you on board."

"Thank you, Deputy Director Collins."

"I have another meeting to go to. Williams will be your supervisor, and you will be working with Agent Franklin. I think you'll be happy working with them. They're two of my best."

Then Collins shook her hand once more and left.

Next, Senior Agent Williams said, "Welcome to the team. I'm Jack, and this is Bob."

"And call me Jean."

Next, Jack jumped right into the details. "The first escaped Nazi is located south of the border in Nogales and is a Col. Franz Schoenfield."

"You're kidding me," Jean said. "I know him." When she looked at her teammates, she saw they were smiling.

Jack said, "We know, Jean. Small world, isn't it? And by the way, after you catch him, you both get to spend Christmas in Phoenix."

"I have a sister in Phoenix who works in Maricopa County as a clerk," Bob said.

After another two hours of briefing, the supervisor announced, "That's it. Your flight to Phoenix leaves tomorrow morning at ten. Good hunting, you two."

Bob asked, "How about lunch, Jean?"

"Why not? I always enjoy a handsome man taking me to lunch." She smiled at her six-foot, good-looking guy with sandy hair and big, blue eyes. She had always been a sucker for blue eyes.

At lunch, Jean found out Bob was raised on a ranch near Pinedale, Wyoming, located on the west side of the Rocky Mountains. He had two sisters: Carol who ran the family ranch for his dad, and Pat, who, of course, lived in Phoenix.

"I take it Carol is a cowgirl," Jean said.

"Oh, yeah. And tough too … What's your story, Jean?"

"Well, my father was a lieutenant in the Marines and was killed at Belleau Woods in World War I, and my mother is executive assistant to the governor of Arizona. I was born in Springfield, Missouri, and raised there as well."

Bob added, "I'm sorry about your father, Jean."

After lunch, Bob headed back to his FBI office to do some last-minute items, and Jean headed home to do the same. They decided to meet at the airport early, have breakfast, and discuss anything that had developed since their briefing. Back at her apartment, Jean made arrangements with the manager about being gone and called her mother to let her know it looked like she'd see her for Christmas.

The next morning, Jean was at the airport restaurant at eight o'clock, and Bob showed up a few minutes later. After they ordered breakfast, Bob filled her in on the latest.

"We'll be meeting the Jewish Nazi hunters in Nogales, Mexico, in two days. When we get to Phoenix, we'll rent a car and stay overnight and visit our relations. So call your mother and let her know. I've already called my sister."

The flight was eleven hours with one stop in St. Louis, Missouri. They arrived at Phoenix at six o'clock, and it was seventy degrees, thirty-five degrees warmer than it'd been in DC. Jean's mother was there, and so was Pat. Everybody met one another, and they all visited in the coffee shop at the airport.

Thirty minutes later, everyone left, and Bob said, "I'll rent a car in the morning and pick you up at your mother's."

It was seven o'clock local time when Jean and her mother arrived home. She already had something in the oven, so they sat down to eat while visiting some more.

Of course, as always, Jean's mom asked, "How much longer are you going to do the spy thing?"

Jean surprised her when she said, "A year from this coming April I'll be thirty years old, and I'm seriously thinking of retiring from my spy job."

Mom replied with a happy voice, "You know I'd love to have you come to Phoenix and stay with me in this big house. And by then, your grandfather would be retired. He's planning on living here as well."

CHAPTER 53

The next morning, Bob and Jean were headed for Tucson and then on to Nogales, Mexico. They arrived at a well-known restaurant on the main drag to meet the Nazi hunters.

While sipping on a cold beer, Bob said, "These guys are supposed to know where our target is located, and they don't consider Colonel Schoenfield as being a war criminal. He's just wanted for questioning. I guess the reason for questioning him is that he was very close to Hitler, and he might help find other war criminals we're after."

Then two men walked in, and Jean could tell they were Jewish. They saw Jean and Bob and headed their way.

They immediately introduced themselves. "I'm Cohen, and this is Rosen," one of the men said, showing their credentials.

Bob said, "Please have a seat, gentlemen, and let Uncle Sam buy your lunch." Not only was the statement a genuine offer to buy lunch, it was also the ID statement. Next, Bob and Jean introduced themselves and showed their credentials. After ordering their spicy Mexican meals, the Nazi hunters informed Jean and Bob that they believed they had a location for their target. And in addition, he was with two more Nazis who were wanted war criminals.

Cohen said, "They're facing hanging, and it won't be easy taking them. So be prepared for a gun battle."

After their spicy lunch, Jean and Bob followed the Nazi hunters. About two miles south of Nogales, there was a road heading west. The lead vehicle turned onto the road, and Bob and Jean followed about four car lengths behind, just in case they all had to suddenly back up.

The lead car pulled over on a dirt driveway to a pasture, and Rosen got out and came to their car. "The house is another sixty yards up this road."

The group of four started walking. On the way, Bob decided Jean should go with Rosen and cover the back because Schoenfield would most likely take off, while the other two would stay and fight. That meant Bob and Cohen would approach the front. If Schoenfield exited the back door, then Rosen could enter and hopefully get the drop on the two bad guys. It was around three o'clock, and the sun was low in the atmosphere, creating some shadows to hide in as they moved from place to place. Bob gave Rosen and Jean twenty minutes to get in position.

Then she heard Bob holler, "This is the FBI. Come out with your hands in the air."

Immediately, the shooting started, and sure enough, the colonel came charging out of the back door.

"I got him. Go for it," Jean said.

Rosen was headed for the back door, and Jean took chase after an old friend. The colonel was using his long legs and moving fast, but so was she. "Stop, Colonel, or I'll shoot!"

Franz stopped dead in his tracks and put up his hands.

When Jean reached him, she said, "Turn around, Franz." His look was precious. "How've you been, Colonel? Move your ass," she said, pointing at the house.

Just as Jean reached the house, one of the war criminals came charging out. When he saw Jean, he started to shoot, but she was quicker and got him first, right between the eyes.

Jean turned to the colonel and said, "Don't move, or you're next." She grabbed the dead man's weapon and entered the house, being careful because there was still shooting going on. Just before reaching the front of the house, she found Rosen, who had been knocked out and was still dazed. She whispered for him to stay put. When she reached the front of the house, the other shooter was facing the front.

"Drop your weapon, or die!" Jean hollered.

Apparently, he had already decided he wouldn't be taken alive and turned, giving her no choice.

"It's all over," Jean called out. "They're both dead."

Next, she retrieved Colonel Schoenfield. The Nazi hunters took the two dead bodies to the local authorities, providing proof they were escaped Nazis. The Nazi hunters accompanied Bob and Jean to the Phoenix FBI field office where they intended to interrogate the colonel. Once they had the colonel behind bars, they retired for the night and agreed to start the interrogation at nine o'clock the following morning. Hopefully Rosen's headache would be gone by then. Bob headed for his sister's house after dropping Jean off at her mother's. Jean had called her earlier at her office to let her know she would have company for the night.

When she answered the doorbell, Jean's mom said, "Hi, dear. Dinner will be ready in twenty minutes."

Jean's mother was a great cook, and anything she fixed always tasted wonderful. That night they were having a chicken casserole made with chicken breast and a spicy sauce on it—just what the doctor ordered. For dessert, it was homemade cherry pie with ice cream. Jean pigged out. She visited with her mom some more and listened to what was happening in Arizona, which was an enormous population growth. Then she asked Jean about Jake.

"He's in Italy with our embassy working with the new Italian government," Jean said, "and I was there two weeks ago on assignment."

Then came the question Jean had been waiting for. "So when are you two going to get married?"

CHAPTER 54

Come nine o'clock the next morning, Jean, Bob, Cohen, and Rosen were in an interrogation room with the colonel. The Nazi hunters started asking their questions. Apparently, the Nazi hunters were after four war criminals, and one in particular. This bad ass was SS Colonel Karl Heller, who ran a concentration camp in Poland and was responsible for killing thousands of Jewish prisoners. When the questioning began, the colonel decided to clam up. Jean excused herself and left the room. Outside, she asked one of the agents if he could find a particular item.

"Let me go look," he said.

Jean returned, and the colonel still wasn't talking. A few minutes later, there was a knock on the door.

"I've got it," Jean said. When she opened the door, the item she'd requested was put in her hand. "Thanks."

When she returned to the table, she said, "Bob, you need to leave the room." Next, she turned toward the colonel and said, "I'm a spy, and I don't have to follow the protocol for questioning a prisoner."

She then jammed the pig sticker into the top of the table and scared the colonel. He quickly leaned back in his chair, almost falling out of it.

Jean said, "Colonel, I want answers, or this room is going to get noisy from you screaming a lot. Now, I want those answers, you SOB!" I looked at the Jewish men and said, "Get on each side and hold him." The colonel stiffened up as Jean grabbed the knife and stood up suddenly.

"All right, what do you want to know?" he asked.

Jean sat back down, and the Nazi hunters started getting their questions answered. They found out three of their targets were in South America, and the one they wanted the most might be in Mexico. Schoenfield wasn't sure. Once the Jewish boys had what they wanted, they were ready to leave.

Cohen informed Jean and Bob, "Rosen and I are headed back to Mexico to look for the SS colonel. Before we head for South America, I will contact you, Agent Franklin."

As Cohen was leaving, he turned toward Jean and said, "Agent Webb, if you ever get tired of working for the CIG, you would be welcome to join us."

Jean answered, "Thanks for the offer, but I don't think I could get used to the food."

Bob reported in to Agent Williams in DC. After his conversation, Bob informed Jean he was instructed to have the colonel escorted to DC. For his cooperation, they were going to send him to wherever he wanted to go.

Before Colonel Schoenfield left, Jean had one last conversation with him. "Well, Colonel, it looks like you get to go free. Where would you like to go?"

He looked at Jean and smiled. "I think I'd like to go to Switzerland where they have a lot of beautiful women. And I'm glad I didn't catch you in France. I would have hated to have had shoot you."

"Yeah, me too, Franz. So long, and enjoy Switzerland."

Later, Bob informed Jean that they had another assignment.

"Where are we going this time, Mr. Franklin?" she asked.

"San Diego, California. A local agent is asking for help going into Mexico to bring back a rapist and murderer."

"It sounds like fun. Here we come, Tijuana, Mexico," she said.

After a short flight to San Diego, Bob and Jean were met by agent Rafael Alvarez, an American-born Mexican World War II vet who was one inch taller than Jean. "Welcome to sunny California," he said.

At the FBI field office, Rafael filled everyone in on what happened. "A Javier Ortiz kidnapped a twenty-two-year-old woman in Chula Vista, and fortunately, we had an eyewitness who saw what happened a week ago. We showed him our Mexican mug shots, and he picked out Javier. Border Patrol found the body three days ago in a ditch on a side road near the border. She had been brutalized, raped, and killed by strangulation."

Jean spoke up. "Any idea where the bastard is?"

"Yes, Agent Webb. I have a contact with a Tijuana state policeman. I saved his life once when we worked together on a case in Tijuana. He informed me there's a place two miles south of Tijuana where all the bad guys hang out and are protected by the Mexican mob. And we can't count on any help from the local officers, because they won't go there."

"I was right. It sounds like fun," Jean said. She got a funny look from Rafael and Bob.

Soon, the three of them were off to Tijuana to meet Rafael's partner, Emilio Santos, another American-born Mexican and ex-Ranger. They met near the Tijuana horse racetrack and headed south. On the way, they developed a plan for once they arrived at the tavern. Emilio parked the car near the tavern, facing a weathered building;

barely standing, based on appearances. Emilio would go in first, as he was dressed in native clothing. The remaining three would watch for his signal. He stepped outside, stood next to the entrance, and lit a cigarette. That was the signal the target was there. Next, Jean would go in and get their attention while Rafael and Bob slipped in toward the back. At the bar, Jean ordered tequila on the rocks with a beer chaser. She was standing next to Javier Ortiz, whom she recognized from his mug shot. He looked just as mean and ugly in real life as he did in his photo. He leaned over and asked Jean what she was doing there.

"Having a drink," she answered. "Do you mind?"

Javier made his first mistake and moved closer. Jean stuck her pistol in his belly and said in a low voice, "You're under arrest, asshole, and if you move, I'll blow your guts all over the bar."

He stiffened up. Apparently he didn't believe her and made a move. Jean rapped the barrel of her gun up against his head, and down he went. Then all hell broke loose as his friends started for Jean. Emilio took one of them out, and Rafael and Bob nailed the others.

Then the bartender pulled a shotgun. Before he could use it, Jean shot it out of his hands and said in a loud and clear voice, "Keep your damn hands on the bar, or the next one will be right between your eyes, asshole."

Bob and Jean covered Rafael and Emilio as they dragged Javier out of the tavern and threw his ass in the trunk of the car, handcuffed. Next, Rafael had made arrangements for a boat anchored near the tavern for a fast getaway. There was a phone at the tavern, and Rafael and Emilio knew they might have to take on the Mexico mob and that wouldn't be good, according to them. They finally reached a dock and found a small rowboat. Everybody was already on board when Jean heard a vehicle coming on fast. The anchored boat was only thirty yards out, and Jean didn't want to be caught on the water if the bad guys showed up with automatic weapons.

She made a quick decision and pushed the boat off from the dock. "Get out of here," she called out. "I'll catch up. Now row your asses off!"

Jean ran to the end of the dock and waited. It was late afternoon, so the sun was in the driver's eyes. Jean, however, could see the driver clearly. Thinking about how she'd been called a modern-day Anne Oakley, she got ready. When the car was close enough, Jean emptied her six-shooter at the driver. Then suddenly the truck flipped over and bounced several times. Men who had been in the bed of the truck went flying in all directions. Once she saw no movements, she ran to the end of the dock and dove in like she was an Olympic swimmer in a race. When she came to the top of the water, her arms were moving as fast as she could go. She reached the boat just as they were pulling up the anchor and starting the engine. She grabbed a towel and received friendly hugs from three thankful men and bad words from another.

CHAPTER 55

South of the entrance to the San Diego Harbor, a harbor patrol boat waited just north of the Mexican territorial waters for a special delivery.

A man on watch sounded off, "I see a boat approaching."

Once the boats were side-by-side, transfer of the prisoner and the Americans were made, and a wave good-bye was given to the Mexican skipper. After Rafael and Emilio made out their report, the supervising Special Agent Rogers congratulated everybody on a job well done and thanked Bob and Jean for their help. Then it was time to catch the next plane to Phoenix. At the airport bar, Jean ordered the tequila she didn't get to drink in Mexico. Bob ordered a bourbon and water, a typical cowboy drink.

"When was the last time you had some time off?" Jean asked Bob.

"Probably two years ago, and it felt nice too."

"It's been three years since I saw my mother, and that was a weekend pass in DC when she visited my grandpa." Jean looked at Bob. "It would be good to see your loved ones every year. Don't you agree, Bob?"

"I agree, Jean."

Then Jean heard the announcement for their flight to Phoenix. It was a two-and-half-hour flight, and they both rested. Jean did ask Bob what his and Pat's plans were for Christmas.

"I'll probably help Pat cook our Christmas dinner and relax and enjoy being with her. She is such a sweet sister."

"That's good, Bob. I'm probably going to do the same with my mother."

At the airport, Pat was there for Bob, and Jean's mom was there for her. They wished one another happy holidays and said their good-byes.

On the way home, Jean got to thinking and asked her mom, "Who are you having over for Christmas?"

"It's just going to be us and dad, who's flying in tomorrow. Why?"

"How about two more people?" Jean asked.

"Who are you talking about?"

"How about having Bob and Pat over for Christmas?"

Jean's mom looked at her and said, "They both seem like very nice people. I think it's a good idea, dear."

The following morning, Jean called Bob. "Good morning, Bob. The reason I called was to invite you and Pat to have Christmas dinner with us. My mom is an excellent cook, and I'm picking up my grandfather today at the airport. He's Senator Howl, and I know he would love the company. So how about it? We're eating at about one o'clock, but come early ... That's great, Bob. I'll let her know. See you tomorrow."

When Jean and her grandpa arrived back at her mom's house, he had some news to share. "I'm retired as of two days ago."

"Oh, Dad, I'm so glad. Then you're here to stay?"

"Yes, I am, Mildred. I could have retired in 1940 at sixty-five years old, but I stuck around until the war was over. At seventy-one years old, I'm ready for a retired life."

After sharing his news, he got hugs from two good-looking women. On Christmas morning, everybody was up having breakfast, and Mildred was getting ready to start cooking and assigning jobs to Jean and Grandpa. Jean's mom always fixed a ham, sweet potato hash with melted marshmallows on top, mixed vegetables, mashed potatoes, and some BBQ sauce on the side. Then she topped off the meal with homemade cherry and pumpkin pies and ice cream.

Bob and Pat arrived about eleven o'clock. Pat wanted to help, and Bob and Grandpa got to talking. Jean noticed that they seemed to be enjoying themselves. After a marvelous dinner, everybody retired to the living room to have a good visit and get to know one another better. Bob told stories about being raised on a ranch in northwest Wyoming with his two sisters. Pat was the youngest, and Carol was the oldest. They heard about his great-grandfather who knew Crazy Horse when he was with the Sixth Cavalry. He also knew men who were in the Seventh Cavalry. Later, he became a US Marshal for the western territory of Wyoming.

Then Grandpa let Bob know he had been with the Rough Riders and Teddy Roosevelt during the charge up San Juan Hill during the Spanish-American War in 1898. Bob congratulated the senator on his retirement and being part of great service to the United States. Then Grandpa asked Bob how he liked the FBI, and Bob said he loved it.

Soon, it was time to say good night. Jean thought everybody had a good time. Grandpa commented, "Those two are very nice people. I wish them the best."

CHAPTER 56

Bob and Jean reported in at the Phoenix field office on January 2 and received their next assignment, which would be in Rio de Janeiro, Brazil. They were told that when they arrived in Rio de Janeiro, they would meet two local FBI agents and team up with them to apprehend two Nazi war criminals.

The next day, Bob and Jean were on the first flight to Mexico City and then on to Panama City, Panama, for a fourteen-hour flight and overnight stay. Next came a fifteen-hour flight to Rio de Janeiro with an intermediate stop in Caracas, Venezuela. The following day, Bob and Jean spent time resting up after their twenty-nine-hour trip and time adjustment. On the fourth day, they met the two local agents.

"Good morning, guys," Bob said. "Let me introduce Jean Webb of the CIG. She's here to help apprehend our targets." Handshaking took place, and Bob continued. "Jean, this is Agent Barbosa and Agent Estevez."

Back in Bob's hotel room, the local agents updated Jean and Bob on the case. "Our informant says he knows where they are hiding, and there's a meet set up for two o'clock tomorrow at this location. We'll meet with him."

"Okay, guys, and we'll all meet back here and decide what our next move will be. And we'll be your backup tomorrow, just in case," Bob said.

The following morning at breakfast, Bob asked, "Because this is your first time here, Jean, how would you like to do some sightseeing this morning?"

"Gee, Bob, that sounds great," Jean said. "What do you have in mind?"

"How about a cable car ride to the top of Mount Corcovado to see the tallest statue in the world? The *Christ the Redeemer*, the seventh wonder of the world. We'll take a lunch and enjoy the view at 2,100-foot elevation of Rio de Janeiro."

Bob and Jean were at the cable car station waiting. Jean sensed they'd been followed ever since they'd left their hotel, the Copacabana Palace. When the cable car arrived, Bob and Jean climbed on board. Just as the car was ready to go, two men jumped on board with them. There were now eight people on board, and the two men seemed to be working their way toward Bob and Jean.

When they were very close, Jean stepped in front of Bob with one hand in her coat and said, "Hi, fellows. *Tun du sprechen deutsch?*"

That caused the two men to make their move, but not before Jean was able to. As soon as her pistol/silencer appeared, they froze.

Then Jean said in German, "Move to the door, or die right here." When they were at the door, Bob forced it open. Jean said in German, "Jump, or I'll shoot."

The two men jumped, knowing they were over water. Jean said aloud, "I hope they can swim. Don't worry, folks. They just tried to rob us."

At the top, Bob and Jean walked around looking at everything and looked up at the ninety-foot statue. After an hour of looking around, they found a place where it wasn't too windy and had an early lunch looking down on Rio de Janeiro. After lunch, it was time for them to head for the meeting place near the downtown business district at a well-known tavern. Bob and Jean had the tavern staked out when their team members went in right at two o'clock.

Jean said, "I hope they can trust this guy."

Barbosa walked in first and a few minutes later so did Estevez.

Barbosa spotted the informant, code name Cajero (teller), and slowly approached him. "Friends come from high places," Barbosa said.

Cajero responded, "And low places also."

When Barbosa and Estevez were seated, a brief conversation took place, and the two agents received the information they were looking for. Then it was time to leave, so Barbosa said his good-byes and left.

Back at the hotel, Barbosa and Estevez headed for Bob's room. Once inside, Barbosa told Bob what the informant had said.

"The two Nazis we want are at a hacienda one mile south of San Paulo," Barbosa noted.

"Jean and I will take the left side, and you two get the right side. We'll leave so when we get there, it'll be dusk. Once we look things over, our plan may change," Bob said.

As predicted, it was turning dark when they arrived. They parked their vehicles about fifty yards from the hacienda and slowly approached their targets. When they cleared the trees, it was impossible to miss the hacienda, because it was lit up like a Christmas tree.

Bob quickly sized things up and said, "We'll go with the original plan. Stay in the shadows as much as you can, and wait for my signal. Okay, Jean. I'll follow you."

When Jean got closer, she spoke. "Bob, I think we are about to bite off more than we can chew. Look at all those damn Nazis."

At about that same time, Bob's walkie-talkie sounded off. "Bob! It's a trap." They heard shooting.

Bob looked over at Jean, but she was already receiving heavy fire.

"Jean! Let's get out of here!" Bob hollered.

"Get going, Bob. I'll cover you," she yelled back.

Bob started to leave but then looked back at Jean and could tell she was pinned down. He ran back to her and hollered, "Jean! Take off when I start firing." With that, Bob emptied his weapon as Jean jumped up and ran for her life. When they reached the road, they met Barbosa. "Where's Estevez?" Bob asked.

"He bought it," Barbosa reported.

Bob, Jean, and Barbosa ran to their vehicle, and Bob said, "Let's get the hell out of here."

"Those are my exact sentiments," Jean said.

Back at Bob's room, everybody was taking a break, and all three had a glass of bourbon and water on the rocks as they thought about what happened.

Barbosa spoke first, "Bob, I swear they were waiting for us."

Jean spoke next. "They had to be waiting, because we saw no one before we got there. Unless they had a lookout in the woods ... That means Barbosa is right, Bob."

Bob was in deep concentration, and his mind kept trying to figure out how in the hell they knew. Then it hit him. "It was the damn informant."

"Yeah, you gotta be right, Bob. It had to be him, but there's nothing we can do about it," stated Barbosa.

Then Jean stood up and faced the two men. "You two can't do anything, but I can."

CHAPTER 57

The next morning, Bob, Barbosa, and Jean headed for the US Embassy to report in. Later, Bob found out he and Jean had orders to head for Caracas, Venezuela, immediately. Barbosa would try to get the local authorities to help him gather up the Nazis they were after.

Jean spoke to Bob. "You head for the airport and make reservations for the two of us, and I'll be right behind you." After Bob left, she turned to Barbosa and said, "I need a ride to the airport, but I have to make a stop first."

On the way to the next stop, Jean thought about what the situation was and contemplated the options she had. If she kidnapped the informant and turned him over to the local authorities, according to Barbosa, he wouldn't be punished for causing the death of an American agent. He would only serve some jail time. That left Jean with her only other option. Barbosa parked in front of the tavern, and she walked in, looking for the informant. She knew what he looked like from a photo.

When Jean spotted him, she casually walked over to him and sat down. "Friends come from high places." He stiffened up, and she added, "Don't do or say anything. I have a pistol aimed at your belly. Now order me a drink, and make it tequila with a beer chaser."

When the drink came, Jean bit into the lime, downed the tequila, and took a drink of beer before speaking again. "This is for Agent Estevez."

With a noisy tavern, nobody noticed the thud sound, and Jean reached over, acting like she was giving him a hug. Then she got up and walked out of the tavern to the waiting vehicle.

On the way to the airport, Barbosa didn't say anything until he dropped her off at the terminal. As she was getting out of his vehicle, he said loud and clear, "Thanks, Agent Webb."

Jean headed for the bar where Bob would be waiting and thought, *Spying is a nasty business, but sometimes it's necessary.*

Bob and Jean finished their business in Caracas and spent several months traveling around South America tracking and apprehending three more Nazis who were hiding in Colombia, Argentina, and Peru. Then it was back to Mexico City to apprehend one more Nazi. Next, they were able to spend a weekend in Phoenix.

This time, Jean and her family had a picnic with Bob and Pat at the zoo. It was a cool day on April 6, 1946. Again, everybody enjoyed being together. Bob and the senator had interesting conversations, and Jean and her mom got to visit with Pat.

Being a nice, good-looking blonde, Pat had no trouble getting men to call on her. "Some of these cowboys are something else, but fun," she said.

"Just don't let them get you riding a bull, mostly their BS," Mildred said.

On Monday, Jean and Bob got their new assignment. They would be traveling through Texas border towns like Juarez, south of El Paso, Acuna, and Del Rio. It took two months, because two fugitives were added to the manhunt. The partners had a few close calls, but they managed to save each other's butts once or twice. Then they wrapped it up at the end of June and were headed back to DC.

At FBI headquarters, Arthur Collins said, "Job well done, Bob and Jean. Jean, anytime you're looking for a job, give me a call. I'll see if I can convince the director to hire a woman."

Jean thanked DD Collins and said good-bye to Bob and gave him a friendly hug.

Once Jean arrived back at CIG, she greeted Chester.

"Come in and have a seat, Jean. It's good to have you back. Are you ready for your next assignment?" Chester asked.

Jean responded in a serious tone of voice. "That's what I want to talk to you about. I've got a personal dilemma to solve."

"What's that, Jean?" asked a concerned Chester.

"I've got to make a decision on whether I'm staying with CIG, and I need time to make up my mind."

"How much time, Jean?"

"I don't know, Chester," she answered. "Maybe weeks or months. It's been bugging me for months."

Jean stood and took out her credentials and handed them to Chester.

"No, Jean, you keep them. I'm putting you on temporary medical leave. When you've made up your mind, come see me."

"Thanks, Chester," she said. "I'll let you know where I'm at."

The next day, Jean got her act together and took care of her apartment again with the manager and made reservations for a flight to Rome. It was a good thing she made good money as a spy, or she wouldn't have been able to pay for her sabbatical.

Jean was busy packing her bags when the phone rang. "Jean speaking."

"Hi, Jean," the voice on the other end said. "I'd like to dine with you tonight. I'll have a car pick you up at seven. See you then."

"Yes, sir, Mr. President," she responded.

Jean still had the receiver in her hand as she wondered what in the hell was going on. Then the receiver started making a buzzing sound, and she hung it up.

Once she was dropped off at the White House and approached the secretary, she waved Jean through. "He's waiting. Go right in."

Jean walked in, and the president got up and came around his desk and said, "Oh, Jean, it's so good to see you, my dear. Please, have a seat."

"It's always good to see you, Mr. President, and thanks for the invite."

"You're welcome, Jean, and it's Harry … I understand you are going to take some time away to solve a personal problem."

"Yes, sir—I mean, Harry. I need to think clearly about what I want to do the rest of my life. I'm not sure I still want to be a spy."

"The reason I invited you here tonight was to make sure you know you have my support, whatever you want to do."

"Thanks, Harry," Jean said. "I really appreciate knowing that."

"Good. Now, Jean, how do you like your Kansas City steak cooked?" the president asked.

"Medium rare would be nice." Jean couldn't believe she was having dinner with Harry S. in the White House.

Next, Harry asked, "How would you like a drink, since we are both off duty?"

Jean answered, "Bourbon and water on the rocks would be great."

After a wonderful dinner, Jean had a wonderful time visiting and hearing Harry remember the first time he met her grandpa and how they became good friends.

Then he surprised Jean when he said, "Jean, you look so much like your grandmother. She was a fine lady and always a pleasure to be around. How's that retired senator from Missouri doing in Arizona?"

"Last time I talked to Mom he was definitely enjoying retirement."

"That's good to hear, and I wish him well. Oh, one thing I wanted to tell you."

"Oh, what's that Harry?" Jean asked.

"Several months back I had lunch with General Clark, and he told me an interesting story about an extraordinary woman he met in Northern Italy."

Jean smiled. "Yes, I turned down his offer to become his intelligence officer."

"That's what he said, and he also said if you had accepted, you would probably have been a colonel or a one-star general by the time you retired."

"He said that?"

"Yes he did, Jean," Harry confirmed. "He also said you earn more than the DSC. So I want you to know you have accomplished what you set out to do, and I'm proud of you, Jean, as are a lot of other people."

After Jean and Harry finished their drinks, she said good night and walked over to give him a big, wonderful hug. "Thanks for being a great president, Harry," Jean said before departing.

CHAPTER 58

By noon the next day, Jean was on the second leg of her flight to Shannon, Ireland, which was scheduled to arrive at about seven o'clock in the evening.

The TWA flight attendant said, "Here's your lunch, ma'am. What can I get you to drink?"

"A Coke with some ice, please," Jean responded. While eating lunch, Jean was thinking about how nice it was going to be seeing Jake.

After lunch, the flight attendant asked, "Can I get you anything else, ma'am?"

"Yes, I'll have bourbon with a splash of water on the rocks."

Once the drink was gone, Jean reclined her seat, leaned back, and closed her eyes. Several hours later, she woke up and realized she had dreamt about the church in Venice and Father Sergio. She decided right there that Venice would be her next destination after visiting with Jake.

The plane landed on time, and Jean headed for the Inn & Tavern near the airport where she had stayed once before. She checked in and headed for the tavern for a nightcap. It was eight o'clock local time, and Jean saw an empty barstool and walked toward it. There was singing, dancing, and, of course, lots of drinking from what she could tell.

When Jean sat down next to an elderly gentleman, he turned to see who it was and said, "Bless my lovely stars. The heavens opened up, and an angel fell through."

Jean smiled at the gentleman and said, "Just for tonight. Tomorrow I get to go back up into the heavens."

"And not only is she beautiful, but witty too. I'm Shawn Cafferty, at your service, ma'am."

"Well, howdy, Shawn. Can I buy you a drink, and then you can tell your life story."

The following morning, Jean managed to get up and have an Irish breakfast with corned beef hash and eggs with potatoes and homemade bread. The coffee was so strong it almost made her stand at attention, but she needed it because she thought Shawn was never going to stop drinking and talking. Bless his Irish heart. After several more cups of coffee, Jean was off to catch a short flight to London and then on to Rome. On the flight to Rome, she had more coffee and then a nice cold beer.

Then she was back to sleeping until she heard, "Rome in twenty minutes."

"Boy, did I sleep," she muttered to herself, "and I feel better."

When Jean deplaned, she saw Jake waving and smiling. When she reached him, there was a hardy embrace and a very long kiss.

When they were breathing again, Jake asked, "How long?"

Jean answered him. "How does two weeks sound?"

That really threw Jake a curve ball, and with a confused look, he said, "What's going on, Jean?"

"Let's go get my bags, and I'll tell you later at your apartment."

When the couple arrived at Jake's apartment, Jean let him know she was starving, so they both headed to the kitchen to fix something to eat. During dinner, she told him what was going on.

"Jean, is there anything I can do to help you resolve this?" Jake asked.

"No, Jake, but thanks for asking," she said. "This is something only I can resolve, and I'm not going to make a decision before I'm 100 percent sure. Now, what can we do for the next two weeks?" Jean asked, smiling at her handsome man.

Jake got two weeks off, after telling the ambassador Jean was visiting. The ambassador had told him to greet Jean for him and let his office know where he would be, if he was needed. Then Jake took Jean sightseeing. Between tours, the couple wound up back in bed. It could be said that both Jean and Jake were getting caught up in that department. Jake helped make it an enjoyable two weeks, and Jean knew she could have easily spent two more weeks with him. He was such a wonderful man. Just before Jean was getting ready to leave, Jake received a letter from Jean's mother. Jean wondered what she was up to now.

Jake read the letter and told Jean what she'd said. "She says there's going to be an opening for a position to head up a unit that will be the Arizona Rangers. If I'm interested, I'm supposed to send her my résumé."

"Sounds like a great opportunity, Jake," Jean said.

"Well, maybe I'll think about it."

Jake took Jean to the train station, and they said their good-byes and enjoyed a long kiss and a big hug along with it. Jean was on her way to Venice and a certain church. She had planned to stay a week, because she wanted to see everything she could of the beautiful city.

Jean arrived at two o'clock in the afternoon and checked in at the Canal Grand Hotel before heading for the café nearby, located on the canal. She ordered the daily special and wine. While waiting for her late lunch, Jean decided that she would visit San Beneto the following morning at about nine o'clock.

Back in her room, Jean was looking forward to a very restful sleep. She thought she'd had enough wine in her system to make that happen. Before falling asleep, she thought about seeing Father Sergio and about what questions to ask. She hoped he could help her with the dilemma she faced.

Jean woke up with the sun shining on her balcony. She enjoyed a hot water bath in the deep tub, where she soaked for thirty minutes. Then she got dressed and headed for her favorite café for breakfast. After breakfast, Jean decided to walk along the canal to the church. The weather was predicted to hit a perfect eighty degrees. She wore shorts and a nice-looking blouse with the top button undone. On the way to San Beneto, Jean received several whistles from some of the young Italians.

When she entered the beautiful church and looked around, Jean felt that same feeling as before. Then she walked to the altar and looked around again. The artwork was so beautiful. A few minutes later, Jean headed for Father Sergio's office. She found his office, and his door was open.

When she entered, he was sitting at his desk. As he looked up, a surprised look appeared on his face.

"Oh, Jean," he gasped, "it's wonderful to see you, my dear." He instantly got up and came around to Jean and grabbed her with both hands.

"It's good to see you too, Father," she replied.

"Please have a seat and tell me what's going on, my child."

"Well, I decided I needed some time off, so I'm on kind of a vacation— or I guess you would call it a sabbatical. I've a serious decision to make. So I came to see you, Father, and to see some more of Venice."

"May I ask what decision?" Father Sergio said.

"I'm not sure I want to be a spy anymore, but I also need to be 100 percent sure before I make that decision," she explained.

"Apparently, Jean, this has bothered you greatly, and I understand with your profession how it could be real trouble for you."

"You're right, Father. I need to stay focused on doing my job, but I'm having strong thoughts about sleeping in the same bed every night and settling down in one place."

"Jean, knowing you, I would surmise that when you were a young woman, being who you are, you wanted an exciting life, and that meant entering into a man's world. Because you are a brave and courageous person, you have accomplished the impossible. But because you have gotten older, you're wondering if you still want to do this. So it's time for you to weigh your options versus your feelings and decide how you want to live the rest of your life. It may also mean setting your emotions aside and considering what's practical and what will make you content and happy."

"Thank you, Father," Jean said. "You've given me a lot to think about, and I think I can now."

Jean said good-bye to a very young and smart Father Sergio and left the beautiful San Beneto. She walked back to her hotel, doing a lot of thinking on the way. During the next six days, Jean paid Father Sergio several more visits, and each time, he helped. Also, during those six days, she spent time touring Venice. Then she decided to go to Milan and left the next day on the train. Jean had called Mario so he would meet her at the train station. This time, he would be able to recognize her.

On the train, Jean thought about how she would enjoy Milan and the people. This time around, she would be able to visit some of the people she knew during the war. When the train pulled into the station, Jean could see Mario waiting.

"Hi, Mario," she called out. She saw Vito was with him.

"Hi, Jean," said the two Italians.

Jean gave each man a friendly hug. Vito said, "Give me your baggage tickets, and I'll meet you in front of the station."

As they walked to the front of the station, Mario asked, "How long do you plan on staying with us, Jean?"

She replied, "I'm not in any hurry to leave … unless you kick me out."

Mario quickly responded, "That's not going to happen."

When Vito showed up, Mario headed for the parking lot and his new car.

"Hey, look at that. She's a beauty, Mario," Jean noted.

Mario said, "Yeah, the apples have been good to me this year."

When the trio arrived at Mario's home, his two teenagers came running out of the house. Jean got hugs from both of them. Then she saw Marie and walked over to give her a hug. Next, Jean saw Angela sitting and realized she was pregnant. She turned around and looked at Vito, who was beaming with a big smile.

"It's about time you quit messing around and got the job done, you big lug."

CHAPTER 59

Jean looked over at Angela and saw she was glowing. Yet, she looked very pregnant with a large belly full of baby and seemed ready to pop.

Jean walked over and sat next to her and said, "You look beautiful, Angela. When, my dear?"

"Any day now, and I hope soon," she replied, sounding like a woman tired of being pregnant.

Marie had fixed a feast and called everybody to the table. Vito rushed over to help his wife up and over to a seat. Jean enjoyed watching Vito be a loving husband. Of course, Italians love to eat too, and the food smelled and tasted wonderful.

After dinner, Jean helped the kids and Marie clean up, and then everybody retired to Mario's large front porch where there was a cool breeze. Mario then served some wine, and the evening was filled with some interesting conversations and just visiting with old friends.

The next morning, after a marvelous breakfast, Mario took Jean around to see more old friends and meet some new ones. Then Mario needed to go check on his orchard, and she went with him.

While walking through the beautiful apple orchard, Mario asked, "Jean, what's going on? I sense something is bothering you."

Jean stopped. "Yes, Mario. I've an important decision to make about my career. That's why I'm on this trip away from work. So you know, I did talk to your brother while in Venice, and he was able to help a lot."

Mario put both hands on Jean's shoulders and said, "You know all you have to do is ask, Jean, and I'll do whatever it takes to help you also."

"Thanks, Mario," she said. "I appreciate that, my friend."

For the next three days, Jean toured the center part of the city and the piazza del Cuomo and the beautiful cathedral. She was enjoying herself, riding in a horse-drawn carriage. On her way to the west side of town, she passed by Piazzale Loreto where she'd seen the terrible site of Benito Mussolini hanging by his feet, dead. When she reached the Spanish walls, she stood where she had on April 11, 1945, before the attack on the Nazis and Italians who were occupying Milan. She noticed in touring the city, the reconstruction was in full swing with multiple-story structures being built. She saw a lot of company offices being built, because Milan was having a large migration from southern Italy. There were factories starting up, which meant jobs.

One day while sightseeing, Jean passed what looked like a hospital. The driver said, "Switzerland has created the hospital until we build one of our own."

Four days later, after the Caruso family had eaten dinner, the phone rang. Mario answered it, and everyone heard, "Okay, Vito, we'll be right there." After Mario hung up, he turned and said, "Angela is having her baby, so let's head for the hospital."

Vito was already pacing when Jean and Mario's family arrived at the waiting room. The waiting area was only half occupied. Maria spent time calming down Vito, a little.

Two hours later, the doctor came out and announced, "It's a girl, weighing 9.6 pounds."

Before leaving for the recovery room, Vito said, "Later, you guys. Come and see Jean Louisa Basso." He looked right at Jean as he spoke.

Later, they were able to see Jean Louisa. She was a pretty baby, and why not? Angela was a good-looking blonde, and Vito wasn't bad looking, just big. And, of course, with Jean being her godmother, she had to be beautiful.

The following Saturday, Mario and Jean went fishing at Como Lake, a trip that lasted all day and part of the night.

"This is great, Mario," Jean said. "I haven't been fishing since I was a teenager in Missouri fishing on the lakes of the Ozarks."

It was a beautiful day, with sunshine, seventy-degree temps, a slight breeze, and the Alps for a backdrop. Mario had brought some wine, cheese and crackers, and a lunch for later. He had told Jean that they would be fishing for bass, crappie, and pike, and Jean let him know bass and crappie were what they had in Missouri. After a couple of hours, they had caught six fish, and Jean was totally relaxed, looking at this beautiful country.

Then Mario asked her, "Jean, have you gotten any closer to making your decision?"

"I think so, Mario. I've been narrowing down my options."

At the end of the fishing day, the duo had eighteen fish. Mario said, "Fish for dinner tomorrow night." With that, they cleaned and iced them down.

Before heading back to Milan, Mario took Jean to a restaurant on Lake Como that was serving trout almandine, and it was wonderful.

Before leaving the restaurant, Jean said, "You know, Mario, I think I could get used to living here."

Mario quickly responded, "The people of Milan would be proud to have you live with us, Jean."

That almost brought tears to Jean's eyes. She gave Mario a big smile and said, "Thank you for that, Mario."

It was ten o'clock when they reached Mario's home, and Vito was waiting for them.

"Mario and Jean, the Russians are back," Vito said. "This time there are three of them, and they are armed."

Jean immediately rushed to the phone and called Jake in Rome. Fortunately, he was home. Jean thought she must have gotten him out of bed, because he sounded like he was still waking up. But when she told him what was happening, he snapped awake.

"As soon as I can gather six Italian government men, I'll be there," Jake said. "Count on me arriving about seven."

Then Mario rounded up six of his men and armed them. He also had Vito get Angela and the baby and bring them to his house, because there would be guards posted all night. Jean had her weapon with her, and Mario had a weapon also, just for this reason.

CHAPTER 60

Mario, Vito, and Jean took turns keeping a lookout in case the asshole Russians decided to try something. Jake did show up at about seven, just as he'd said, and just in time for breakfast. Maria fixed food for everybody, including the six government men.

After the eating was done, Jake asked, "Where are they staying, Vito?"

Vito said, "On the east side of town at a small, rebuilt hotel. I'll be glad to show you."

When Jean, Jake, Mario, and Vito reached the hotel, Jake sent one of the Italian G-men in to scout around. The man returned shortly and reported back to the others.

"They're having breakfast and are almost done," he said.

"Good, let's surround the entrance and wait for them to come out. Stay hidden the best you can," Jake said. "I'll give the signal, and hopefully they won't put up a fight."

Mario, Vito, and Jean were with Jake. They waited, not saying anything. About thirty minutes later, the Russians exited the hotel, and when they were out in the open, Jake gave the signal. In a matter of seconds, the Russians were surrounded and being hollered at.

"Hands up, and don't move," one of the G-men said.

The Russians found themselves with nine weapons being pointed at them and did as they were told. When the lead Italian G-man checked their papers, it was obvious they had crossed the border illegally and were arrested. Mario, Vito, and Jean walked up to where Jake was standing. The G-men were searching the assholes and getting ready to cuff them when the Russians broke free, and knifes suddenly appeared.

Jean quickly realized they were charging at her and Mario. Jake managed to shoot one of them in the leg, and Jean took after the lead charger going after Mario. Vito quickly stepped in front of Jean and took out the other charger with very little effort. Jean had the bigger SOB, and she slid like she was going for second base just as he swung his blade at her and came up on her knees. She then planted a karate blow to his balls, and he let out a yell, bending over. Next, she hit him with a karate blow using her knuckles into his chest, and he went down. When he looked up, he was staring at the barrel of a pistol.

Later, during interrogation, the two chargers refused to talk. Jean pulled her weapon and informed them, "I once threatened to shoot off a German captain's balls, so maybe I need to shoot off your balls, since I didn't shoot his off, assholes."

It didn't seem to bother either of the men until she had Vito pull them away from the table so she had a clear shot. Then Jean calmly started reciting eeny, meeny, miny, moe. When she finished, she found herself pointing at the smaller Russian. "Smaller balls I bet," she said as she cocked her pistol.

With that, he started singing like a bird. The larger Russian started hollering at him to shut up, and Jake coldcocked him. They soon found out it was as Jean had suspected. They'd been sent to assassinate Gustavo, Mario, and her too if she were there. When they were done talking, Jake informed them they would be in an Italian prison for a long time.

Before Jake left for Rome, Jean let him know she was headed to Paris in four days.

He smiled. "I'll try to get a four-day weekend. It shouldn't be a problem when I tell the ambassador it's you I'm seeing. He still thinks you're the cat's meow."

Jean still wanted to try to see everybody she knew in Milan from the war before leaving. Of course, Mario and Maria made it easy for her by having a feast and inviting everybody. When it was time to leave, Mario escorted her to the train station.

Before boarding, Jean gave Mario a very hardy hug, kissed him on the cheek, and said, "Good-bye, you wonderful man. Take care of everybody. I know you will. And if you ever need me, you know where to find me."

"Good-bye, Jean," he said. "I may have to call you once a year, so you can come and solve my problems." He was smiling from ear to ear.

Once the train was moving, Jean poured herself a glass of wine from a bottle Maria had given her, along with some cheese and crackers to go with it. As she enjoyed her snack, she got to thinking that she had just had the two best weeks of her life. Maybe? She just might take Mario up on his offer and go back.

In Paris, the agency had made a reservation for Jean at a luxury hotel. As she checked in, she wondered what Chester was up to.

The next day, she found out why that hotel had been selected. She had to go to work, because the US ambassador had lunch with the French prime minister and General de Gaulle. Apparently, the general had asked about Jean and Jake. The US ambassador asked to see Jean.

So, she reported in. "I'm Agent Webb, and I understand the ambassador wants to see me."

She saw a well-dressed man show up, and he said, "I'm the ambassador's assistant. Please follow me, Agent Webb."

When Jean entered the large conference room, she saw two gentlemen. One of the men got up and came over to her. She thought maybe she had met him before.

"Hi, Agent Webb. You probably don't recognize me without the mustache and beard. I'm Yves Le Noir."

"Yes, you're right, Yves," Jean said. "I like you better without the facial hair." She received a friendly gesture in return.

"Come, Jean, and let me introduce you to Ambassador Leon Gibbons," Yves said.

The ambassador got up and said, "It's indeed an honor to meet you, Agent Webb. Please come and have a seat." He shook Jean's hand before sitting back down. "I understand you know why you're here."

"Yes, sir, I do. Did the general say why he wanted to see me?"

"Not exactly, but he did describe you as an extraordinary woman and said he would love to see you and Major Blakely also. Because we are trying to keep the general in our corner in joining the United Nations, which replaced the League of Nations back in April, we decided to have this dinner with him and the French prime minister, who would like to meet you also."

"Well, it looks like I'm going to dinner tomorrow night. I do have one favor to ask," Jean noted.

The ambassador asked, "What's that, Agent Webb?"

"I'd like for Agent Blakely to stay in Paris for at least four days."

Yves spoke up. "It's already been taken care of, Jean. Tomorrow we'll go pick up Jake and then pick out a dress for you and a tux for Jake to wear to dinner."

Chapter 61

Yves picked Jean up at her hotel at nine o'clock, and they headed for the airport. Jake was arriving a ten o'clock via US Army Air Corp. At the gate, Jean saw Jake and waved at him. He rushed over and gave her a big hug as Yves watched. Jean then introduced him to Yves.

"Glad to finally meet you, Yves," Jake said, "and thanks for your help."

"It's all part of the job, Jake. Now let's go find a dress for Jean and a tux for you."

While out looking at clothes, Yves explained a few things to Jean and Jake. "Try not to get in a conversation with the general about politics, if you can help it. Right now he is still not happy with us."

Jean spoke up. "Yeah, I remember he wasn't happy about being left out about Normandy until the last minute."

"He still holds a grudge against Roosevelt and Churchill over that, and now he and our president have had words," Yves informed them.

"Having known Harry S. since I was a little girl, I know he wouldn't put up with any baloney from any foreign power," Jean said.

The dinner party was being hosted at the US Embassy, and twenty guests were invited. At the receiving line were US Ambassador Gibbons, Jean, and Jake. Jean's dress was the latest French design. It was a coral color that looked very nice with her wavy auburn hair, and of course, it was low cut, exposing a lot of her beautifully full figure.

Jake looked marvelous in his tux; being six foot two and handsome didn't hurt.

As Jean stood in the line, she began to think to herself. *Here I am, standing in line, and all I'm supposed to do is smile and be nice. I feel like a pawn in a chess match, being moved around to block the opponent's moves. And the opponent is Charles de Gaulle, a French aristocrat and warrior.*

After most of the guests had arrived, Jean heard the announcement, "Prime Minister Georges Bidault and Mrs. Bidault."

When the prime minister reached the receiving line, Ambassador Gibbons introduced Jean and Jake.

The prime minister said, "Miss Webb, it is an honor to finally meet you."

Jean thanked him for coming, and then he introduced his wife. Jean shook her hand and received a smile in return. She then turned to see who was next in line, and there he was—the opponent, Charles de Gaulle, along with his wife. When Jean went to shake his hand, he took it and kissed it like a gentleman and Frenchman.

Then he introduced his wife, and Jean shook her hand with both of hers and said in French, "Welcome, Mrs. de Gaulle. It's an honor to meet you. Please enjoy the evening."

Next, de Gaulle thanked Jake again for saving his life. At the head table, Jean sat next to Charles, and his wife sat next to Jake. On the other side of Jake was the prime minister, who spoke English.

Next, Jean and the general engaged in a general conversation, like what she had been doing since the war.

"Hunting Nazis in Mexico and South America and helping run the Russian Communists out of Northern Italy," Jean said.

That caused him to shake his head and turn to his wife, saying, "See, my dear. I told you she's a warrior like me."

Jean leaned over and said to Mrs. de Gaulle, "May I ask what you have been doing since the war?"

She answered, "Worrying a lot less." The two women talked in French for fifteen minutes, and then dinner came.

During dessert, Charles asked, "May I call you Jean?"

She said, "Yes, Charles." Jean wanted to enjoy the evening with Jake and Charles, so she said to de Gaulle, "I'm supposed to convince you to quit messing around and join the United Nations, but knowing you, I'm sure you will do what's best for France. Now, Charles, let's enjoy the evening."

Charles then said, "I agree, Jean."

And they did enjoy the evening, which included dancing and joyful conversations.

Jean danced with Charles, Prime Minister Bidault, Ambassador Gibbons, Yves Le Noir, and finally Jake, as well as with half the other men. Sometimes it's not always good to show a lot of cleavage.

CHAPTER 62

The next day, Jean declared herself back on vacation and said good-bye to everyone. Then, for the next four days, Jake and Jean did Paris, day and night, and sometimes in bed. During the day, they managed to visit the Eiffel Tower and see Paris from the top observation deck. The next day, they went to the Louvre and looked at magnificent art for two hours. Over the next two nights, they hit several nightclubs, shows, and the bed. One night, they went to see a headliner show at the Moulin Rouge, followed the next day by a relaxing time at Notre Dame Cathedral, which was beautiful. On the fifth day, they both checked out of the hotel and headed for the airport.

Jake had a nine o'clock flight to Rome, and he let Jean know, "I did send my résumé to your mother."

"Good, Jake. It sounds like a great job." Jean gave Jake a long kiss and a hardy hug before saying, "See you, handsome."

At ten o'clock, Jean boarded her flight to London and then took a bus to Southampton and a hotel. She had booked passage on the USS *Washington* ocean liner, leaving the next day. She was looking forward to seven days on the high seas and total relaxation. The weather was a little chilly, being the middle of September and in the north Atlantic, but sitting on the sundeck with a blanket and a hot drink sounded just fine to her. On the fifth day, Jean had pretty much made up her mind on what the future was going to hold on the sixth day, she spent part of her day in the bar and lounge, celebrating her decision. The rest of the day was spent in her cabin preparing for her meeting with Chester Thurston, which was in two short days.

After arriving in New York City, Jean took a two-hour train ride to DC. She arrived at her apartment midafternoon and made a few calls. Then she unpacked her dirty clothes and headed for the laundry room. Later, she had dinner at a nearby restaurant. Before going to bed, she fixed herself tequila on the rocks with some lime juice and a beer chaser and then turned on the radio to listen to the news, followed by some soft music. Jean woke up about midnight in her easy chair and staggered to bed.

In the morning, Jean took her sweet time getting up and making herself presentable and then headed for a nearby restaurant for a nice breakfast. Once at CIG headquarters, with a solemn spirit, she headed straight for Chester's office, carrying a document. When she reached his office, she knocked on the open door.

Chester jumped up and came around, saying, "Oh, Jean, welcome back. Come and have a seat."

"Thanks, Chester," she said. "I'll make this short and to the point. Here's my resignation." Jean handed the paperwork over to Chester, who had a surprised look on his face.

After catching his breath, he asked, "Are you sure, Jean?"

"Yes, I'm sure. It's the hardest decision I've ever had to make. I do want to thank you for being a friend and a good supervisor, Chester."

"I take it would be a waste of time to try to talk you out of this?" he asked.

"Yes, it would," she noted. "Here are my credentials and weapon. I'm leaving for Phoenix tomorrow night on a train."

Chester stood up and came around his desk. "Good luck, Jean. I really mean that."

The two colleagues shook hands, and Jean left feeling some sadness, but that was behind her now. She spent the rest of the day taking care of things so she could leave the following night. When she arrived back at her apartment, Jean called her mother and told her what she had done and when she would arrive in Phoenix. Of course, Mildred was ecstatic to hear the news.

PART THREE

A CIVILIAN ... AGAIN

CHAPTER 63

It was just after dusk when Jean arrived at track three. It was so damn cold she thought perhaps the bottom of the thermometer must have fallen off. Her nose felt like icicles were forming on it, and she was glad she was wearing her winter coat and gloves.

Then she noticed it had started snowing. "Good-bye, DC," she gladly muttered.

On her way to the baggage porter, Jean saw steam engines breathing steam onto the platform, where crowds of people were walking through it like they were walking through clouds. There were all kinds of noises—like train engine noises, PA announcements, and porters and conductors hollering. After checking her bags with the baggage porter, Jean's Pullman porter took her small traveling bag and led her to her cabin.

He placed the bag in the cabin and asked, "Is there anything I can get for you?"

Jean thanked him and gave him a tip. She decided to change into something comfortable and slipped into a pair of slacks and sweater. Now it was time to get warm from the inside out. Jean headed for the bar and lounge car. She sat at the bar and figured it was a good place to relax and think about what she might do in Phoenix. She had several options to think about.

* * *

Meanwhile, someone else barely boarded the train in time, looking for Agent Jean Webb. He tipped his porter and looked in the mirror, making sure his disguise was good before setting out to find Jean Webb.

"I have to find her and kept an eye on her, because I'm determined to put an end to the situation, once and for all."

*   *   *

Back in the bar car, Jean was ordering a drink. "Bartender," she said, "I'll have a shot of tequila with a beer chaser." She noticed that the young, good-looking bartender had a cute ass.

While waiting for her drink, she looked around and only spotted one couple sitting in the lounge. Then she noticed a man sitting at the end of the bar; his eyes seemed to be glued on her. Then the barkeep showed up with Jean's drinks, and she noticed something was missing. She started to say something when suddenly the man at the end of the bar sat down next her. She could tell he'd had several too many, and there was a ring on his left ring finger.

Jean figured he was probably a traveling salesman. He looked to be in his thirties, had a full head of hair, and wasn't bad looking.

"Lady, I'd like to buy you another drink," he said.

Jean looked at him and responded. "No thanks, mister. I'm fine."

Then he made a big mistake and moved closer and started to put his arm around her. Jean took his hand and slammed it onto the bar and barked, "If no isn't good enough for you, I suggest you take a cold shower or make wonderful ravishing love to your wife when you get home, asshole."

Jean saw his face flush before he started getting angry, so she stood up and got ready to handle the situation. The man looked up at Jean and saw a firm look on her face and her hands ready for action. Then his angry look turned into a sheepish look, and he quickly got up and returned to the end of the bar. The man then downed his drink and left.

Jean was smiling when she noticed the bartender was too. "What are you smiling at?" she asked. "And where's the damn lime?"

The young man made a quick move, and Jean had her lime. She bit into it, downed the tequila, and chased it with swallows of beer. Then she looked at the barkeep and said, "I'll have another shot of tequila, and don't forget the damn lime."

She heard, "Yes, ma'am."

Welcome back to being a civilian and having to put up with a bunch of dumbass male idiots, Jean thought to herself. *Hopefully, the war will help change that, but it may take decades, and I'm not going to wait. Even if I have to kick a bunch of male assholes, so be it, because I'm not going to put up with anymore male supremacy acts.*

With that off her chest, it was time for Jean to relax and think about Phoenix, Arizona, and what the hell she was going to do when she arrived. One thing she knew for sure was that she wanted to buy one of those new French bikini swimsuits she'd seen in Paris. *With my big boobs, my cup will probably overflow*, she thought with a chuckle. *So I'll enjoy lying in the sun, watching the male mouths drool. Dream on, you male idiots.* Then Jean sucked on the lime, downed the tequila, and chased it with the beer. Now she was feeling warm inside and out.

Suddenly, Jean felt like there was somebody behind her.

"I'll have what she's having, and make it two shots. I'm buying."

Jean instantly turned around, and there was Jake, big as life. She popped off her barstool into his arms and planted a big kiss on his lips.

When they were breathing again, she asked him, "What are you doing here?"

"Well, I'm here because your mother got me the job working for the governor of Arizona."

"That's great, Jake."

When the bartender brought their drinks, Jean and Jake clinked their shot glasses together and toasted to Arizona. Then they enjoyed bar snacks, appetizers, and a friendly conversation. And the train keep moving down the tracks. *Click-a-de-clack. Click-a-de-clack.*

After some serious drinking had been accomplished, Jake asked, "What's a beautiful, unemployed lady like you going to do in Phoenix?"

"Well, let's see," Jean said. "I've been thinking about becoming a high-priced prostitute."

The bartender dropped a glass of beer, and the lounge got quiet.

Jake muttered to himself, "I guess I asked the question wrong. Come on, Jean. Get serious."

"All right. Your cabin or mine?"

Jake saw it was time to go, because the alcohol was making her both silly and ornery, which he had seen before. "Your cabin, sweetheart."

"Okay, lover." Jean slid off the barstool into his arms, and Jake heard, "Thank you."

Next, Jake pointed Jean in the right direction and barely heard the bartender say, "There goes one lucky son of a gun."

On the way to her cabin, Jean spoke. "Jake, this sure is a rough train ride, because I keep bouncing off the walls." Jake chuckled and grabbed her so she'd quit hitting the walls. "Thanks, Jake," she said.

Once inside Jean's cabin, Jake started undressing her. When he was down to her bra and panties, she started to undo her 38D bra strap. Jake picked up her five foot nine body, which weighed a solid one hundred and forty pounds, and lifted her into the overhead berth. "Good night, darling," he said. Before he left, he could tell she was out like a light.

The other person who had boarded the train in DC kept his distance so Jean wouldn't see him. He had his reasons and would be ready when the time came. He returned to his cabin for the night.

CHAPTER 64

The next morning, Jean was dreaming she was hearing voices, howling, and all kinds of others sounds from outside of her cabin. Suddenly, she woke up from a deep sleep and realized she wasn't dreaming and had an awfully nasty headache from a terrible hangover.

"Oooh … damn! What the hell did I run into last night?" she said, grabbing her head. "It wasn't the train, because I'm on it." Then she remembered. *Tequila, with beer chasers.*

"It must have been bad limes, or I'm getting to damn old to do this crap anymore," she mumbled. "Oh! Damn! It even hurts to move. And what the hell is that noise outside?"

Finally, Jean got up enough courage to move and almost fell out of the overhead berth, but she managed to land on her feet like a cat. "Hell! I need coffee."

Then she looked at the lavatory three steps away and slowly took one step at a time, keeping one hand on her forehead and moaning with each step she took. It seemed like it took forever to reach the lavatory. Jean rinsed the bad taste out of her mouth, splashed lots of water on her face, and straightened up, holding on to something before drying off her face.

"Now I have to go pee." She sat on the toilet gently and relieved herself, commenting, "At least this doesn't hurt."

Next, Jean carefully staggered back to the couch and sat down easy like, avoiding hitting her head on the overhead berth, and then leaned back.

"That's a little better." Jean still wished she had lots of black coffee. "Why in the hell has the damn train stopped? That's why I woke up, and that damn noise outside didn't help either!"

Every time her head moved, it hurt, so she tried not moving it. Despite her stillness, she was still suffering and moaning and wishing for coffee.

Then there was a knock on her cabin door. "Who's there?" she managed to say.

"It's just me, and I've got coffee."

Thank God for Jake, she thought. *Wishes do come true.*

Jake's words helped force her to her feet, and she didn't even bother to put anything on. She just unlocked the cabin door and headed back to the couch, sitting down slowly with one hand still on her forehead.

"Good morning, Sleeping Beauty. Wow! Even first thing in the morning, you still look good in your bra and panties, sweetheart."

"Quit talking and give me coffee before I attack you."

"Ah, I see we're just a little hungover, darling," Jake noted with a smile. He poured her a cup of black coffee and handed it to her with both hands, trying to show he wasn't as bad off as her.

After downing several cups of coffee, Jean asked, "Did I get laid last night?"

"No, you were too drunk to enjoy it, darling."

"Oh well. Later, handsome. I've always wanted to get screwed on a moving train."

Jake just shook his head. "Get dressed, and I'll buy you some breakfast."

After another cup of coffee, she got up and removed her bra and panties for fresh ones. Jake just shook his head again. "You are one gorgeous woman, Jean."

"You should know, lover," she replied.

Jake continued enjoying the view and commented, "Yes. And if you would've said *yes*, we'd be married by now."

And all he heard was, "Uh-huh."

When Jean felt up to navigating, the couple headed for the dining car.

On the way, she asked, "Where the hell are we, Jake?"

"We're in Chicago, darling," he said.

When they entered the dining car, a very hungover Jean still turned men's heads. She had natural beauty, a tall, picturesque figure, and beautiful wavy auburn hair. She was wearing slacks and a sweater that showed off some of her best assets. Before reaching their table, Jean noticed a cowboy with a big hat and thought he looked familiar. She was sure she had seen him before, except this man had a mustache and beard. Once Jean and Jake were seated, the cowboy got up and walked right past Jean. She looked again, but nothing registered.

When the waiter took Jean's order, she picked the biggest breakfast on the menu, along with orange juice and a pot of black coffee. "And bring the coffee now," she added.

While waiting for breakfast and downing lots of coffee, Jean didn't even bother to look outside into the bright Chicago sunlight.

After getting some food in her, Jake asked, "Seriously, Jean, what are you planning on doing in Phoenix?"

"Seriously, Jake, I'm thinking about becoming a private investigator— you know, a PI."

Jake's face showed he was a little surprised, and yet, he came back with, "You'll probably be good at it, knowing you, Jean."

After inhaling her large breakfast, Jean still felt tired and a little hungover and let Jake know. "I'll see you later, Jake. I need more rest, and later, I'm buying lunch."

Jake watched her carefully head for her cabin, still a little wobbly.

After more sleep, coffee, and a hot shower, Jean started feeling better and decided to sit in the small lounge next to her cabin to look out the window, as the train was moving again. She had ordered a beer, commenting, "I need a little hair of the dog." Meanwhile, she watched the Illinois countryside fly by. After downing some of her beer, she noted aloud, "That helped."

She then sat back and relaxed, knowing Missouri was just down the track. Missouri was her mother's birth state, and she realized how much she had missed her mother. Jean finished the beer and returned to her cabin. "Now it's for time a nap," she noted.

Soon, Jean heard a knock at the door. Then a voice said, "I'm ready for lunch, sweetheart."

And Jean said, "Okay, Jake. I'll meet you in the dining car in twenty minutes."

He replied, "Hurry up, darling. I'm hungry."

While getting ready to go, Jean though about Jake and what he had said. "If I were the marrying kind, I'd have married Mr. Jake Blakely after the war," she whispered to herself.

237

CHAPTER 65

A westbound train's steam engine was pulling hard across the continent, allowing Jean to relax and enjoy the countryside's beautiful scenery. Now she was on her way to the dining car, wearing slacks and a button-up blouse with the top button undone, showing some cleavage. She looked sexy and felt good as she turned men's heads.

"Good afternoon, handsome," she said to Jake when she found him.

Jake looked up. "Wow! Do you look good … nice and rested too."

"Thanks. I do feel better." Jean looked out the window as she sat down and asked, "Do you know where we are?"

"Yes, we're just leaving St. Louis and on our way to Springfield, Missouri."

"Hey, that's my mother's birthplace, and I was raised there. I still have a great-aunt living there. I always liked Springfield, because it was a nice, easygoing town."

"I always figured your mother for a Show-Me-State girl. Even at fifty, she's still a good-looking woman and almost as tall as you, Jean."

Jean quickly answered. "Fifty-three and an inch shorter."

Jake shook his head and announced, "Our next stop is Oklahoma City."

A waiter showed up, and Jean ordered lunch. "I'll have the Mexican food plate, tacos with beans and plenty of hot sauce."

Jake just shook his head again and ordered. "I'll have a ham sandwich on wheat and hold the mayo, with a class of milk."

"You're not still hungover? Are you, darling?" Jean said, grinning at her tall Texan.

The food came, and the two travelers watched the Ozark hills of Missouri come and go while enjoying their lunch. After passing through Joplin, Missouri, Jake commented, "Oklahoma, here we come."

"When will we know we're there?" Jean asked.

"It's easy, darling. After we cross the state line, all you have to do is just watch the oil wells fly by and take in the smell of oil."

Jean gave him a smirk look and came back with, "You mean black gold, don't you, smarty?"

Jake gave a slight grin back.

"Why don't you tell me about your job, Jake," Jean said.

Jake finished his sandwich, drank the rest of his milk, and said, "I'll be heading up a new security group to protect the governor and his family, plus any special assignments handed to me by the governor."

Jean gave Jake a serious look and asked, "Why the change? Is there something I'm missing here? Isn't that the job of the state police?"

"Not anymore. Since the war, the state has been growing in leaps and bounds, and according to your mother, the state now wants a better-trained and more organized unit in place, similar to the Texas Rangers. So, she recommended me, and since she's the executive assistant to the governor of Arizona, I got the job."

"Great. It sounds like a good move, Jake. I wish you the best."

"Thanks, Jean. By the way, what plans do you have for laying your head down at night?"

"You got any suggestions?" Jean questioned.

"Yes. All you have to do is say *yes*, Jean," Jake answered.

"That's not going to happen, Jake."

"How about sharing an apartment?"

"Sorry, Jake. That isn't going to happen either. When Grandpa and Mom came to Arizona, Grandpa bought a large house. Now he's in a senior residence care center, and according to Mother, he's happy."

"Yeah, and knowing the senator, I'll bet there are lots of single women there too," Jake joked.

Jean looked at Jake, shaking her head. "All you men are just alike ... thank goodness. So Mom invited me to stay with her in the big house."

Jean saw a disappointed look on Jake's face before he moved on. "What kind of cases are you going to take on as a private eye?"

"In the beginning, probably anything that comes along," replied the future PI.

With lunch finished, Jake said, "My cabin or yours?"

"I'm still a little tired, Jake, and I've got some more thinking to do. So later, when you're buying dinner, you can ask that question again, handsome."

Back at her cabin, Jean ordered some refreshments—tequila, beer, lime, and ice. She tipped the porter and fixed herself her first drink of the day. Then she stripped down to her bra and panties, and this time, she put on a bathrobe. Then she sat down next to the window and watched the Oklahoma oil wells and countryside come and go.

Jean thought of four guys she had a lot of admiration for: Carlos, Joe, Howard, and John. When she had arrived at Army Headquarters in DC, she had eventually found out they were assigned to a Ranger company, and their mission was to be the first ones to reach the Chancellery in Berlin and hopefully take Hitler alive. Of course, that didn't happen. She hoped they had all survived the war.

Then her mind shifted to Phoenix, and she thought about becoming a private investigator, wondering if that was really what she wanted.

CHAPTER 66

The westbound train reached its next stop, Oklahoma City, and Jean and Jake were able to disembark. They stretched their legs and watched the beautiful sunset happening in the western skies.

"This is nice, Jake," Jean said, holding hands and enjoying the comfortable evening, breathing plenty of fresh air with a slight scent of money, *black gold*.

"I agree, Jean. The West has its moments—warmth, fresh air, and charisma … even romance." Smiling at Jean, he added, "Although, sometimes it can be rough—extremely hot and cold from the desert to the mountains."

"In other words, Jake, it's beautiful but dangerous, including cowboys and Indians?"

"You're right, sweetheart. Hopefully, friendly Indians, but you gotta watch out for those cowboys." Jake wrapped his arms around Jean and gave her a big hug and a kiss.

*　*　*

"There you are, Agent Jean Webb," a man nearby whispered to himself. "You're lucky you have someone with you. I better get on board, and then I'll find out where your cabin is. Later, I'll settle my business with you, bitch."

*　*　*

Before long, the couple was back on the moving train and having a few drinks in the lounge before dinner. Jake commented, "We should enjoy our dinner tonight, especially since we'll be eating as we pass through the worst part of Texas—the Texas panhandle. Hell, it's so bad even the Indians won't take it back."

Jean and Jake continued to enjoy the evening with wonderful conversation, remembering exciting times they'd had together. After a nice dinner and after-dinner drinks, Jake asked, "Your cabin or mine?"

Sporting a big smile, Jean said, "Yes, it's time for some serious love making, so I can get screwed on a moving train … Click-a-de-clack … click-a-de-clack."

After a wonderful evening, Jean and Jake found themselves enjoying an early-morning breakfast with pleasant scenery as they entered the western half of New Mexico.

"The hills and snow-covered mountain peaks are beautiful," Jean said.

"Yes, you're right, my dear lady."

After an enjoyable, scenic breakfast, Jean and Jake relaxed while watching the picturesque scenery.

The train conductor came by and announced, "Next stop Flagstaff, Arizona, in one hour. Phoenix passengers will transfer to the southbound train."

"Well, I guess we need to get ready," Jean said.

"Right behind you, as always, dear lady."

Jean was on her way to depart the train with her small bag when a man holding a pistol suddenly appeared. "Hello, Agent Webb," he said. "Let me introduce myself. I'm Galeno Morales, and you killed my brother in Rio, you bitch! And now it's time for you to die."

Jean threw her bag at him and reached for her derringer, but she could tell she was going to be shot.

Bang.

Jean saw the assassin fall forward on his face. When she looked up, she saw that tall cowboy coming toward her with a smoking pistol. "Hi, Jean," he said as he pulled off his mustache and beard.

"Bob Franklin!" Jean yelled as she hurried over to her hero and gave him a big hug and a kiss on the cheek.

Moments later, Jake showed up with his pistol in hand. "Meet Bob Franklin," Jean told him.

Later, Bob made arrangements with the conductor to have the body put in the baggage car for pickup in LA. Jean, Jake, and Bob boarded the train to Phoenix.

Now, with everybody in the lounge, Bob began explaining what had happened. "Barbosa got a tip about the teller's brother who swore to get even and was headed for the states to find his killer. The brother had ties with a cartel in Colombia, and they helped him with their contacts in Chicago. So Barbosa wired me a description, which I received the day you left. I barely caught your train."

"Now I owe you, Bob," Jean said.

"So do I," Jake said.

When the train pulled into the Phoenix station, their enjoyable, endearing, and exciting trip ended. While collecting their baggage, Jean heard her name. She turned around and saw a tall, good-looking blonde woman headed her way. "Hi, Mom," she called out, and a family embrace took place.

"Oh, Jean, I have missed you so much, darling."

"And I've missed you too, Mother."

"Hi, Mildred," Jake chimed in. "It's good to see you again."

"Oh, hi, Jake … Did you come with Jean?" Mildred asked.

"Yes. We just happened to be on the same train from DC," replied Jake.

Mildred looked at her daughter, smiling, "Oh, how nice you both had company all the way from DC."

With a sophisticated tone, Jean added, "Yes, Mother. Jake was very comforting on the trip."

"Uh-huh," Mildred said with a smile. "Come on, you two. I have a car waiting."

"Oh, Mother. You remember Bob Franklin," Jean said as Bob walked up.

"Yes. Hi, Bob. You were on the train as well?" Mildred asked.

Jean spoke up. "Yes, Mother, and Bob saved my life in Flagstaff. You need to give him a hug and drop him off at his sister's place."

Mildred said, "No. We'll go and pick up Pat, and Bob, you and Pat are having lunch with us." On the way home, Mildred asked, "Jake, where do you plan on staying?"

"I have a hotel room until I can find an apartment," he answered.

"Nonsense. We'll cancel your room, and you can stay with us until you do find an apartment. We have plenty of room now that Dad is in a home."

"Thank you, Mildred," Jake said.

Jean got a serious look on her face as she stared at her mother. *You, matchmaker, you. Now what are you up to?*

CHAPTER 67

Mildred, having lived in Arizona since 1939, had become an excellent cook of Mexican food. "Hope you like Mexican food," she said to her company. "I didn't make it too hot so you could enjoy it."

She heard, "I appreciate that, Mildred," from her three guests.

Ignoring her guests, Jean jumped right in and poured hot sauce all over her food. The others took it a little more conservatively with the hot sauce. When everybody had tasted their food, Mildred heard, "It tastes great, Mildred."

During lunchtime conversation, Mildred asked, "So, what's this business about becoming a private investigator, Jean?"

"Yes, Mother. I want to give it a shot and see if I like being my own boss."

"Mildred, you know it's no use trying to change her mind. I should know," Jake said.

"Okay, darling, if that's what you want," Mildred said.

"Yes, Mother. That's what I want." Jean continued eating her hot and spicy food.

Bob spoke up. "I think Jean will make an excellent PI." Jake agreed.

Jean stopped eating and said, "Thanks, guys."

When lunch was almost over, Mildred informed everybody, "Save room. There's cherry pie and ice cream."

When everybody finished eating, it was time to sit back and relax.

Then Bob said, "Mildred, if you're ever looking for a husband, I'm volunteering." That got some laughs.

"Oh my, I'll have to think about that, Bob." Mildred smiled and then added, "Jean, you're right. I like them young."

Jean popped up. "Boy, are you in trouble now, Bob." Everybody was smiling after that comment.

Then Mildred said, "Why don't you young people go and listen to some music while I clean up."

Instead, the young people cleaned up and sent Mildred to the living room with a bourbon and water to listen to some music. Later, when the young people showed back up, there was some dancing. Bob danced with Jean, and Jake danced with Pat, as Mildred enjoyed watching. Then Jake went over and invited Mildred to dance. Next, Bob danced with Mildred also. Then it was time to visit with Bob and Pat.

Mildred asked, "Pat, how's your job going, dear. Have you met anybody yet?"

"The job is fine, and I haven't met anybody yet, Mildred."

Mildred reminded Pat, "Just remember what I told you about those cowboys."

And Bob chimed in, "That's what I've been telling her, Mildred."

Jean asked, "Bob, how long can you stay before going back to work?"

"I'm afraid it's tomorrow, Jean. I've got to call LA and wire Barbosa and let him know what happened and where the body is in case somebody wants to come and take it back to Brazil. Then I'm headed back to DC."

Jean walked over and gave Bob a big hug, and Mildred walked over and gave Bob a hug and a kiss on the cheek and said, "You take care of yourself, Bob."

Then it was Jake's turn. "I'm not going to hug or kiss you, but thanks for saving Jean's life." Jake gave him a hardy handshake.

After her guests left, Mildred said, "There goes two nice people." Both Jean and Jake agreed.

Later that night, Mildred said, "It's my bedtime. Jake, breakfast is at six o'clock, and then I'll take you to see the governor. Good night, you two." Mildred received a good night back. When Mildred reached the top of the stairs, she stopped and looked back down into the living room and saw Jake and Jean dancing and muttered, "Now that she's settling down, maybe she'll get married, so I can have some grandkids."

CHAPTER 68

Dawn was starting to break through the night as a tall, handsome, well-dressed man came down the stairs wearing a sports coat, shirt and tie, and nice-looking trousers. It was six o'clock, and Jake smelled coffee, eggs, and bacon and heard a blonde lady humming and singing an old tune, "Seems Like Old Times."

"You have a nice voice, Mildred," Jake said as he entered the kitchen.

"Thanks, Jake. How do you like your eggs?"

He looked over at hers and said, "Just like yours, my dear lady."

"Do you always say such nice things to a woman, Jake?" Mildred asked.

"Only when they're lovely and gorgeous," Jake responded.

"Oh, go sit down, you charmer."

Mildred brought over the eggs, bacon, toast, and coffee, and Jake said, "This looks great."

The two went on to enjoy their breakfast while chatting.

As they were talking, Mildred surprised Jake with a question. "When are you going to marry my daughter?"

It only surprised Jake a little, because he knew she was hoping he'd become her son-in-law.

"When she says yes," Jake told her.

"Well, how many times have you asked her?"

"More than I care to remember, starting when the war ended."

"Well, maybe someday she'll decide to get married. I hope," Mildred said.

"Yeah, someday," Jake said. *But when? For Pete's sake.*

"Good morning, you two," Jean said as she walked into the kitchen.

"Oh, good morning, dear. Do you want some breakfast?" Mildred asked her daughter.

"No, Mom. I'll just have some coffee and toast."

"Good morning, darling," Jake said.

And Jean responded, "Good morning, Jake."

Mildred asked, "What's your schedule for today, dear?"

"Well, I think I'll go get my license for becoming a private investigator and a permit to carry a weapon."

"Good, dear. And if you happen to meet a Chief Bailey, I think you'll like him. He seems to be a nice man. I met him several months ago at a state function. You can tell him hi for me. You ready to go, Jake?"

"Almost, Mildred," Jake said. "Give me another five minutes."

Mildred said, "Get rid of the tie. This is Arizona, and ties are only worn at official functions. See you later, dear."

Jean had a mouthful of toast and jam, so she waved good-bye.

On the way to meet the governor, Mildred informed Jake, "Tom Russell is a down-to-earth kind of guy and a damn good governor. You two should get along great."

"That's sounds good, Mildred," he said. "That always helps make the job worthwhile."

Mildred reached over and turned on her car radio to catch the early-morning news. "Looks like another beautiful day in the Valley of the Sun. Well, it looks like President Truman will have to deal with what could be the worst maritime strike in US history. The longshoremen have stopped shipping on all the coasts, and meetings have already been scheduled to meet with the longshoremen's officials."

"I think the longshoremen are about to find out how tough Harry S. can be," said a confident-sounding Mildred.

Jake replied, "I believe you're right about that, Mildred."

Once they arrived at the state capitol building, Mildred spoke to the receptionist. "Hi, Sally. He's expecting us."

"Yes, Mildred. He's waiting. Go right in."

"Good morning, Tom," Mildred said once inside the office. "I'd like to introduce Mr. Jake Blakely. Jake, Governor Russell."

The two gentlemen shook hands, and the governor said, "Welcome to Arizona, Jake. I've been looking forward to this. Please be seated, and let's visit for a while. And it's Tom in private."

"Thank you, Govern—I mean, Tom."

Mildred excused herself and said, "Jake, when you're through with your visit, come and see me, and I'll show you around."

CHAPTER 69

As she drank the last of her coffee, Jean glanced at the kitchen sink. "Looks like I need to earn my keep and do some KP." Next, Jean headed upstairs and jumped in the shower. After having a nice, hot wake-up shower, she put on a nice skirt and blouse and applied some makeup before heading back downstairs to finish reading the newspaper.

"At least there isn't a crime every hour of the day and night here like in DC," she muttered to herself. "Maybe that's why I slept so well last night—no sirens."

Mildred had left a city map so Jean could find her way around Phoenix, and Jean checked it out before calling a cab.

When the cab arrived, Jean informed the driver, "Phoenix Police Headquarters."

Jean remembered how cold DC was when she left. "I don't need a heavy coat in sunny Phoenix in October, since the paper indicated seventy-five degrees today."

Twenty-five minutes later, her cabbie said, "That's three dollars, miss."

Jean handed him four. When Jean entered police headquarters, she saw a police station like any other she had been in before. It had a desk sergeant who was busy answering questions, handling people, and doing anything else that came his way.

When she had completed the paperwork, turned it in to the desk sergeant. After looking it over, he said, "Wait right here, Miss Webb." He then had a clerk deliver her applications and informed Jean, "Chief of Detectives Sam Bailey requires an interview with all PI applicants."

Jean thought, *This ought to be good.*

Shortly, a large, portly, nice-looking man entered the front desk area and introduced himself. "Miss Webb, I'm Chief Bailey." They shook hands, and he said, "Please come with me."

Jean followed him to his office, and he closed the door. "Please have a seat, Miss Webb."

"Thank you, Chief," she responded.

"So, you are serious about being a PI, Miss Webb?" the chief asked.

"Yes, Chief Bailey. I'd like to give it a try."

"I see you have listed Mildred Webb as a reference."

"Yes, she's my mother, and she said to say hi."

"Yes, I met your mother at a function the governor had several months ago. Nice lady."

That's interesting, Jean thought. *Mother said the same thing.*

He looked a little further at the application and said, "I see you were with the CIG for sixteen months. You mind if I ask why you left?"

"Yes, I wanted to settle down," Jean answered.

"What? The spy business not exciting anymore?" questioned Chief Bailey.

"Yes, Chief. Something like that."

"Oh," said a surprised chief. He hesitated before asking the next question. "I see you were a major in army intelligence, and you were well decorated."

"Yes, Chief. I was with the OSS and had assignments in France, Norway, Germany, and Italy."

"You were an OSS operative?" he asked.

Jean replied with a firm, "Yes, Chief."

Chief Bailey hesitated again. "May I call you Jean? And may I say that it's an honor to meet you."

"Yes, I prefer Jean, Chief. And thanks."

"It's my guess you had to put up with male domination in the army, but you didn't let it interfere in accomplishing your goals. And that was probably because you achieved a stature that required their respect," the chief noted.

Jean's face expressed he was right on. "Yes. During the first two years, until I joined the OSS," she confirmed.

Chief Bailey continued. "I have a daughter at the Phoenix Police Academy, and she has this male domination problem almost every day. It's unfortunate that law enforcement is a man's world and women are so new to it. But I admire you for trying, so if you have any problem with my people, please let me know."

"Thanks, Chief Bailey," Jean said. "I appreciate that, but I'd prefer to handle it myself."

Chief Bailey commented, "There's no doubt in my mind that you would be able to handle it, Jean. I do have a question for you."

"Yes, Chief. What's that?"

"I've a need for another detective," he noted. "Would you be interested?"

"Thanks, Chief, but I want to try this PI thing on my own," she responded. "I do appreciate the offer, and I'll definitely keep it in mind."

"Okay, Jean," he said. "Look, from time to time we get complaints and domestic issues where we're limited to help. If you don't mind, I'd be happy to refer some of them to you, Private Eye Webb." With that, Chief Bailey signed her application and permit papers.

"I appreciate what you said, Chief Bailey," Jean said. "And I'd like to meet your daughter sometime."

Chief Bailey replied, "I'd like that too, Jean."

As Jean was about to leave, the chief spoke up. "Oh, there is one last thing I'm supposed to do. That's to give you a lecture about cooperating with the police and keeping your nose clean with the law. Consider it done, and here is a copy of our statues. Read it, and you'll do just fine."

CHAPTER 70

After a pleasant and productive visit with the governor, Jake now had a very good idea what was needed and where to get started, handling things sooner than later.

"Jake, I'd like you to meet my family. How about dinner tomorrow night?" the governor asked.

"Yes, sir. Uh … I mean, Tom. I'd love to."

"Fine. Sally will give you all the details, so we'll see you tomorrow night. Oh, I understand Mildred's daughter is here. She's welcome to come also."

"Thanks, Tom. I'll let her know." After getting the information he needed from Sally, Jake headed for Mildred's office.

"How did it go, Jake?" Mildred asked.

"Great, Mildred. You were right. Tom seems like a great guy. In fact, I'm having dinner with the governor and his family tomorrow night."

Mildred said, "That's great, Jake."

Jake added, "Jean is invited too, that's if she'll go. Of course, you probably already knew about it, right?"

Mildred smiled and then got a firm look on her face, "Oh, she'll go all right. Now, come and let me introduce you to the rest of the staff."

Jake spent the next hour meeting everybody, and then Mildred showed him to his office. Jake sat down and took a deep breath. "I guess I need to make some notes and start developing a game plan. I need to review existing staff and evaluate. Then I plan to visit the Texas Rangers in Austin, which will help me start up the Arizona Rangers."

Later that night at dinner, the Webb household became interesting as Mildred listened to Jean and Jake talk about their first day in Phoenix, Arizona.

When Jean finished, she said, "I kind of like that Chief of Detectives Bailey."

Mildred answered, "That's nice, dear."

That answer seemed to bother Jean for some reason.

Jake wrapped up his day by saying, "I'm going to like working for Governor Russell, and Jean, you and I are invited to dinner tomorrow night at the governor's home."

Jean said, "I don't know, Jake."

Mildred quickly said, "Please don't disappoint the governor, dear."

CHAPTER 71

In Phoenix, it was a cool, comfortable evening as the governor's guests arrived for a casual dinner.

"Welcome, Jake," Tom said as they entered his home, "and this must be Jean."

Jean was wearing a nice casual evening dress.

"Yes, Tom," Jake said. "Let me introduce Miss Jean Webb, who's now a private eye."

"It is indeed a pleasure to meet you, Jean. I've heard so much about you, and it never hurts to have a private investigator in the family." He smiled as he shook her hand.

"Thank you, Governor Russell," Jean said, smiling back and then jabbing Jake in the ribs when the governor wasn't looking.

Governor Russell introduced his wife, Terry, and their children, Tom Jr. and Nancy, to their dinner guests. Then he asked, "Anybody care for a cocktail before dinner?" In response, he got three yeses from his two guests and his wife.

During the getting acquainted time, Tom said, "Jean, I think it's amazing you were with the OSS during the war. Being a spy had to be awfully dangerous."

Before she could say anything, a wide-eyed fourteen-year-old Tom Jr. asked, "You're a spy? How many Germans did you kill?"

Before the governor could say anything, Jean answered, "I lost count after two dozen." Her response caused the young man's mouth to drop open.

Jake spoke up. "But she's really a nice person. Just don't get her upset," he said as he smiled at the kid's parents.

The governor went along with Jake's statement and said, "Well, you two better behave from now on, or I'll just have to hire Jean, who's now a private eye, and have her come and straighten you two out."

Little Nancy walked over and said, "Are you really a nice lady?"

Jean looked down at her and smiled. "You bet I am." She picked her up and set little Nancy on her lap.

Then they had their own little conversation until Tom Jr. came over and joined them. A little later, the cook entered the room and announced, "Dinner is served." Everybody gathered around a long table with a large roasted chicken and all the fixings for an impressive-looking table.

Jean said, "This looks wonderful, Terry."

Terry responded, "Thank you. Please, everybody be seated and enjoy."

Governor Russell gave grace and said, "Let's dig in," and then started carving the chicken.

During dinner conversations, Jean said, "Terry, the food tastes wonderful."

"Thank you, Jean. I'm glad you're enjoying it."

Jake commented, "Jean's right, Terry. It's wonderful."

"I noticed you have some beautiful Indian art," Jean added.

"Thanks, Jean," Terry said. Jean's comment apparently reminded Terry of something. She looked at her husband and announced, "Tom, Jean just reminded me that I have decided to make my annual trip to Santa Fe the weekend after next, before it gets too cold. I'll take the kids, and they'll just miss one day of school."

The two kids became visibly excited.

"Oh no," said Tom.

Terry looked at him and asked, "Now what?"

"Well, dear, I'm not going to be able to go with you. There's a governors' meeting in San Diego on October the eleventh, and I've already committed to it. Sorry, dear."

Terry looked at Jake, "Well, Jake, I guess you have a problem. Which one of us are you going to protect now?"

"I guess you're right, Mrs. Russell," Jake said as he looked over at Jean. "But I have a solution."

Governor Russell said, "Oh? What's that, Jake?"

"I'll hire Jean to go with Terry, along with one of my men. Jean is more than qualified. And besides, it'll give Terry some company on her trip. I can work out the details with Jean next week in preparing for the trip to Santa Fe."

"Excellent idea, Jake. What do you think, dear?" Tom asked his wife.

Terry looked at Jean and smiled. "I think it's a great idea."

CHAPTER 72

On October 18 at ten thirty in the morning, a twin-engine Beechcraft 18 landed at Santa Fe airport and taxied to private hanger A.

An anxious Jean, who still hated flying, departed first and saw her advance guard waiting. "Hi, Dick," she said. "Let me know when we are ready to go."

"Yes, Jean," he answered, "as soon as we get the baggage loaded."

When it was time, Jean boarded the aircraft and informed Terry and the kids, "We're ready to go. Let's get into the vehicle."

On the way, Dick drove and updated Jean. "The hotel is two blocks from the downtown square. It's an old three-story building that has recently been renovated with first-class Spanish décor, both outside and inside. There's a nice restaurant, and I have briefed hotel security."

Jean admired the Spanish décor as she proceeded to the check-in desk. "The Russell party is here, and I'm security," she said. "I'd like to meet with your house detective ASAP. Thanks."

Once everyone was settled in their rooms, Jean returned to the check-in desk to meet with the house detective who had called her earlier.

"Miss Webb, I'm Joe Franks, house security. What can I do for you?"

Jean led him to an unoccupied part of the lobby. "I have Governor Russell's family here, and I understand you have been briefed."

"Yes, ma'am," he said. "I was yesterday by your man, Dick, and I also briefed the hotel staff."

"Good. If you see any unusual activities or people, please let me know right away."

"You got it, Miss Webb." The two shook hands.

And Jean said, "Thanks, Franks."

Before returning to her room, Jean performed a survey of the hotel, locating all exits and sort of getting a lay of the land, just in case. Back in her room, Jean checked out her firepower. She brought her military-issued Colt .45-caliber automatic for close-range rapid fire, and in Phoenix, she'd found a Colt PEA .41-caliber six-shooter, with a six-inch barrel for accuracy.

Then she knocked on the adjoining room door, and Terry opened it. "Hi, Terry. Everything okay?" Jean asked.

"Yes. Thanks, Jean."

"Let me know when you're ready to go shopping."

"Okay, Jean, probably after lunch."

At the hotel restaurant, everybody had good-ole US of A food except Jean, of course. Everybody watched her pour hot sauce on already hot and spicy New Mexico Mexican food and shook their heads. Then the Russell party was on the square, hitting every shop and dragging along an eleven-year-old and a fourteen-year-old. Dick had the responsibility of watching the kids, while Jean stayed close to Terry.

It turned out to be a nice, comfortable day to shop on the old Santa Fe town square. From her college days, Jean knew parts of the square were built in the late fifteenth century, and Santa Fe was the first capital city in the United States, which the Spaniards established in 1610. That's the same year the San Miguel Chapel was built and is the oldest church structure still standing.

Now the city square was home to historic monuments, restaurants, small businesses, and galleries. Jean found out there were markets, souvenirs shops selling Indians goods, jewelry, clothing, and inexpensive art pieces to the tourists.

When Terry saw Cesar's shop, an upscale establishment, she said, "Here's my favorite shop that has pieces from my favorite artist for sale."

Jean walked in first, as usual, and Terry followed.

When Cesar saw one of his best customers, he quickly came from around the counter to meet her, saying, "Oh! Mrs. Russell, it's so good to see you again."

"Hello, Cesar. It's good to see you too." Terry took a moment to introduce Jean.

"It's nice to meet you, Jean," Cesar said.

As the two continued to chat, Terry started looking around. Then Terry saw the wedding vase. "Cesar, please tell me the beautiful wedding vase is Esteban."

"Yes, Mrs. Russell. It's his." Cesar retrieved it and set it on the counter.

"Jean, look at this. It's got to be one of his best pieces."

Jean looked and said, "It is beautiful, Terry." Jean saw the price, but she knew Terry came from money, so it wasn't a problem for her to buy it.

"Oh, Cesar, I'll take it … and make sure you pack it carefully."

"I will, Mrs. Russell. I'll have it ready later, and I'll deliver it myself," he said.

Later, back at the hotel, there was a knock at Jean's door. "Who is it?" she asked, quickly buttoning up her blouse.

"It's Franks, and I have a package for Mrs. Russell."

Jean opened the door with one hand; the other hand held a weapon behind her back.

"Hi, Franks. Come in and put the package on the table." Jean directed. "Thanks for bringing it up."

"No problem." Then Franks saw the weapon. "Loaded for bear, Miss Webb?"

"I don't take chances, Franks. Good night."

Jean let Terry know her wedding vase had been delivered, and Terry then informed Jean, "I would like to go to Taos tomorrow for a day. I understand it has become an art center for established and beginning artists."

"Okay, Terry. I think we'll need to put your purchases in the hotel safe," Jean suggested. "They're worth over a thousand dollars."

Terry said, "Good idea, Jean."

CHAPTER 73

At the newly renovated hotel, the Russell party had already finished breakfast and was leaving for their trip to Taos, New Mexico.

Thirty minutes later, little Nancy asked, "Jean, how long will it be before we reach Taco?"

"You mean Taos, Nancy," Jean said. "Probably about an hour, sweetheart."

"Can we have tacos when we get to Taos?" asked Tom Jr.

Jean responded, "I don't know why not, Tom, but you'll have to ask your mother."

Terry said, "If that's what you want, it's okay with me."

"I want one too," announced Nancy. Everybody smiled at her response.

The previous night before going to sleep, Jean had remembered that Carlos Sanchez lived in Santa Fe. *Maybe I'll get a chance to look him up*, she thought. Then Jean saw the Taos city limit sign. It was about ten o'clock when the Russell party arrived at the Taos town plaza.

Jean said, "It looks like it's going to be a nice warm, sunny day."

Being an unusually warm day was fine with Jean, who peeled off her sweater and tied it around her waist. Then everybody was off to see the artists, displaying their skills and wares. Jean could tell Terry was excited to start touring the plaza as she looked for outstanding pieces of art. Jean stayed close, because Terry had several thousand dollars in cash on her.

After looking around for almost an hour, Terry spotted something. "Jean, look at this. It's one of Esteban's pieces."

The young artist nearby said, "Yes, ma'am. He was here the other day and left me some of his pieces to sell. He's a very good friend and a nice man. He also has helped me improve my skills."

"I'll take this one, and I like this one too," said Terry.

The young artist replied. "Thank you, ma'am. This one is mine."

Terry looked at him and said, "Yes, I know young man." She reached in her purse and pulled out a handful of bills. "Here's five hundred, young man, and two hundred is for you."

Showing that much money was making Jean nervous, causing her to keep a watchful eye on everybody around them, as Dick was busy taking care of the kids, who were starting to get impatient and restless.

"But, ma'am, I'm only asking one hundred for my work."

"And I like your work very much," Terry said.

"Thank you again, ma'am."

Terry continued to tour the remaining displays, and Jean had Nancy with her. It was almost one o'clock when Terry saw a large painting she apparently liked very much.

"Oh, Jean, it's beautiful, and it's only three hundred and fifty dollars."

Jean continually watched the people around them and particularly three young men who were following them separately and now were gathering. Jean was getting an uncomfortable feeling, so she gave Nancy back to Dick and alerted him.

"I think we're going to have company," Jean said. "Look to your right."

"Huh? Oh, I see what you mean," Dick said, moving the kids behind him and reaching for his weapon, just in case.

Jean moved so she was between Terry and the three potential thieves. When Terry reached for her purse, that's when they charged. Jean didn't see any weapons, so she decided she needed some exercise. When the first one reached her, she stiff-armed him and shoved him to Dick. The next one took a swing at Jean. She blocked it, put a foot between his legs, and chopped the back of his neck.

"One thief, down and out," Jean said as she turned toward the last one who pulled out a knife, causing Terry to scream. Jean quickly grabbed her sweater from around her waist and muttered, "Why's it always the big, tough one who has the knife? But that's good, because they're usually the slowest." Then she braced herself, and the thief swung the blade at her. She easily blocked it, surprising her attacker.

When they squared off again, Jean said, "Drop the knife, or tell me where you want me to stick you with it." That seemed to make the thief angry, which was what she wanted.

He charged again. Jean decided it was time to quit playing with him and easily disarmed him by blocking his move and twisting his hand, making him drop the knife. She then put her elbow in his face and stomped him with a bunch of karate blows, including one to his head. He went down hard and was not moving too well. Next, she bent over, picked up the knife, and stuck it in his face.

"Now, tough guy, where do you want it?" Jean asked.

With the knife in his face, the thief started crawling backward until he bumped into something. He looked up and saw a police officer.

267

"I'll take over, ma'am, if you don't mind," the officer said.

"Be my guest, Officer. And thanks," Jean said, handing him the knife.

Dick had his weapon out, and it was pointed in both of the other two young men's faces. "Let's go, you two," Dick said as he escorted them to the police officer. "Here's two more."

Jean now had the kids with her. Terry was still in a momentary state of shock. Jean looked at the kids and said, "Terry, I think it's time for lunch. Right, kids?"

"Yeah, Mom," the kids agreed.

"And the Hotel La Fonda is right here," announced Jean.

Tom Jr. and Nancy said in unison, "It's time for tacos."

"Dick, would you please escort Mrs. Russell for some tacos?" Jean requested.

CHAPTER 74

Having recovered from their adventurous trip to Taos, the Russell party was near the square enjoying an early Mexican dinner at a famous restaurant called Loretto. At least one was enjoying it, Terry and the kids, along with Dick, were drinking a lot of water, because they weren't used to New Mexico's hot and spicy food. Of course, Jean was having no problem at all.

"Jean, you must have a stomach made of cast iron. How can you easily eat this hot food and not have to drink a pitcher of water?" Terry said.

"I guess I'm just a natural to eating hot and spicy food. I must have inherited it from my Spanish side of the family. Oh, I would recommend everybody order lots of ice cream for dessert."

Later, in her room, Jean heard a knock at her room door. She proceeded to answer it, with a .45 automatic pistol in her hand behind her back. "Who's there?" she asked.

"It's Franks, Miss Webb."

Jean opened the door slowly. "Come in, Franks. What is it?"

"Our sheriff is down in the lobby and wants to talk to you about an incident you had in Taos earlier today." Then he saw the pistol and added, "Loaded for bear again?"

"No ... maybe venom. Let's go see what the sheriff wants."

Once in the lobby, Franks introduced Jean to Sheriff Geraldo Torres. "Sheriff, this Miss Webb, security for the Russell party."

"Good evening, Miss Webb. Sorry to bother you, but I think I need to warn you about something I heard from Taos late this afternoon."

"What's that, Sheriff?" Jean asked.

"The thieves you dealt with today have people here in Santa Fe. I understand the one with the knife is the brother to a gang leader here in Santa Fe, and we know him. He's dangerous, and we're trying to find him, because a Taos deputy overheard his prisoners talking about getting even with your party."

"Sheriff, we're leaving first thing in the morning," Jean said. She thought for a moment and added, "Sheriff, here's what I'd like you to do, because this is probably not over yet."

"I like it, Miss Webb," the sheriff responded. "And I'll take care of it. Good night."

"Thanks, Franks," Jean said before heading back up to her room.

And she heard, "Yes, ma'am. Anytime. I'll see you in the morning."

CHAPTER 75

After Jean made it back to her room, she thought about things and decided not to tell Terry what had happened in the lobby, but she did brief her partner, Dick. When dawn came pouring into Jean's room, she had already been up getting ready for the trip home. She had both weapons out, checking and cleaning them, along with all her extra ammo. She had a feeling she might need it, if what she was told proved to be right. Two hours later, there was a knock on the adjoining room door, and Jean opened it.

"Is it time for breakfast, Jean?" little Nancy asked.

"Yes, darling. Get your mother and brother up, and we'll go."

"Okay, Jean. I can handle that." Jean knew she could.

An hour later, everyone was having breakfast, and Dick made his desire clear to the waitress. "No hot or spicy food for me," he said.

Jean said, "What? Not enough ice cream last night, Dick?"

Dick forced a grin back at her, and Terry chuckled a little.

Then Jean saw Franks. "Excuse me," she said before joining him. "Good morning, Franks. How are we doing?"

"Everything is set, Miss Webb, and so you know, Sheriff Torres's men are already there." Before Jean could say anything, he added, "I have a favor to ask, Miss Webb."

"What's that, Franks?"

"I would like to shake your hand and tell you it's been a real pleasure knowing you."

Jean smiled and stuck out her hand. "Me too, Joe," she said.

Back at the breakfast table, when everybody finished, Jean said, "Let's be ready to go in an hour, and Dick, in a half hour, would you bring the car around to the front entrance? I'll load up first and stand guard."

"You got it, Jean."

While standing guard outside the hotel entrance, Jean saw a large sedan pull up and park a block away. "Well, good morning, gentlemen," she said.

Shortly, Dick showed up with a bellhop and baggage, "You load up, Dick, and keep an eye on the sedan behind us." Dick looked as she added, "I'll go get the items out of the hotel safe."

When everything was finally loaded, Jean said, "Dick, why don't you go bring down the family, while I stay here."

"Right, Jean."

When everybody showed up, Jean said, "Let's hurry. We've a plane to catch."

As they left for the airport, Jean watched the parked sedan start to follow. "Dick, when we clear the city limits, punch it. We're being followed. Head for hangar D."

"But I thought our plane was in hangar A."

"Hangar D, Dick," Jean repeated.

"Yes, ma'am," Dick said.

When Dick cleared the city limits, he sped up and said, "They're coming on faster, Jean."

"Then punch it hard, Dick."

Now Terry and the kids knew something was going on, and Jean updated them. "We're being followed, and I'm not taking any chances. So hang on."

Now the kids were excited, but Terry wasn't.

"We're almost there," Jean said.

Dick saw hangar D and headed for it. Jean said, "When you enter the hangar, head for the back and stop."

As their vehicle passed by the entrance, the big hangar doors started closing, and Dick stopped at the rear of the hangar.

Jean turned to Dick and said, "Now, head for hangar A and get them on board and wait. I'll join you when the sheriff has everything under control. Now go!"

When Jean got out, the rear hangar doors opened, and Dick took off. Jean ran to the front of the hangar and stepped through the small door to meet her aggressive pursuers. The sedan pulled up about twelve yards away, and four men got out, weapons drawn.

The apparent gang leader said, "We want all your money and purchases, or somebody's going to get hurt."

Then the leader started to make his move, and Jean put a round from her six-shooter into the windshield next to where he was standing. The shot caused him to back up. Next, the hangar doors opened, and three policemen showed up next to Jean with their weapons pointed at the pursuers. Then Jean heard police sirens and saw two sheriff cars had pulled in behind the bad guys.

"Drop your weapons now! And hit the ground, belly down!" The pursuers quickly dropped their weapons and fell to the ground.

Then one of the vehicles pulled up next to Jean, and Sheriff Torres said, "Jump in, Miss Webb. You've got a plane to catch."

CHAPTER 76

The following morning, Jean was sleeping soundly when the phone started ringing, ending a deep slumber. Jean slowly rolled over to answer it, saying, "Now who the hell is calling? Can't a woman get some sleep once in a while? ... Hello?"

"Get up, sleepy head. The governor wants to see you right away," said Jake.

"What the hell for?" Jean asked.

"Can't answer that, but he's expecting you within the hour, darling."

After she hung up the phone, Jean said, "Well, I guess I better get my butt in gear and go see what our governor wants."

After a quick shower, breakfast snack with some coffee, and barely dressed, she jumped in her mother's car that was left for her use and headed for the capitol. As Jean approached the governor's office, Sally said, "Go right in, Jean. They're expecting you."

As Jean approached the door, she muttered, "Who's expecting me?" When Jean walked in, there was a room full of people, including Terry and the kids, Jake, Mildred, and, of course, the governor. *Now what?* she thought.

Governor Russell got up to meet Jean in the middle of his office and shook her hand. "Thanks for coming, Jean. Please have a seat. Jean, I'd like to take this opportunity to personally thank you for protecting my family. After listening to them, your performance was outstanding. I just want to thank you for it and congratulate you from the bottom of my heart."

Everybody started clapping, which made Jean speechless and very much surprised her. She was also slightly embarrassed.

"Jean, do you have anything to say?" Jake asked.

"Well, I ..." As she looked around the room, she found her words. "I really don't know what to say except I just did the job I was hired to do, and thank God nobody got hurt. I do thank you, Governor Russell, for your comments."

Terry and the kids jumped up, and the kids ran over to Jean to give her a big hug.

Terry said, "I'll go shopping with you anytime, Jean." She then gave her a friendly hug.

Mildred walked over and said, "Job well done, daughter." She gave her a hug too.

Then the governor dismissed everybody except Jake and Jean. Once everybody had left, he said, "Jake, I want you to put Jean on a retainer for future services, as needed."

"Yes, sir, Tom. Right away," Jake agreed.

Jean said, "Thanks, Tom."

"You're welcome, Jean."

CHAPTER 77

Before long, Jean found an office space to rent. It was one hundred and sixty square feet with a window, evaporative cooler, refrigerator, and ceiling fan. But she had to buy a desk and three chairs, a typewriter, a file cabinet, a phone to put in. She also had her office door sign painted.

"It's a good thing spy's make good money so I can weather the storm just starting this agency," she said to herself.

Then she was open for business, and people started showing up.

Looks like Chief Bailey kept his word, she thought.

All kinds of cases walked through the door, from wife beating, divorce issues, and a store having product being stolen. After several weeks, Jean was busier than she ever imagined. Jean had a meeting with the wife beater and his wife. During the conversation, he started hollering at Jean and threatened to kick her ass, so she kicked his ass instead.

When he'd had enough and succumbed, she hollered at him, "You leave her alone, or I'll be back, and we can do this all over again, asshole."

Next, Jean got the divorces to parley, and Jean acted as arbitrator. She eventually got them talking decently to each other and felt there was a chance of reconciliation. Jean then went undercover and caught the employee who was stealing from the store. A few days later, while taking a break, Jean was in her office, and a lady walked in, interrupting her thoughts. Jean saw she looked like she had been hit by a Mac truck.

"What the hell happened to you?" Jean asked.

The lady hesitated and then replied, "My husband."

Jean jumped up. "Come in and have a seat."

The lady introduced herself. "I'm Mary Bates."

Jean asked, "Have you reported this to the police?"

"Yes, I have, but they let him go. They said they didn't have enough evidence to hold him."

"Your word against his, right?" Jean said.

"Yeah, it was something like that."

"Call me Jean, and what's your husband's name?" The woman answered it was Henry. "How can I help you?" Jean asked.

"Well, I think I may need protection. He has a quick temper, and that's why I look like this. The next time he could kill me if I can't get away. I just need somebody I can call immediately in case he starts the rough stuff again."

"All right, I'll take your case," Jean said. "It's sixteen dollars per day plus a twenty-five-dollar retainer and expenses."

After Mary left, Jean had a new, crisp hundred-dollar bill in her hand, "Wow! I don't see too many of these babies."

Chapter 78

Jean decided it was time to pay a visit to a friend and thank him personally for all the business he had sent her. When she entered the station, the desk sergeant recognized her. "Hello, Miss Webb, and congratulations."

"Huh? Oh, thank you, Sergeant," Jean said." Is Chief Bailey in?"

"Yes he is, and do you remember where his office is?"

"Yes, I do. Thanks, Sergeant."

Jean knocked on the open door, and the chief looked up. "Oh. Hi, Jean. Please come in."

"Chief, I came by to thank you for all the clients you've sent me."

"You're welcome, Jean. I'm glad to do it. And congratulations on your first big job. I'm surprised you're not working for the governor now."

"Oh, you heard?" Jean asked.

"Hell yes, it's all over headquarters what you did. Good job, Jean."

"I was just doing what I was hired to do, Chief."

"Yeah, but you did it so well. If the governor doesn't hire you, and if you're ever interested, I will," the chief said.

Now Jean was wondering how he knew so much about it. "I know. Thanks, Chief Bailey … I do have a favor to ask you."

"Just name it, young lady."

"I had a visit from a Mary Bates."

"Oh, yes. The wife beating case."

"Would it be possible for me to talk to your detective handling the case and get a little more insight on it?" she asked.

"You got it, Jean." The chief pushed a switch on his intercom, and said, "Janice, send in Detective Hays."

Det. Jeff Hays stuck his head in the chief's office. "You want to see me, Chief?"

"Yes, Jeff, come in and meet Jean Webb."

"Oh, hi," Jeff said. "I'm glad to meet you, Miss Webb."

"Call me Jean, Jeff."

"Okay, Jean. Chief Bailey has told us so much about you that I feel like I already know you."

Jean looked over at her friend who had an innocent look and shrugged his shoulders. "Jeff, Jean has Mary Bates as a client," the chief explained. "Would you fill her in on what we know?"

"It'd be my pleasure, Jean."

As Jean was leaving, the chief added, "Jean, please tell your mother hi for me."

As a suspicious PI, Jean thought, *It helps to know people in the right places. Right, Mom?*

Jean followed Jeff, admiring his build and cute rear end, because he wasn't bad looking for a police detective. She figured he was probably in his midthirties; he was about six foot tall, had brown hair and blue eyes, and seemed nice.

Once they were at his desk, Jeff pulled out a file marked Bates. "I interviewed Henry Bates, and I felt he was telling the truth when he said, 'I didn't beat up my wife.' And yet, when I interviewed Mary, I sensed she wasn't telling me everything."

"That's interesting, because she was very positive and swore that her husband did the beating," Jean said.

"I strongly suggest you interview Henry. Here's where he lives now and his work address."

"Thanks, Detective Hays. I think I'll take your advice and do just that."

"Call me Jeff, and you're welcome, Jean. Good luck."

CHAPTER 79

Jean decided to visit Henry Bates at his new address. She sat and waited in her brand-new maroon-colored Chevy convertible that she'd brought with her fee and bonus from the governor. She'd taken the $400 and added $900 of her own money, and now it was all hers. Again, spies do make good money.

It was about five thirty that evening when Henry showed up. Jean knocked on the front door, and a woman appeared. "May I help you?" she asked.

"Yes, my name is Jean Webb, and I'm looking for Henry Bates. A Detective Hays suggested I talk to him."

"Why are you here?" the woman questioned.

Suddenly, a man appeared. "It's okay, Mom. Detective Hays did call. I'm Henry. Please come in, Miss Webb."

Already, Jean sensed Henry was a nice man and a gentleman. They wound up in the living room, and Jean asked, "Henry, your wife hired me to protect her in case you get angry again. Do I need to be concerned about that?"

"No, but I do … I think she wants you to kill me."

"What!" questioned a surprised Jean.

Henry then explained what had been going on. "I have a temper, but I've never hit a woman in my life," he said. "But lately, Mary has been pushing it for some reason."

Suddenly, a voice from behind Jean said, "And he never will. I should know. It's not in him," said Mrs. Bates. "It's like she wants to pick a fight."

Jean asked, "Why would your wife lie, Henry?"

Henry replied, "I don't know. It was about six months ago when I started getting suspicious about what she was doing while I was at work. Every time Mom would ask her to go shopping, the answer was always no, or when Mom would go by to visit, she was never there."

Jean could understand why he was suspicious and asked, "Did you ever ask her where she was?"

"Yes, I did, and that's when the screaming and hollering started. Then it seemed like we were arguing all the time. It's like Mom said. She acted like she wanted to fight all the time."

Now Jean could see why Detective Hays wanted her to listen to Henry's side of the story. "Henry, how long have you been married?" Jean asked.

"It's been about a year now," he answered.

"What was your wife's maiden name?"

"Davies," Henry said.

"And where was she from?"

"The Dallas, Texas, area."

"One last question, Henry. Do you have any insurance?"

"Yes, at work. I have medical and life insurance, plus GI insurance."

"You mind if I ask how much?" Jean probed.

"No. It's a hundred thousand at work and ten thousand GI," he answered.

"And who are the beneficiaries?"

Jean could tell by the looks on Henry's and his mother's faces what they were thinking. Henry answered, "I changed only the beneficiary at work to Mary."

Jean thought for a moment and looked at Mrs. Bates, "Do you have another place to go to that Mary doesn't know about?"

"Why, yes," she said. "I could go visit my cousin in San Diego."

"Good. I suggest you start packing."

"But why, Miss Webb?" asked Mrs. Bates.

"Because I don't like taking chances, and I want time to check things out, especially when Henry gives her the good news about changing beneficiaries. Right, Henry?"

The next day Jean got a call from Henry, "Miss Webb, it's done, and I decided to change both beneficiaries."

"Okay. Henry, has your mother left?"

"Yes, I put her on a bus first thing this morning."

"Good, Henry. And watch yourself," Jean said. "There's no telling what she might do next."

"Yeah, I will, because when I told what I had done, she got hopping mad on the phone, making threats already."

Jean decided it was time to check up on Mary and see what she was up to. As Jean approached the front door, she could hear a loud voice inside. Apparently the phone was near the front door.

"Yeah, the son of a bitch changed the beneficiaries! Yeah, I'll be right over."

Then Mary slammed down the phone. Jean quickly ran back to her vehicle and pulled several doors down the street. Shortly, she saw Mary leave the house, jump into her vehicle, and speed away. Jean followed her to another house. Mary ran into the house, and it wasn't long before Mary came out with a man, and they left together.

So she got another man, Jean thought. Again, Jean followed them to a nearby restaurant and watched them go inside to eat and talk, as Jean watched them being seated next to a window.

Jean thought aloud, "I think I'll go invite Detective Hays for lunch."

Just before noon at police headquarters, Jean surprised Jeff. "Hi, Detective. Are you hungry? I'm buying."

"Oh, hello, Miss Webb. What's the occasion?"

"Quit being so polite. It's Jean, remember? And we're celebrating your gut's intuition, so I thought we'd go feed it."

At lunch, Jean told Jeff what she had found out after talking with Henry and his mother.

Jeff responded, "I'm glad you decided to check things out. Is there anything I can help you with?" He had a sincere look on his face.

"I'm glad you asked, Jeff. Could you run a wanted list and check these two out? Here's the description of the man she was with."

"Not a problem, Jean."

When they got ready to leave, Jeff said, "I'm buying the next time."

Jean smiled. "If you insist, Detective Hays."

The following day, Jean got a call from Detective Hays. "Congratulations on your hunch, Jean. I'm definitely buying lunch. Same place in an hour?"

At the restaurant, Jeff told Jean what he'd found out. "Well, here's the report from the FBI. It looks like our couple is wanted by the FBI for questioning involving fraud and possible murder. Their names are Larry and Lisa Brown, brother and sister. And they've been busy, because they're wanted in Utah and Kansas."

"A brother and sister act," stated Jean.

Jeff handed Jean the file and started eating. In between bites, Jean scanned through the report. Twenty minutes later, she said, "I think I know what their next move might be, but she's not available."

"Who's that?" Jeff asked.

"Henry's mother. I talked her into leaving town. That's means they've got to figure something else out that will irritate Henry to the point where he wants to kill her."

So Jean told Jeff her plan on how to nail them in the act and make the FBI's case easy to convict them.

"Are you sure, Jean?" Jeff questioned. "It sounds dangerous for Henry and you."

"I know." Jean agreed. "That's why I need to talk to Henry first, but I have a feeling he'll go along with it."

Later that night, Jean paid Henry a visit at his mother's home and explained her plan on how to catch the bad guys. "Yes," he said. "I'm willing to help nail these good-for-nothings, Miss Webb."

CHAPTER 80

Earlier, at Mary's home, she and her brother had been planning their next move. "We need to make Henry so mad that he acts like he wants to kill me. And we need to make sure the private eye bitch is there to stop him—permanently."

"What do you have in mind, Lisa?" Larry asked his sister.

"You'll attack his mother. That worked once before in Kansas, and it should make him mad enough to come after me. Then I'll call the private eye bitch."

Later, Larry Brown had conveniently parked down the street to do his job—spy on Henry. "Well, look what we got here," Larry whispered. "It looks like Lisa's private eye bitch just paid Henry a visit. Lisa will just love hearing about this."

Larry returned to inform his sister, "Henry's mother appears to be gone, and Henry had a visitor … your private eye bitch."

"What! That bitch," Lisa yelled. "I wonder how much she knows."

"Maybe we should pull out before it's too late," said a concerned brother.

"No way. We've gone too far to quit, and I didn't take this beating for nothing. We're just going to have to come up with a different plan." Lisa quickly figured out something else. "I'll talk Henry into coming over and follow the first part of the original plan. When the private eye shows up, we'll kill Henry and her."

Larry asked, "What good will that do?"

"Well, dummy, when his mother shows up, she'll have an accident, and then the inheritance will be ours."

The next day Mary called her husband and wanted to kiss and make up. "Please, Henry. Give me another chance to make things up to you. I was wrong, and I promise to be a good wife."

"All right, Mary. I'll be there," Henry said.

Mary didn't bother to call her private eye, because she knew Henry would. Later, when it was dark outside, Henry showed up. "Please come in, Henry. I'm so glad you came," Lisa said.

Jean followed Henry until he went inside, and then she started snooping around outside, listening for the hollering and screaming to start so she could rush in.

Suddenly, a voice said, "Why don't you go inside so you can hear everything better? Oh, and I'll take your pistol." It was brother Larry.

"Well, Larry, I see you found a prowler. Welcome, Miss Webb," Lisa said. "I'm glad you could drop by. Oh, I hate to tell you this. I don't need your services anymore, and I'm afraid that's too bad for you, dearie."

"Don't dearie me, you little bitch." Jean scowled. "I know who you two are, Lisa."

"Well, that makes it easier killing you then. It's called self-preservation. Larry will take you outside and shoot you as a prowler—in self-defense, of course. Larry, make sure you put her weapon back in her hand. Now, Henry, I'm going to shoot you in self-defense, dearie."

"No you're not, Lisa," said a voice behind her.

"What!" said a startled Lisa. Henry quickly knocked the pistol out of her hand, causing her brother to be distracted momentarily.

Then Lisa watched as Jean quickly disarmed her brother and clobbered him at the same time.

Detective Hays appeared and said, "Hi, Jean. Need a little help?" He started cuffing his prisoners and added, "I got everything recorded."

"That's great, Jeff. Good job, and great timing," Jean said.

When Jean walked over to Lisa, she asked, "How did you know?"

Jean answered, "I didn't, but I don't take chances either, dearie. Earlier, when you were gone, Detective Hays obtained a search warrant and planted some recording/listening devices. Then he made sure the back door was unlocked, dearie."

Jean looked at Jeff and said, "They're all yours, Detective Hays, and you can tell my friends at the FBI that I said, 'You're welcome.'"

Before she left, Henry said, "Thanks, Miss Webb."

And Jean replied, "You're welcome, Henry." She left with a satisfied smile on her face.

CHAPTER 81

It had been a busy two weeks for Jean, so she decided to relax by going to the gym next door. "I could use a good workout and meet my neighbor," she said, taking her packed gym bag and heading next door.

"Hi, I'm Maggie," the woman at the desk said. "Welcome to Maggie's Gym. We take men and women."

"Hi, Maggie. I'm Jean Webb your next-door neighbor."

"Oh, yeah. You're the private eye. Glad to meet you."

"What's the deal on using the gym?" Jean asked.

"It's five dollars per two-hour visit, which includes a shower and a towel."

"Good," Jean said. "Here's my five."

"Thanks, Jean. Here's a lock and key for your locker, and there's a sign by the door that says WOMEN IN THE LOCKER ROOM."

About that same time, a young, tall blonde walked in, and Maggie said, "Hi, Sarah."

"Hi, Maggie." The woman then headed for the locker room and put up the sign.

As Jean walked toward the locker room, she thought, *What a nice gym.* It was early, so the gym was empty, and Jean saw it had an area for the boxers to train, including a boxing ring, punching bags, weights, and a running track. She guessed the gym was about the size of a basketball court.

When she entered the locker room, Jean introduced herself to the other woman. "Hi, Sarah. I'm Jean." *What a nice, tall, good-looking blonde,* Jean thought to herself.

"I'm glad to meet you, Jean." The women shook hands, and Jean noticed she had a strong grip. Walking out of the locker room, Jean and Sarah were talking.

"Well, there you are, Sarah. We've been waiting for you," said one of two young men.

Sarah responded, "Look, I'm not at the academy now, so leave me alone."

Jean quickly thought, *Academy. This must be Sarah Bailey.*

Then the other man said, "Why don't you introduce us to your girlie friend, Sarah."

That's when Jean walked up to the smart-ass young man and said, "You know what, asshole? You just insulted us women."

"So what, girlie friend?" he replied.

"Wrong answer, asshole." The man got a quick shot to his chin with Jean's open palm, sending him sprawling across the gym floor.

When his partner started to make a move, Sarah gave him a left-hand punch to his stomach and then a right uppercut to his jaw. Then there were two assholes on the floor. The two men jumped up and made their moves. Jean planted a karate kick to the stomach. She then swung around, delivering another kick to her opponent's chin, knocking him down hard. Meanwhile, Sarah ducked and planted her next blow on her opponent's chin again and finished off with an uppercut that sent him back to the floor. Jean made a quick move and planted her knee in her opponent's stomach and placed the knuckles of her right hand against his throat. "You move, asshole, and I'll shove your Adam's apple to the back of your miserable throat," she said, putting pressure on the Adam's apple.

Maggie came running over with a sawed-off double-barrel shotgun and said, "Don't move." She handed the weapon to Jean.

Jean got up and turned to Sarah. "Are you Chief Bailey's daughter?"

Sarah looked surprised and said, "Why, yes I am. How did you know?"

"I'm Jean Webb."

"Oh, yeah. My father told me about you. You're ex-OSS, ex-CIG, and now a PI."

"That's right." Jean looked at the two clowns on the floor and asked, "Are these the only male pigs that bother you at the academy?"

"No. Most of them do," Sarah answered.

Jean pointed the shotgun at the two pigs and said, "Get up, you two, before I change your voices to girlie sounding." She dropped the barrel to a forty-five degree angle and aimed it between their legs.

They quickly got up, saying, "We're sorry, Miss Webb. We didn't know it was you."

"Well, you do now. Chief Bailey told me to let him know if any of you clowns gave me a bad time." The two clowns looked at each other. "But I told him I can take care of myself. Isn't that right, gentlemen?"

"Yes, ma'am," answered the two concerned future police officers.

"So listen up. If I hear of any more of you male pigs harassing Sarah, I'll come down to the academy and start parting some pig's hair, starting with you two. Understand? Gentlemen!"

"Yes, ma'am," answered the two male pigs. Then Jean started poking one of them in the gut with the shotgun. "Now, you two get the hell out of here!"

And two future police officers took off in a hurry.

Maggie started clapping and said, "That's the best show I've seen in years, Jean. Don't worry about the five dollars. Just come over anytime."

"Thanks, Maggie," she said, handing back the shotgun.

Sarah and Jean worked out together for two hours and then decided to go for a malted shake at the corner drugstore. That way, they could get better acquainted.

After chatting back and forth, Jean learned Sarah had lost her mother to cancer five years earlier. "I'm sorry, Sarah. That would have been tough at sixteen."

"It was. How old were you when you lost your father?" Sarah asked.

A surprised Jean thought, *How did she know that?*

Then Sarah said, "I guess you're wondering how I knew that."

"Yes, I am," Jean admitted.

"Your mother told Dad and me."

"When did she tell you that? And I was a baby—just a year old."

"The last time they went on a date," replied Sarah.

"What! My mother is dating your father?" Jean started laughing.

"What's so funny, Jean?"

Jean stopped laughing long enough to ask, "Was it right after I showed up?"

"No, months before," Sarah said.

Jean thought, *You're a foxy old lady, Mother.* Jean looked at Sarah. "Just wait until I see that father of yours."

Sarah suddenly got nervous and said, "You're not going to shoot him, are you?"

"Hell no," Jean said with a chuckle. "I'm going to give him a big hug and kiss."

That surprised Sarah, and she didn't know what to say, so she just asked, "Why?"

Jean grabbed Sarah's hands and looked her in the eyes. "Wouldn't it be nice if we became stepsisters?"

Sarah smiled. "Yes. That would be very nice."

While still at the drugstore, Jean decided it was time to expose the hidden relationship. "Sarah, do you know when our parents are having their next secret rendezvous?"

"As a matter of fact, I do. It's at a restaurant near the South Mountain Speedway on Friday night. I think they're going to watch the midget cars race after dinner. My dad knows Bobby Ball, one of the drivers."

Jean thought for a moment. "Here's what we're going to do ..."

When Jean and Sarah left the drugstore, the soda jerk said, "Gosh, I hope I meet someone as beautiful as those two women are."

That afternoon at five o'clock, Jean stopped by Jake's new apartment and waited for him to show up from work. Jean was feeling horny after her workout.

"Well, hi, sweetheart. This is a nice surprise. What's the occasion?" Jake asked.

"I'll tell you later," she said. Once inside, Jean started undressing Jake.

Later, after an hour of good sex, they jumped in the shower together. "Mom is dating Chief Bailey," Jean said.

"Good for her," Jake said, scrubbing Jean's back.

"But why be so secret about it?" she asked.

"I don't know, Jean. They must have a good reason for doing it."

"What! To hide it from me?" Jean turned around and got her 38Ds done.

After they got out of the shower and dried off, Jean told Jake about her plan. "So here's what Sarah and I want to do …"

Jake said, "You sure you want to do that?"

"You're damn right I do," said an upset daughter.

Later that night at dinner, Jean asked her mother, "Are you busy Friday night?"

"Why, dear?" Mildred asked.

"Well, Jake and I are going out and thought you might join us."

"Oh no, dear. I'm just going to stay home and relax. It's been a busy week at the governor's office."

"Oh. Well, maybe the next time, Mother?" Jean asked.

"Yes, dear. Let me know ahead of time, and I'd love to go," her mother said.

"Okay … good night, Mom." Climbing the stairs to her bedroom, Jean thought, *Staying home Friday night. Right, you foxy lady.*

Chapter 82

Friday night came, and Mildred started listening to the five o'clock news when a car horn sounded off.

"That's Jake," Jean said. "You have a nice, restful evening, Mom. See you later." *But sooner than you think, foxy lady.*

Jean and Jake had a nice cool drive out to South Mountain while enjoying the sunset and the orange-yellow sky with a background of the scattered clouds and mountain peaks.

Jean spoke up. "This is part of that wonderful, beautiful West we talked about on the way out here from DC."

Jake said, "Yes. It's like looking at a beautiful painted picture, dear."

After enjoying the beautiful scenery some more, Jake asked, "Are you still wondering why your mother and Chief Bailey were keeping their dating a secret from you."

"A little, but I intend on finding out tonight," stated a determine daughter.

"Well, there's the Hi-Speed Steak House," Jake said.

Once inside, Jean looked around and saw western décor, including a wooden floor with tables and chairs, an indoor cooking wood fire grille, and a large bar and dance floor. Also, there was a small band playing western songs.

Then Jean saw Sarah and Jeff. As they walked toward Sarah and Jeff, Jean remembered asking Sarah if she had a date for Friday night, and Sarah said she didn't. So Jean called Jeff Hays. When they reached the table, Jean saw a beautiful-looking blonde, because Sarah was a good-looking woman like Jean and had a full figure like her possible future stepsister. Both were wearing low-cut dresses, exposing some of their best-looking assets.

"Wow, you look marvelous, Sarah," Jean said.

"What about me?" asked Jeff.

Jean quickly replied, "Oh, Jeff, you always look marvelous. Jeff and Sarah, this is Jake Blakely."

The men shook hands, and Jake said, "Jean's right. You do look beautiful tonight, Sarah."

A slightly embarrassed Sarah informed Jean, "The hostess knows to seat them at this table."

"Great, Sarah. I'm going to enjoy this," said a get-even daughter.

The two couples ordered their favorite poison and got better acquainted.

"So, Sarah, what made you think about becoming a police officer?" asked Jake.

"I don't know," she said. "I guess after we lost Mom, I always liked the idea of protecting people. Since it was good enough for my father, why wouldn't it be good for me?"

"Good answer, Sarah," Jean said and added, "Here they come. Everybody act surprised."

Jean watched as the dating couple were busy talking and not looking where they were about to be seated. When they neared the waiting foursome, the hostess said, "Here's your table."

A surprised-acting daughter said, "Well, look who's here. Strange meeting you two here, and I see you got your second wind, Mother."

Jean got a firm look from her mother, and Mildred replied with a firm answer. "Well, you know how it is, Jean, when a good man comes along and asks you out." Knowing her daughter was probably upset with her, everybody looked at Jean.

Jean had forgotten where her sharp orneriness and stubbornness came from. "Okay, Mom. Have a seat, and let's enjoy the evening together."

Jake leaned over and said, "Good move. Let's dance."

Then Jeff and Sarah followed suit and got up to dance also.

"Sam, doesn't Sarah look beautiful tonight?" Mildred said.

"Yes, she does."

"I have a feeling Jean had something to with that," commented Mildred.

Sam Bailey looked at his lovely date. "Are you going to tell her why we didn't let her know about us?"

"I'll have to now."

CHAPTER 83

Jean and Jake returned to their table, and Jake excused himself. He looked at Sam and gave him a tilted come-with-me look, and Sam joined Jake as they headed for the men's room.

"Okay, Mom. What the hell has been going on?" Jean asked.

"Okay, Jean, just calm down, and I'll tell you … I met Sam several times during the past year, and he called me three months ago and asked if I would go out with him. I said *yes*. We both decided to keep our dating low profile, with both of us being in high-ranking political positions. Then I told him about you and that you were on your way to Phoenix, and he let me know he could use another good detective."

"And I said I wanted to be a private investigator."

"That's right, and you wanted to do your own thing and try it on your own."

"Right, but you two couldn't leave it at that."

"Yes, because of what Sam saw happening to Sarah at the academy, we didn't want you to know Sam would be helping you. But after meeting you, he tried to get me to tell you anyway, because he felt you could handle it."

"He's a good man, Mom."

"Yes, I know."

The men returned, and Jean said, "Sam, let's dance." He glanced at Mildred and got an okay nod. On the dance floor, Jean asked, "What are your intentions in regards to my mother?"

Sam looked Jean right in the eye and said, "What any red-blooded man would do with a good-looking woman like your mother."

"Good … And by the way, you are one hell of an actor, Chief." The smiling Sam got a big hug and kiss on his cheek.

The three couples enjoyed their steaks, conversation, and just having a good time. Jean noticed Jeff had his arm around Sarah quite a bit, and she smiled at Sarah.

Before dinner ended, Chief Bailey let Jean and Sarah know he'd heard about what had happened at the gym. "I would've paid big bucks to have seen that show," he said. Then he went ahead and explained it to the others.

Jake and Jeff both said, "So would I."

Mildred noticed Sarah and Jean were smiling at each other. Then it was time to go watch the midget cars race and hopefully watch Bobby Ball win.

CHAPTER 84

Monday morning Mildred was up and ready to go to work. "I feel great after a marvelous special Friday night and a wonderful weekend," she said.

While having her usual breakfast, she had a clear mind, knowing everybody was happy about her and Sam dating. While driving to work, Mildred had on her radio and was listening to the morning newscast. She was enjoying the cool November weather when she happened to glance in her rearview mirror and noticed that a car seemed to be following her.

Mildred knew she needed gas and commented, "I'll stop at my usual gas station." When the attendant came to the vehicle, she said, "Joe, fill her up, and can I use your private phone in your office? It's very important."

"Go right ahead, Mrs. Webb," Joe said.

Mildred went into the office and dialed Jake's number. "Good morning, Jake. I think I'm being followed ... I'm at Joe's Gas Station ... Okay, I will." Mildred paid Joe and said, "Thanks, Joe. See you later."

Back on the road, Mildred made a left turn at the next stoplight. She then traveled five blocks, turned right, and traveled another six blocks. "It's the same vehicle, and it's definitely following me," she said to herself.

When she passed a certain apartment building, she honked twice and kept on going. Mildred then reached for the glove compartment and said, "I better get ready." She pulled out a revolver and then checked the rearview mirror and saw what she wanted to see.

"It's time to extend the proper welcoming, whoever the hell you are." Coming to a complete stop, Mildred turned slightly sideways and crawled out the passenger's side as she prepared to meet her pursuers.

When the other car stopped, she saw two men getting out of their car with weapons in their hands. Suddenly, another vehicle came to a squeaking stop and turned sideways. She knew it was Jake.

"Thank goodness," she said with a sigh of relief.

Jake jumped out of his vehicle and hollered, "Drop those weapons! Get your hands up, now!"

Instead, Mildred watched the pursuers start shooting at Jake. "No you don't," she screamed as she started shooting at them.

Now the surprised pursuers jumped in their vehicle and peeled rubber. As they flew by Mildred, she ducked just before they fired a shot in her direction, shattering her passenger's side window. "Damn you, assholes," she said.

Now an angry blonde stood up, took aim, and fired, hitting their rear window as they sped away. Jake came running over and said, "You okay, Mildred?"

"Yeah, I'm okay … Damn it! I missed the driver, but thanks to you, Jake, I'm still here."

"You okay to drive to work, Mildred?" Jake asked.

She replied, "Oh, yeah."

Jake said, "I'll follow you." As soon as Jake reached his office, he called Jean. "Jean, I think someone just attempted to kidnap your mother."

Jean responded with shock. "What! You're kidding, aren't you?"

Then Jake explained what happened. "She's okay, but I'll have one of my men with her from here on out until we catch whoever these bastards are."

"Thanks for calling, Jake," Jean said.

After hanging up the phone, Jean got up and started pacing around her office. *Who in the hell is trying to kidnap my mother?* she wondered. Shortly, her phone started ringing. "This is Webb Detective Agency. Jean speaking."

"Jean, it's Bob Franklin! I just received an urgent message that somebody has put a hit out on you and your mother."

"Yeah, they just tried, but she's safe, thanks to Jake. Do you know who the bastards are?" Jean asked.

"Not for sure, but I've got more intel coming in. I'm catching a military flight first thing in the morning, so I'll see you late tomorrow afternoon, hopefully with more information. Please take care of yourself and your mother," Bob said.

"I will," she promised. "Thanks, Bob, and I'll see you tomorrow."

PART FOUR

A SPY AGAIN

CHAPTER 85

Jean called Jake to let him know about her call from Bob and to ask him to definitely keep a man with her mother until they knew more. "Jake, please be available for a meeting late tomorrow afternoon with Bob and plan to dine with us."

Jean closed up shop and headed home to make sure everything was okay and to wait for her mother to arrive. Then she started thinking about who could be after her hide. Then she fixed lunch. Jean had just finished eating when there was a knock at the front door.

She approached the door armed. She saw a uniformed officer whom she recognized.

"Hi, Jean," the officer said. "Jake sent me to watch your house."

"Come in, Tom," she said, opening the door. Tom was one of Jake's Rangers. "How about a cup of coffee?"

Tom replied, "I'd love one, Jean."

Jean and the Ranger enjoyed a cup of coffee while Jean surmised who might have put the hit out on her. "I don't think it's anybody from Brazil or South America." Concentrating more, she said, "It's got to be the Mexican mob."

Then Jake called. "Jean, is Tom there? ... Okay, and so you know, I'm having a Ranger meet Bob's flight at Luke Field."

"Thanks, Jake," Jean said. "And let's have the meeting here, so Mom can hear what's going on … Good … See you then."

Next, Jean called her mother and let her know about the meeting. Of course, Mildred told Jean she would be home early so she could fix dinner for everybody and had already planned a dinner for the following night. When she arrived home, Mildred started dinner, and Jean jumped in and helped her out.

During dinner, Jake told Jean, "We found the car at the airport. It had a bullet hole in the rear window just where you put it, Mildred. It was a rental car. We're running the information at the rental agency, because they had to have a driver's license on file."

"Good, Jake, but it's probably a fake ID." Jean pointed out. "So maybe they left, and maybe not all of them left."

"Yeah. Maybe, Jean, but we're not taking any chances. We're going to be watching the border and incoming flights from Mexico since you think it might be the Mexico mob, and we are notifying customs and Sam," Jake said.

"Sounds good, Jake," Jean said. Mildred liked what she heard too.

CHAPTER 86

The following morning after breakfast, Jean called DC. "Chester Thurston please. Jean Webb calling."

"Oh, Jean, I'm glad you called," Chester said as soon as he picked up the line. "DD Collins called and told me what's going on. Is your mother all right?"

"Yes, she's fine. Jake managed to fight off the attackers. Chester, I want back in so I can legally go after these bastards."

"I expected your call, Jean, and the paperwork is already started. And Bob has your credentials. Let me know when you have a plan and if you need anything from me. Also, just so you know, in the near future, we are going solo from the current chain of command. The new name will be CIA, for Central Intelligence Agency. And finally, your operation will be sanctioned under illegal trafficking of heroin into the United States per the Harrison Act of 1914. We know the Mafia is involved, and so is the Mexican mob. Good luck, Jean."

"Thanks, Chester," Jean said. "I'll call if you can help. Thanks again."

Next, Jean placed a call to the Santa Fe, New Mexico, information operator. "How can I help, ma'am?" the operator asked.

"I need a number for the sheriff's office ... Thank you."

Jean dialed the long-distance operator and gave her the number. "Santa Fe Sheriff's Office."

"Sheriff Torres, please … Jean Webb calling."

Shortly Jean heard, "Hi, Miss Webb. What I do for you?"

"Sheriff, by any chance do you know a Carlos Sanchez?"

"I sure do. I know two—Carlos and Esteban."

"Esteban the artist?" Jean questioned.

"That's right; they're both friends of mine."

Then a lightbulb went off in Sheriff Torres's head. "By any chance, are you Major Webb, formerly with OSS?"

Jean replied, "Yes, guilty as charged."

"Let me reintroduce myself. First Lieutenant Torres of the Second Rangers. Carlos's CO."

"Well, I'm glad to meet you, Lieutenant … I need to get in touch with Carlos."

Sheriff Torres gave Jean Carlos's phone number, and she thanked him. Jean decided to call Carlos later that night, hoping to catch him at home after her meeting with Bob Franklin. She had a feeling she might need his help, along with Joe, Howard, and John.

Mildred arrived home early with groceries for dinner and saw that Jean was uptight and anxiously pacing as she waited for Bob and more information.

"Jean, why don't you help me fix dinner. It'll get your mind off trying to figure this situation out."

"Okay, Mom," Jean agreed.

Bob and Jake finally showed up. "Hi, Bob," Jean said. "Come in and sit down. Can I fix you a drink?"

"Yeah, I could use one, Jean," Bob replied.

Jake said, "Jean, go head and visit with Bob. I'll fix the drinks."

"Make that one more, Jake," Mildred said.

After visiting for a while, Mildred said, "Let's eat. I've got barbeque pork chops and beans and cornbread." Four people immediately headed for the table.

Tom said, "Good. I've smelled those chops for two hours." He grinned as he made his way to the table.

During dinner, things were quiet, because Mildred's food tasted awful good.

Bob said, "You keep this up, Mildred, and I'm just going to have to marry you."

"Now you're in big trouble, Mom," Jean said.

Smiling, Mildred replied, "Oh my goodness. Not tonight, Bob."

After dessert, everybody retired to the living room where Mildred said, "I'll do dishes later."

Bob retrieved his notes and began explaining what he found out. "I'm afraid it's not much, but tomorrow I'll know more. Jean, you remember our friend Javier Ortiz ... Well, he escaped while working on a road gang between Chula Vista and the border."

"How the hell did that happen?" Jean asked.

"Two trucks armed with men came driving in; the men killed the two guards and took Javier. A witness said they took off heading east. Then two weeks later, Agent Emilio Santos heard a rumor that one of the men killed during the capturing of Javier in Mexico was the younger brother of the mob boss Tito Cardoza, and Javier is his kissing cousin."

Jean piped up. "It's a small world, isn't it?"

Bob continued, "Yesterday when I got the call from Rafael Alvarez, he said they checked on Javier's visitors, and one of them was Chico Garcia, a lieutenant in the Cardoza mob. So Rafael figured that's where Javier is, and of course, he told his cousin what happened, naming you. Finally, Emilio is trying to find out more and will be in San Diego tomorrow. I have already booked two tickets for the first flight out."

"Thanks, Bob. I'll be ready," Jean said positively.

Chapter 87

At eleven o'clock the next day, Jean and Bob entered the San Diego FBI field office and met with Rafael and Emilio.

"Good morning, gentlemen. What do you have for us?" Bob said.

"Well, first of all, the Border Patrol found the abandoned trucks at an airstrip near the border, so we can assume Javier is in Mexico," Rafael said.

Next, Emilio reported his findings. "It's obvious the Cardoza mob was behind this planned escape. The intel I have locates the Cardoza compound in the San Luis Potosí area in the hills between the towns of Aguascalientes and León. That locates it east of Puerto Vallarta and west of Tampico."

Rafael jumped in. "We know the Mafia in the States has supported the Cardoza mob that has illegally been shipping heroin into the states. Based on the Harrison Narcotic Act of 1914, these guys are subject to a maximum of ten years in prison and twenty thousand dollars in fines. Well, that's what we have so far."

Then the three men looked at Jean. "All right, gentlemen," she began. "Here's the ball game. This operation is sanctioned and based on the Harrison Act, so we can bring these guys to justice or eliminate them if they resist. Next, we know that the Cardoza mob is being supplied heroin by the Colombians, according to our resources. We don't know for sure which one. So, Emilio, do you think you could find out which one or ones are supplying?"

"Yes, but it will take some time."

"That's all right, because we have some planning and some recruiting to do," Jean said.

On the flight back to Phoenix, Bob asked, "Who are you planning on recruiting?"

"Four wonderful guys who helped me kick the Nazis out of Milan, Italy. I hope ... Let's schedule a planning meeting in Phoenix after I talk to Santa Fe, New Mexico."

Jean acquired a large map of Mexico, and she and Bob started memorizing the area where the Cardoza compound was located and the possible routes to it from both the east and west coasts. Bob was in contact with the San Diego field office on a daily basis, while Jean flew to Santa Fe after making an important call. Carlos was waiting at the Santa Fe Airport when Jean's charted flight landed.

At the gate, Jean departed and immediately saw Carlos. When she reached him, she gave him a big hug.

"It's good to see you, Jean," Carlos said.

"And it's good to see you too, Carlos ... How about coffee and a donut?"

"Okay, we can get one at the coffee shop."

While enjoying their coffee and donut, there was some catching up to do. "So you're a private eye now. And how's that working for you?" Carlos asked.

"I'm busy, and so far I'm enjoying it ... What kind of trouble have you been getting into?"

"Part-time deputy sheriff and part-time treasure hunter," Carlos said.

"Have you found anything worthwhile?" Jean asked.

"Yes, I have. I found some treasure and some artifacts, and the museums pay pretty good. So, Jean, what's this important issue you have?"

Jean looked Carlos in the eye. "I've got a price on my head."

"What!" Carlos gasped. "You're kidding, aren't you?"

"No, I'm not. A Mexican mob boss has a hit order on me and my mom. They already attacked Mom, but Jake fought them off. Carlos, I've been sanctioned to go after him, and I need your help. The agency will pay five thousand dollars plus expenses for each man. This guy is a major smuggler of heroin into the United States."

"What do you have in mind, Jean?" Carlos questioned. "Or do I dare ask?"

"I have three FBI agents, me, and your team of four makes eight. We're on our own. It's kind of like being in the war behind enemy lines."

Carlos asked, "Where does this bad ass hang his hat at night?"

"He has a secured compound in the San Luis Potosí area near León, Mexico," Jean said.

"That's deep into Mexico. How do you plan to get there?"

"That hasn't been decided yet. There's going to be a planning meeting in Phoenix soon," Jean said.

"All right. Let me do some checking, and I'll get back to you in a couple of days."

A smiling Jean said, "Thank you, Carlos." And she gave an old friend a big hug.

CHAPTER 88

On her flight to Phoenix, Jean's mind was busy organizing and planning her next moves. *I'll need to call Chester and let him know what I need and who will hopefully be going with me. Then I need to study the area map for possible routes to the compound and where the drop site might be, and that means I get to jump out of a damn airplane. And I thought the war was over.*

Next, Jean hoped Emilio would be able to find out who the supplier was in Colombia. She trusted he was being very careful while in the lion's den. Suddenly, the plane started bouncing around, and Jean's hands quickly grabbed the armrests, squeezing them with a white-knuckle grip. Then the plane quit its dancing around almost as fast as it started.

Jean heard the pilot yell, "Sorry about that, Miss Webb, but sometimes we hit air pockets flying over these mountains."

No more air pockets, please, she thought.

Bob Franklin was waiting when Jean's plane landed and was there when she put her feet on the ground.

"Hi, Jean," he said. "I've got good news. The Border Patrol and the DEA caught two of Cardoza's assassins crossing the border."

"That's great, Bob. Now maybe we can extract more intel from the bastards."

Later that afternoon, Jean and Bob, along with Jake, started interrogating the assassins.

"I know why you are here. I want answers, and I plan on getting them one way or another," Jean said, speaking in Spanish and sticking a big pig sticker into the tabletop. By the looks on their faces, it looked like she was getting someone's attention. Speaking in Spanish again, she added, "Bob and Jake, you two probably ought to leave." Jean grabbed the pig sticker.

When the two got up to leave, one of the assassins started talking. Jake quickly removed the other one.

Then the questions started, but not before Jean made a statement, speaking in Spanish with anger in her eyes. "I'm CIG! And you, you son of a bitch, you came to kill my mother and me, and I don't have to follow the rules. If you don't give me the answers I want, I will skin you alive, and you will disappear, asshole." Jean stuck the blade hard into the table again. "Now, is Javier Ortiz at the compound?"

Jean received a quick yes in reply.

"Now you're going to describe the layout of the compound and the security, manpower, and exits."

An hour later, Jean had what she needed and told the assassin, "For your help, I'll see you get a break and not be returned to Mexico, if that's your desire."

CHAPTER 89

A few days later, Jean was in her office doing some paperwork when the phone rang. "Webb Detective Agency. Jean speaking."

"Hi, Jean. It's Carlos … Well, you got your team."

"Oh, thanks, Carlos. Please tell the other guys' thanks for me … I'll give you a couple of days' notice before the planning meeting, and then flight arrangements will be made."

"Great, Jean. We'll be waiting."

About an hour later, Bob showed up. "Hey, Bob. Anything new?" Jean asked.

"Yeah, I talked to Rafael, and he received a telegram from Emilio. Once it was decoded, it said he was zeroing in on a family he suspects, and he understands there's a German with them who's their new enforcer. And he'll be in contact in a couple of days. I asked Rafael to send a reply, asking for the name of the German."

"Well, I've got some good news," Jean said. "I have my team … Carlos called an hour ago."

"That's great, Jean," Bob said. "Things are shaping up. I see you've been studying the compound's layout."

"Yeah, the one thing we need to do is get above the compound in the hills so we can observe the situation before going in," Jean explained.

"I agree, Jean. Well, I better get back and call Rafael ... Oh, Collins is aware of everything and said to tell you the FBI is behind you also."

"Bob, the first chance you get, please let Collins know I appreciate it."

"I will, Jean. Bye."

*   *   *

In Bogotá, Colombia, Emilio had just left and was headed for a compound approximately two hundred miles northwest. His designation was Medellín, Colombia. From there, he would travel eighty miles northeast to where there was a secure compound located in the foothills of the Andes Mountains and above a large valley along the Magdalena River. The location was perfect for growing the opium poppy plant that is used to produce heroin.

It was one o'clock when Emilio reached Medellín, and he began looking for a restaurant. While eating, he made some inquiries about a shop that sold mountain-climbing equipment. An hour later, Emilio was on his way to the valley and the foothills of the Andes Mountains.

Emilio looked for a hidden spot to park his vehicle. After he found one that would be well hidden from the road, he made his way to a location above the compound where he could observe their operations. Just before dusk, Emilio reached a spot above a ledge and a crevice to descend in. There, he'd be hidden from the compound. By the time he reached the ledge, it was dark and cold, so the first thing he did was put up his shelter and eat something with a cup of hot coffee. Next, with a long-range infrared nightscope, he began observing the activities in the compound and took notes.

When the sunrays hit the valley, Emilio had eaten his breakfast made from packaged food and drank some hot coffee. "Damn it's cold this morning," he mumbled. "I'll be glad when that sun is shining on me." Then it was time to go to work. "There's their process plant, and it looks like they're getting ready to ship some product. Ah, I think I see the German, and he's well-armed with a pistol and rifle. And that must be the drug lord with him, along with a couple of men. I better write down some descriptions of the German and the drug lord."

Emilio noted the entrances and exits and the number of security guards. About two hours later, he heard a helicopter and then watched it land in the valley below the compound. When Emilio could see the person who arrived, he recognized him right away, "Chico Garcia—bingo! I got the right one. Time to get the hell out of here."

Emilio packed up, hooked onto the anchored line, and climbed back up through the crevice to the top and proceeded to descend the way he'd come up the mountain. Four hours later, he came to a platform and took a break. He could see his vehicle from there, and just as Emilio was about to leave, two men showed up. They had automatic weapons. They broke into the vehicle, and Emilio decided it'd be best to join them.

Just before reaching his vehicle, he hollered, "Hi there, guys. Boy, did I have one hell of a climb. In Bogotá, they told me this was the best climb."

He startled the two men, and they immediately pointed their weapons at Emilio, who put up his hands and said, "Is there a problem here?"

One of the men said, "Who are you, señor?"

"Oh, I'm a friend of your president and a salesman who likes to climb mountains."

That must have confused them, and when they looked at each other, that's when Emilio nailed them with his pistol/silencer. Next, he hooked up their vehicle to his own, towed it to the river, and pushed it in.

"I need to go like a bat out of hell and get on a plane ASAP before they catch me," he said to himself.

It was later that afternoon when Emilio reached the airport and managed to catch a flight to Panama City scheduled to leave in twenty minutes. Emilio was walking to the aircraft to board when he saw a helicopter land. Two men got out and were joined by two policemen. He then saw them point in his direction and start coming his way.

Once everybody was seated on the plane, the four men showed up. The policemen said, "Everybody have out your passports for inspection." Emilio was hoping they didn't have a good description of him from the car rental place. When they reached him, he handed them his passport, and they asked, "Why were you here, señor?"

"I was here on business and made several calls yesterday and today, and now I'm on my way to Panama City to make my next one." He handed the mean four of his business cards.

"Thank you, señor."

"You're welcome, señores."

Now Emilio was glad he used a fake passport and driver's license to rent the vehicle. *Sorry, fellas*, he thought to himself. *Maybe the next time we can dance.*

Earlier at the compound, Chico had been talking to the drug lord Manuela Escobar, a ruthless woman. She heard her second-in-command say, "We have a problem. I just found two of my men in the river, dead."

"What! Juan! Search the foothills to the south of us immediately and get two men in the helicopter headed for the airport. Hopefully we can catch whoever was here." Next, she turned to her foreman and said, "Get those damn trucks loaded and out of here, pronto!"

Chico said, "I'll go with the product. We'll let you know if we find out anything."

"Do that, Chico," Manuela said firmly.

CHAPTER 90

In Panama City, Emilio called Rafael in San Diego. He made his report and booked a fight to San Diego with a stop in Mexico City. Once on board he had a gin martini, saying, "I needed this."

In Phoenix, Jean got the word and scheduled a planning meeting in three days in Phoenix. Then she called Chester and let him know who was going. Chester had a problem with the FBI men going along and would need to clear it with Collins. When Jean told him about the German at the drug lord's compound in Colombia, he didn't have a problem because he assumed he was a wanted Nazi.

"I'll call you after our planning meeting and let you know if there's anything you can furnish," Jean told him. "Bye, Chester."

When Bob found out about the scheduled meeting, he reserved a conference room at the Phoenix FBI field office. Three days later, Bob picked up Rafael and Emilio at the airport, and Jean picked up her team as well. Everybody was introduced to one another, and each person gave a short history as to who they were, what their qualifications were, and what their involvement had been in the war. Then, after lunch, the group visited for thirty minutes before Bob and Jean called the meeting to order.

"We have prepared a topo map of the area, showing the elevations of the terrain where the Cardoza compound is located. The first order of business is to determine which way we should approach it. Carlos, have you been in this area on your exploring trips?"

"Yes. I was through there once. It's pretty much open terrain coming from the east, but I'm afraid they would see us coming before we crossed the fields below, making us sitting ducks."

"Thanks, Carlos. Anybody else?" Jean asked.

Rafael responded. "I'm sure they would be watching the north, and it looks like they have a clear line of sight to the south. It looks like the west is the best route, and besides, we want to be above them."

"I agree, Rafael. Anybody else have any comments? Now is the time to bring them up," Jean said.

Bob looked at everybody and said, "Then we all agree ... good. Jean, I suggest we fly into Puerto Vallarta in two groups of three, and two of us will drive vehicles across the border and rendezvous at a designated location for a drop that will have our equipment and weapons."

"Good idea, Bob," Jean said. "We'll pick the hotel as our base and proceed when everybody is present. Any other comments, gentlemen? ... Yes, Joe?"

"Who flies and who drives?" Joe asked.

"I'll drive since they know me," Carlos said.

"I'll drive," Emilio said. "They know me also."

Jean continued. "Carlos, I'd like you and Joe to give some thought to an attack plan once we're there. Bob, would you do the same? Okay, now we're going to hear from Emilio about his wonderful, exciting trip to Colombia."

"Thanks, Jean. Gentlemen, this is where the Escobar compound is located," Emilio said, pointing at a map of Colombia. "The target is two hundred miles northwest of Bogotá and eighty northeast of Medellín. The drug lord is none other than Manuela Escobar, one of the largest in Colombia. She is a ruthless woman and a killer. As you can see, the compound is located on the western slope of the Andes Mountains. I recommend we fly to Venezuela and enter Colombia in a helicopter, landing on the eastern slope and climb above the compound. I found a ledge overlooking the target, and it's perfect for a sniper. Then I have a layout of the compound and the entrances and exits. Security is tight, and yes, there is a German who is now in charge of security. Finally, while I was there, Chico Garcia arrived by helicopter, apparently to escort a large load of product. Unfortunately, I did not get away clean. I had to kill two of their men."

"Thanks, Emilio, for gathering this intel, which was a very dangerous effort," Jean said. "I do have one question. Did you find out the name of the German?"

"No, I did not."

CHAPTER 91

Carlos picked Burns to be the sniper. He was on his way to Quantico, Virginia, for a one-week crash course in sniper training by Marine Recon. Meanwhile, Bob and Jean were making arrangements for transportation and accommodations for their teams into foreign countries unannounced. Jean called Chester to let him know they had a plan developed, and he set a time for her to call back so his experts could listen in. After a very long phone conversation, Jean got an okay from the experts, who noted it was "a well-thought-out plan." Bob continued with the details, while Jean had to play PI during the day and spy at night, which made for long days.

* * *

In Colombia, the loaded trucks arrived at the Port of Cartagena, and the product was loaded on a ship, which immediately set sail for parts unknown. Chico Garcia was on board. He instructed the captain to head for Veracruz, Mexico, where he would be given further instructions later.

* * *

Meanwhile, in Mexico, at the Cardoza compound, one of Tito's lieutenants informed him, "Our two men have not returned, and we have not heard from them either. I can't find out anything as to their whereabouts."

"I don't like it," Tito said. "You better tighten up security—twenty-four hours. Have we heard from Chico?"

"Yes, he has left Colombia, and we should rendezvous in three days."

"Good, I want product on the road to the States in one week."

CHAPTER 92

After having a busy week, Jean decided to temporarily close her agency until further notice. Jean had made arrangements with a local mountain-climbing club to have everybody brush up on their skills. So when Burns returned, it was mountain climbing time.

The instructor had everybody doing strength-building exercises, eating a special diet, and learning how to use the basic equipment. After a week, it was time for actual climbing exercises. Joe was issued the rock-climbing gear, and everybody else was issued mountain-climbing gear. Jean's judo and karate training and her diligence in going to the gym once a week helped her keep up with the men. And because of her OSS training in mountain climbing, she was one of the first on the practice wall and a local cliff. Pathfinder Joe's practice was scaling a sheer cliff face, and everybody watched, knowing he had to reach the safe haven for everybody as they ascended to the top of the mountain.

During a lunch break, Jean announced, "We go next week and leave from the Tucson Airbase."

Then everybody went home to spend time with their families and loved ones. Jean called Chester and let him know when they were leaving. Jean spent most of the week visiting with her mother, including going out to eat at a nice restaurant and to the movies. Dinner with Jake and Mildred on Jean's last night home was a little tense when Jean broke the ice.

"If everything goes according to plan, I should be back in three days. Once I hit stateside, I'll call you, Mom."

Mildred responded, "Remember what your grandfather always told you. Don't forget to duck." With that, Mildred left the dinner table, knowing how dangerous this mission was for her daughter. She had tears in her eyes as she made her way to her room.

"Jean, I wish I was going with you. This is going to be one of your toughest assignments ever," Jake said.

"Yeah, but I have no choice, Jake," Jean said. "Take care of Mom for me."

The following week at the Tucson Airbase, Jean had a meeting with her team. "Joe, Bob, and I will leave tomorrow for Puerto Vallarta. Carlos and Emilio will leave today in their vehicles headed for the rendezvous and the drop in four days. That means Rafael, Burns, and Carter need to leave in two days. Any questions? … Good. Good luck, everybody, and don't forget to duck."

On the plane, Jean and Bob were checking their passports. "Well, Mrs. Joan Davies, how do you like being married?" Bob asked.

"Well, Mr. George Davies, just remember these are just aliases."

"I can tell you aren't going to be any fun at all, Mrs. Davies," Bob said, smiling at Jean.

"That's right, Bob. You get the couch."

Jean thought if Bob wasn't like a brother to her, she'd consider the good-looking cowboy joining her in bed. Joe's alias had him as a wealthy rancher from New Mexico who was on a vacation to do some sports fishing. Jean had reservations at the Coastal Inn overlooking the Pacific Ocean for five rooms in the names of each of their aliases.

Chapter 93

Carlos and Emilio crossed the border at Nogales, traveling south along the western slope of the Sierra Madre Occidental mountains heading for their first overnight stay, Guaymas, located on the coast. After a tasteful dinner, two ex-rangers sat on the patio watching the waves hit the sandy beaches while they sipped on some Mexican beer.

"This is nice, Carlos," Emilio said. "I'm glad you showed me this place ... So you were on a mission with Jean during the war? How was she?"

"She was cool and had nerves of steel. And don't ever get into a fight with her, because she'll kick your ass."

"Yeah, I saw how easy she made the mountain climbing."

The next day the pair was headed for Mazatlán, again on the coast. They'd spent two days there and planned to make a short trip to pick up the team in Mazatlán and then head for their rendezvous. Carlos had stayed at this inn before, and they knew him as an explorer. This time, he introduced Emilio as his partner. Then Carlos took Emilio to a good restaurant where they had food and drink, but not too much drink. There was entertainment with dancers and song, and one of the dancers recognized Carlos. After the show, she came over and joined them with a girlfriend.

"Hi, Carlos," the dancer said. "How long are you here this time? And who is your friend?"

"Hi, Conchita. This is Emilio, and we are here for two days."

"Hi, Emilio. This is my friend Eva. And I like the sound of two days, Carlos," Conchita said, smiling at Carlos.

There was some dancing and drinking before they all retired to the room. The four adults enjoyed the rest of the night playing adult games. The next day, four hungover adults went to a nearby restaurant and had lots of coffee and a big breakfast. Then the four got in one of the vehicles, and Conchita played guide while they saw some of the new construction that was happening. Large hotels, a new marina for sports fishing, and new nightclubs for tourists. Then Carlos paid Conchita for her services as guide, buying her and her friend lunch.

"So, Carlos, where are you going treasure hunting this time?" she asked. "And are you still looking for the lost Aztec treasure."

"Probably southwest of Mexico City near the Sierra Madre del Sur mountains."

"Don't let that jungle get you, handsome, and don't be so long before Conchita gets to see you again."

That night the two Rangers hit the sack early, because they planned to be up before dawn and on the road by daylight to Puerto Vallarta.

CHAPTER 94

That night, Jean let Bob share the bed with her, because there wasn't a couch or a big chair in their room. They took turns using the bathroom and putting on their pajamas.

Once in bed, Jean rolled over and said, "Good night, Bob." She kissed him on the cheek.

"Good night to you, Jean," he said, giving her a brotherly hug.

Before falling asleep, Jean's mind was busy thinking about the mission and about Bob. Having worked with Bob for more than a year, she had fallen in love with him—not as a boyfriend, but as a brother. She knew that could be dangerous being a spy. They both needed to look out for themselves and not worry about the other. However, during that year, they had saved each other's butts more than once.

The next morning, Jean was up before dawn thinking about the mission. When the sunlight came through the window, Jean went over to the bed, laid down next to Bob, and took her thumb and forefinger, and wiggled his nose. "Time to get up, sleepyhead," she said.

When Bob's eyes opened, he looked at Jean and said, "Oh, Jean, why so early?"

"We have to get going and play husband and wife, handsome."

There was a knock on the door, and they heard, "It's Joe, and I've got coffee and sweet rolls."

While enjoying their early-morning treats, Jean thanked Joe and asked, "Did you stay out of trouble last night?"

"Yes, I did. Until I met this nice-looking señorita," he said, smiling at Jean.

Then the three decided to meet for breakfast in an hour and then tour the city, with Joe being their shadow. Being near the water, Mr. and Mrs. Davies walked down to the marina to watch the fishing boats leave for a day of fun or disappointment. Next, they headed for a plaza nearby, acting like tourists. Occasionally, Jean would walk into a shop and casually buy something.

During their walk to the plaza, Joe noticed that someone else was following Jean and Bob. So he held back and watched the man, closely. While Jean was standing in front of a shop, the man pulled something out of his pocket and looked at the couple and then at what was in his hand. That's when Joe decided he'd better find out what was going on and who their shadow was. Joe walked up to the man who was out of sight, putting a cigarette in his mouth.

"*Señor, hacer tu dar a luz?*" (Sir, do you have a light?) After lighting Joe's cigarette, he knocked the shadow out and grabbed the item that was in his hand. "Damn," he said. "It's a picture of Jean."

Joe stepped out so Jean could see him and motioned for her to come to him. When Jean and Bob saw the man, Joe handed her the picture. "He was tailing you, and then he took this out of his pocket. What do you want to do with him?" Joe asked.

"Let's wake him up and take him someplace where we can be alone—in an alley out of sight," Jean said.

Jean started questioning the shadow. "Who the hell are you? And where did you get this picture?" Jean was speaking Spanish.

The shadow's lips didn't move, so Joe grabbed him by the neck and shoved him up against the wall. When his mouth opened, Jean stuck her derringer in it. She began speaking Spanish again. "Start talking, or I'll blow your damn head off!"

Then he started singing like a bird.

Once Jean found out he was a Cardoza lookout, she excused Joe and Bob. "Let's take a walk" she said to the shadow. *Bang.*

Spying is a nasty business, Jean thought.

It was just before noon when Carlos and Emilio arrived at the hotel and joined the rest of the team in Jean's room. Some visiting took place before they began. Then it was time to go.

Jean began. "Bob, Joe, and I will ride with Carlos, and the others will go with Emilio."

The group stopped at a restaurant on the east side of town so the team could grab a bite to eat. When asked what they were out doing, Jean answered for the group. "We belong to a climbing club in the States, and we're here for a good climb."

Then it was time to move on to the rendezvous. It was late afternoon when the aircraft appeared and made the drop. Not long after, the team was now ready for action and headed for the climb.

Joe spotted a plateau and said, "I can reach that before dark. It looks like a good place to spend the night."

Everybody watched Joe climb except one, who served as a lookout. Once Joe reached the plateau, he drove in some anchors, tied off a rope, and gave a signal to climb. At the top, there was a cave just big enough for eight people. So they rigged up a blind at the cave entrance and turned on a light while they ate. Bob, Rafael, and Emilio were entertained by Jean's team telling about some of the events that had taken place during the war. One story was when she kicked the big Italian's ass. Then Joe told them how Jean was a dangerous weapon dressed up in a low-cut red evening dress.

Jean started to get embarrassed and said, "Pipe down, you guys, and let's get some rest. We have a hard climb tomorrow."

The next morning after a camper's breakfast, Joe started out, making his climb to the next landing. After two more intermediate stops, Joe finally reached the top, staying out of sight of the compound below. Once everybody was together, Joe scouted the area and the eastern slope down to the target. He found a route down to the compound and a place for Burns to position himself as the backup sniper. Then Jean, Bob, and Joe watched the activities in and out of the compound.

That night after eating, they discussed what they'd seen with the team and decided on a plan of action. Then it was time to crawl into their sleeping bags for a cold night. Before dawn, Joe helped Burns get to a ledge about two hundred feet above the compound. Then just before dawn, Joe woke up the rest for a quick snack and then proceeded to lead them down the mountain north of the compound and storage building. Jean was team one, and Bob was team two. Jean's position was about fifty feet above the compound walls, and her team was armed with Thompson submachine guns, one rifle grenade launcher, and one bazooka with two projectiles. Bob had the same weaponry. Bob had reached his position by the storage building one hundred feet from the main compound entrance.

Jean looked at her watch and got on her walkie-talkie. "Do you read me, Bob and Burns?"

They responded. "Roger."

She came back with, "Five minutes."

When the time came, the plan began to unfold. Bob blew open the main entrance, charged in, and held a position just inside the main gate, while Jean's bazooka knocked out the barracks. Burns started killing any men leaving the barracks. Then Bob blasted the armory with his other projectile and penetrated into the compound, eliminating anybody who wasn't surrendering, along with Burns as backup. Jean then used her last projectile to blast the storage building and proceeded to the compound. By the time Jean was inside, Bob already had at least a dozen unarmed men. Apparently, there was still a small force remaining in the only standing building, returning fire.

Jean hollered, "Rifle grenades," and four grenades hit their targets.

A white flag appeared. Jean heard, "Don't shoot. We're coming out."

Jean hollered, "Keep your hands above your heads."

Six men walked out with their hands held high. Rafael saw Javier Ortiz, and when Joe spotted Tito Cardoza, he immediately grabbed him and forced him in front of Jean. Rafael arrested Javier.

Joe pulled his knife and put it against Tito's throat, saying, "Just give me the word, Jean, and this SOB is dead."

"No, Joe," Jean said. "I'm going to give this bastard a chance to go free." She disarmed herself and said, "Give him your knife, Joe." Jean then armed herself with a knife and said, "You kill me, you bastard, you go free … I kill you, you're dead, asshole."

Jean could see anger in Tito's eyes. He saw the same thing in hers.

"Jean, you don't have to do this," Bob said.

Jean stepped out to face Tito, and Joe spoke up. "Jean, let me do it."

"No, Joe," she said. "It's my fight."

"Now, Tito, you bastard, tell me where you want me to stick you with this," she said, holding up her blade.

That caused Tito to charge Jean. She was too fast for him and sidestepped him as he lunged forward, allowing her to cut him in the back.

He let out a yell, "Oh! Damn, you bitch!"

Jean then started for him, swinging her blade in all different directions, forcing him to back up and fall to the ground. He quickly got to his feet and swung his blade at Jean. When he swung it back at her, she grabbed his arm lightning fast and twisted it behind him. She put her blade next to his throat before speaking. "Now tell me where you want it, Tito."

"Then do it, bitch!" he yelled.

Instead, Jean pushed and tripped him, making him fall to the ground. "You aren't worth it," she said. "I'm going to let your Colombian connection take care of you, asshole." With that, she walked away.

"I'll kill you yet, bitch." Tito quickly jumped to his feet and charged at Jean.

Bang! Bang! Bang!

When Jean turned around, she saw Tito falling to the ground. She looked back toward her team and saw three smoking weapons in the hands of Bob, Carlos, and Joe. "Thanks, guys," she said. Then Jean faced the two dozen captives and said, "Do any of you want to kill me? If not, I suggest you get the hell out of here."

There was a stampede out of the compound.

Then Bob hollered, "Let's make sure everything's burning and then get the hell out of here. Carter, contact Mother Hen for extraction."

Chapter 95

Back at the Tucson Airbase, Jean reported in to the CIG. "Yes, Chester. Tito Cardoza is dead, and his cartel disbanded. None of my team members were injured."

"Good job, Jean. When do you think you'll hit the Colombian cartel?" Chester asked.

"Probably in two weeks or less."

"Good. I'll let the president know what's happening. Talk to you soon."

Next, Jean let everybody know about the plan. "We'll meet in Phoenix in one week. See you then."

Rafael and Emilio headed for San Diego with their prisoner, and the New Mexico team headed home.

On the way back to Phoenix, Bob and Jean spoke.

"Jean, once the Colombian cartel finds out what happened, they'll be hopping mad, and so will the Chicago mob. I'm afraid you're going to become very popular."

"I know, Bob," she said. "I'll need Jake and Sam to keep a close watch for assassins from both directions. Hey, how about the FBI cracking down on the Chicago mob, keeping them busy until this is over."

"I'll call Jack Williams when we get to Phoenix," Bob said.

* * *

Meanwhile, in Colombia, the bad news reached the Escobar compound and Manuela heard what had gone down. "What! How can this happen? What do you mean there was a raid! By whom? Damn it!" she yelled.

The nervous lieutenant was trying to tell her, but he had seen what she could do when she was angry. "I believe it was the Americans and the Mexican governments," he said. "They even managed to confiscate our shipment to Cardoza."

Now calming down, Manuela said, "So Tito is dead, and his cartel has disbanded ... That was a million-dollar shipment ... Pablo, I want to know who the raiders were. You find out, no matter what it takes."

"Yes, Manuela, right away." He hurried off, breathing easier.

"Now I have to worry about my American connection. That heroin was at least three million on the streets, and they are not going to be happy," Manuela said.

* * *

During the week, Jean spent more time with her mother and Jake, going to movies and out to dinner.

They also played cards with Mildred, the card shark. "Mildred, if you keep winning, I'll have to give Tom a raise to be your bodyguard," Jake said. Everybody was laughing.

Then Mildred spoke up. "Okay, who's ready for cherry pie and ice cream?" Three hands were raised.

* * *

In Chicago, a meeting was being held by a Mafia criminal boss. "We need to find out who raided the Cardoza compound and why the FBI is all over us suddenly."

Then one of the capos spoke up. "I managed to find out the operation is in Phoenix, Arizona, but I don't know who yet."

"Then stay on it until you find out who they are."

"Yes, boss. I'm leaving tomorrow for Phoenix, and I'm taking two soldiers with me."

"Good. You report in daily and be careful. These people are no dummies to be able to hit Tito like they did."

CHAPTER 96

It was back-to-work week, and at the FBI building, Bob brought everybody up to speed on what had been going on. "First of all, the Mexican Coastal Guard seized the heroin shipment from Colombia north of Veracruz, Mexico, estimated at one million dollars. Next, the president called the Mexican president, and now the Mexican authorities are cracking down on the Mexico mob. The Chicago FBI office informed me that three men left Chicago yesterday headed for Phoenix. They were identified as Mafia soldiers. That's it."

"That's enough … At least we got somebody's attention," Jean said. She heard some grumbling but continued. "All right, guys. Let's come up with a plan of action for the Colombians, who are probably hopping mad. Emilio, let's go over your observations and see what develops."

After an all-day discussion about suggestions, disagreements, and debates, the action plan had been narrowed down to two possibilities.

"Okay, guys, let's pick it up tomorrow," Jean said. "Good night."

Bob stayed late with Jean, and she made a statement, "Bob, I think we need somebody inside the compound before the attack. But how?"

By noon the next day, they had decided on a plan of action, and it was the more complicated one. It required Jean to call the CIG to help set up a sting.

Jean made the call later that day. "Chester Thurston, Jean Webb calling ... Hi, Chester. Here's what we want to do about the Colombians. I know you will need the president's help to make it happen."

After hearing here out, Chester responded the only way he could. "Jean, I'll let him know and get back to you."

"Thanks, Chester," she said. "And tell him hi for me ... Yeah, I've known him for a long time."

After hanging up, Jean addressed her crew. "Well, it looks like there's going to be a wait, gentleman, so let's go over the details again."

Jean was surprised when she received a call the next day. "Yes, Jean," Chester said. "He agreed with your plan, and I'll let you know when the Mexicans are on board."

The plan of action was a three-prong mission that involved sending people to Mexico City, to a secret CIG airbase in Venezuela, and to Bogotá, Colombia. Also, while all that was happening, the FBI arrested the three mobsters from Chicago and began questioning them but not getting any answers. When Bob let Jean know what was going on, she and Joe paid the three gentlemen a visit. Within an hour, Jean had her answers, thanks to Joe's methods of questioning someone who didn't want to talk.

Jean informed the FBI supervisor, "Bury them until Bob or I tell you otherwise. Eight lives are at stake if they talk to anyone."

The FBI supervisor guaranteed Jean the men would be isolated. Two days later, the plan was put in motion. Two men flew to Mexico City; five men flew to the secret airbase in Venezuela; and a good-looking blonde photographer boarded a flight to Bogotá, Colombia.

CHAPTER 97

Earlier at the Escobar compound, Manuela was updated on the latest information. "Yes, someone in the Mexican government wants to sell our confiscated heroin at a reasonable price, delivered safely."

"I don't like it," she said. "Pablo, you need to go to Mexico City and check this out. We'll offer not more than three hundred thousand greenbacks."

"I'll leave within the hour," he agreed. True to his word, Pablo boarded their privately owned aircraft for Mexico City to meet the seller.

The next day, at a remote warehouse, Pablo met the seller and his two men. "Welcome, Pablo, I'm Juan, and this is Carlos and Rafael … Now, what's your offer?"

"I'm authorized to bid two hundred and fifty thousand," Pablo said.

"If that's the best you can do, I have another bidder coming this afternoon," the seller said.

"All right, three hundred thousand."

"Okay, Pablo, you just bought some heroin, and I'd guess you recognize your packaging."

"Yes, I do."

"All right, my men will accompany the product to Colombia, making sure your purchase makes it safely to your compound. Once delivered, they will be paid in cash. If not, then I'll ascend upon you with a force big enough to wipe you out."

"Not a problem," Pablo said. "The cash will be waiting."

"All right, where do you want the heroin delivered?" the seller asked.

"It's next to our compound north of Medellín, Colombia. It's our private airstrip."

The seller turned to Carlos. "When will you be ready to deliver?"

Carlos answered, "Two days."

"Good, well, there you go, Pablo. You might keep me in mind for any future shipments to the States. Adios."

Once Pablo left, Carlos and Rafael loaded up the product with one difference. Only the top layer had the real heroin in the packages. The rest was full of sugar.

Rafael said, "I hope they don't dig down below the top layer, or we could be in a lot of trouble, compadre."

* * *

Meanwhile, the five-man team had landed at the secret airbase in Venezuela and were greeted immediately.

"Welcome, Agent Franklin. I'm Agent Howard. If you'll follow me, we'll feed you before you leave tonight for Colombia. You will be flown to your designated location by helicopter in time for your climb tomorrow at dawn."

"Thanks, Agent Howard," Bob said. "We could use some rest also."

*   *   *

In Bogotá, Colombia, a flight arrived from Mexico City. A photographer departed the plane and headed to a rental agency.

"Yes," Jean said, "I'd like to rent a car for three days. I will be staying in Medellín at the Inn, and that's where the car will be left."

On the way to Medellín, Jean noticed she got a lot more looks than usual and thought, *Maybe blondes do have more fun.* Then Jean's mind reviewed her part in this sting.

Tomorrow I'll take some pictures of the town and go north toward the valley along the river, or so it will be seem. Then the next day I'll head for the valley, and my vehicle will have a convenient breakdown, forcing me to walk to the compound and ask for help. Once I'm inside, I'll expose my cover.

CHAPTER 98

As a helicopter hedgehopped over the Venezuelan countryside, the crew chief informed his passengers of their status. "We're thirty minutes from your drop, Agent Franklin."

"Thanks, Chief. Let's get ready, men." Bob instructed his crew.

Once the copter landed, the equipment and weapons canisters were unloaded, and five men hit the ground running.

"Let's head for cover," Bob said. While the canisters were being emptied, Bob checked his map. "Looks like we have a twenty-minute walk to the climb area."

Once the team reached the climb area, they found a two-hundred-foot sheer rock face to climb.

"Joe, it looks like a tough one, so take your time and be careful," Bob said.

"Yeah," Joe agreed. "Roger that, Bob."

Joe immediately put on his climbing harnesses and hooked on the required devices he would need, including climbing shoes. Then Joe started his climb using pitons being hammered into the rock surface or cramming devices in the cracks. With carabineers, a spring-loaded loop attached to the anchors in the wall, and a rope is inserted. Once secured, Joe had a safety backup if one of his anchors failed.

Two hours later, Joe was halfway up the two-hundred-foot climb. Then it happened. One of the anchors pulled out, and Joe dropped twenty feet before he could stop his descent.

"Damn! That was a thrill," Joe said. Joe pulled himself back up to the failed anchor spot and hammered in another piton, making sure it wouldn't pull out this time.

On the ground, Bob commented, "That was scary. I hope it doesn't happen again."

The four men with him all responded, "Amen."

After another two hours, Joe reached the top of the rock face wall onto a ledge. He drove in anchors and dropped two hundred feet of rope. Now, four men were climbing, and Joe continued his climb, which was much easier. Four hours later, Joe reached the top of the mountain. Right behind him, four more showed up, all exhausted. Joe found a good spot to rest that was out of sight from below.

After a thirty-minute break that included taking in food and drink, Joe, Bob, and Emilio proceeded to the spot where they could observe the activities in the compound. Bob had a sketch of the compound that Emilio had made and was adding notes. Emilio showed them the ledge two hundred feet above the compound where sniper Burns and his equipment would be and the way down the mountain out of sight.

"Okay, guys. I've seen enough. Let's have one more review before tomorrow's action. Now, let's get ready for a cold night," Bob said.

CHAPTER 99

Jean had completed her first day of taking pictures and was back at her room wondering how everyone else was doing. "I hope the climb wasn't too much for the team," she said to herself. "I'll know before I enter the compound. That sure was a beautiful valley those assholes have, but after tomorrow, it will be better looking after we are done with the bastards. Now it's time to go eat. I think I'll enjoy a plate of tamales with hot sauce and a cold beer."

* * *

Meanwhile, Carlos and Rafael had completed the first leg of their flight and were scheduled to reach the compound by midafternoon the following day.

Once they arrived at their accommodations, Rafael spoke up. "I hope everybody is in place, or our asses will be cooked."

Carlos assured him they would be fine. "They will be there. You can count on it, Rafael."

* * *

The next day it was like a movie when the director hollers, "Action."

Jean was up early and headed for the café for some eggs, frijoles, and a grilled flank steak and watered down strong coffee. After a good breakfast, Jean got ready and headed out for the compound. Diving slowly and stopping casually to take pictures, Jean was looking for a signal as she glanced toward the mountain. When she got within a hundred yards, that's when her car quit running. She got out and looked under the hood. Now it was time for the long walk, which seemed like she was walking the last mile.

Then she saw the signal. "Great, they made it," a happy photographer said to herself.

As Jean approached the main gate, two men exited from the compound and halted her.

"What do you want?" they asked, speaking in Spanish.

"Well, my car broke down. I was wondering if I could call the inn in town and get some help."

"Si, señorita. Come with me," said one of the soldiers.

Once inside, Jean met Manuela. "Who is she?" she demanded to know. Her soldier quickly explained what had happened.

Then Manuela introduced herself, and Jean stuck a derringer in her face. "Nice to meet you, Manuela. It's no wonder you lost a shipment. You need to tighten up your security." Jean shifted, putting the derringer back between her tits.

Remaining cool, Manuela said, "Nice tits, and just who the hell are you?"

Jean was quickly being surrounded by armed men. "I work for the Ricca family in Chicago, and I was in Phoenix checking out a rumor when Capo Giorgio Volpe, whom you know, called and wanted to meet me. While waiting at the airport for Giorgio's flight to arrive, I spotted some blue suits also waiting for the flight. So when the flight arrived, I laid back, and sure enough, when Giorgio and two soldiers deplaned, they were arrested. I called the Ricca family, and Joe the Batters informed me that a crooked Mexican government official is selling the confiscated heroin. So he sent me here to make sure you acquired the heroin and you shipped the product safely to the States since Cardoza is out of the picture. So you start talking, Manuela, and convince me, or the .45 automatic in my purse will fill you full of holes."

Manuela noticed her hand was in her purse and smiled. Manuela was still smiling when she spoke. "So I see, señorita …"

"It's Juanita," Jean replied.

Manuela said, "It's all right, men. She's okay. So you know my security chief is out recruiting some qualified men."

"Would that, by any chance, be the German I heard about?" Jean asked.

"Yes, and he's very efficient. His name is Colonel Heller, formally with the SS Corp, and he should be back tomorrow."

"Good. Then I'll get to meet him." In Jean's head, she heard bingo. He was the one the Nazi hunters wanted so badly.

"Now, where were we, Manuela," Jean continued.

Manuela explained how she planned on shipping the product to Tijuana to a freight company that smuggles product across the state line.

"Yes, we are familiar with him. Good choice, Manuela."

"Good then. Now, would you care to have lunch with me?"

"Yes … Oh, one more thing. When is the product due to arrive?"

"Should be right after lunch, Juanita."

Jean noticed Manuela put a lot of hot sauce on her food. Jean did the same, which impressed Manuela. Then the two women got to talking girl talk and getting to know each other better.

"So, Juanita, how many hits have you done?"

"I don't know, Manuela. I lost count after two dozen." Jean downed another shot of tequila.

Not to be outdone, Manuela informed her guest, "I've killed more than two dozen men … and women." She looked her guest in the eye as she smiled and downed a shot of tequila.

Jean thought, *Not this time, bitch.*

CHAPTER 100

Arriving as predicted, a cargo plane landed and parked just below the compound, a quarter of a mile away. Carlos opened the cargo door and saw a large flatbed truck on its way.

"Well, here we go, Rafael," Carlos said.

"I hope they have plenty of fresh meat," Rafael responded, causing Carlos to laugh.

Once the truck backed up to the aircraft and a ramp was put in place, four men entered the cargo area and pushed the pallet of product onto the bed of the truck. Then Carlos and Rafael crawled into the cab with the driver. Once inside the compound, the ramp was put in place, and the pallet was pushed onto the ground.

"Welcome, gentlemen," said Manuela, turning to her man Pablo. "Check it," she ordered.

During that time, Carlos got an okay look from Jean. Fortunately, Pablo checked the top layer only, and Manuela got the okay sign from him. No one noticed, and Rafael was breathing easier.

"Good, gentlemen," Manuela said. "We will fuel your plane while you enjoy some food and drink, and you'll be my guests for the night. You as well, Juanita. And, gentlemen, you'll have your money in the morning before you leave."

"Thanks, Manuela," Carlos said. "It will be an honor to join you tonight, ma'am."

Manuela smiled and said, "What nice men we have, Juanita."

Then her guests were showed to their accommodations. Jean warned Carlos on the way. "No talking in the rooms. Probably bugged."

Later, a feisty celebration was happening, and Manuela had women brought in for her men and guests. Manuela was being a gracious host and knocking down tequila shots with her new friend Juanita.

"I like you, Juanita," she said. "You're okay in my book."

"Thanks, Manuela. You're okay too." The women clicked their shot glasses together before taking another drink.

Later, in the middle of the night, Jean took a walk. She told the guard she needed some air and smiled at him.

"Si, señorita," the guard said.

With her large purse slung over her shoulder, Jean inspected the facilities and hid some surprises in it.

The next morning at dawn, there was an explosion at the main gate. The gate was destroyed, and in rushed four attackers as the guards on the wall were being picked off by sniper fire. When the men came rushing out of their barracks, a flash grenade exploded, temporarily blinding them.

"Drop your weapons now!" the two attackers hollered.

Carlos and Rafael joined their teammates and were given their weapons. Carlos called out, "Rafael and I have the process center."

When men came rushing out of the process center, they were cut down immediately, and charges were placed inside. The timer was set

jumped to her feet and was about to throw it at Jean, but before she could release it, there was another sound. Manuela had this strange look on her face as she fell to the ground. Sniper Burns had saved the day, and Jean waved back at him.

Carter had rushed to Manuela. He let Jean know Manuela wanted to speak to her.

"It's too bad we were on opposite sides," Manuela whispered. "I think we could have been friends." And then, gasping for air, she died.

Jean said, "Yes, Manuela, I think we might have been."

Jean couldn't help thinking, *Spying is still a nasty business.*

*   *   *

From a high vantage point, SS Colonel Karl Heller observed the attack. "I warned you this could happen, Manuela," he said. "Now I have seen this notorious Jean Webb in action, and I'm looking forward to matching wits with you, Fräulein. Another place and another time."

for three minutes. "Let's get the hell out of here," Carlos said. They were able to clear the facilities just in time.

When guards came rushing out of Manuela's quarters, another flash grenade exploded, and the guards were immobilized. Then Manuela came staggering out, still drunk. When she saw what was happening, she began to sober up quickly. "What the hell is going on!" she yelled.

Jean walked up to Manuela and said, "You're through, Manuela. I'm Jean Webb. Now do you think you can kill me, bitch?"

Manuela went over to a hand pump, filled a bucket full of water, and poured it over her head. Then, with her adrenaline pumping fast, she was sobering up quickly. She drew a knife and charged at Jean, screaming.

Jean drew her knife and got ready to take Manuela on to the death. Both women faced each other, and then it began—the slashing and swing of blades.

Minutes later, Jean drew first blood and said, "You can quit, Manuela, and live."

But the offer seemed to make Manuela fight harder, and she drew blood from Jean.

Jean's fan club was hollering. "Be careful, Jean!"

Minutes later, Manuela shouted, "It's time for you to die, bitch!" She charged at Jean.

Jean waited for the last minute and surprised Manuela with a unique move, hitting her stomach hard, causing her to fold up. Jean then gave a mean uppercut to the chin, and Manuela fell to the ground, slightly stunned.

As Jean was walking away, she heard something hit the ground. When she turned around, Manuela had a knife in her hand. She'd

Printed in the United States
By Bookmasters

ABOUT THE AUTHOR

TR Garrison is a retired president/CEO with a successful fifty years of experience in construction. The author of numerous published articles and written manuals, he now lives in Apache Junction, Arizona, and has four children and five grandsons.

Sam walked over to Jean and informed her, "It looks like you're going to be busy now that you are back being a PI. I have lots of people who need your help."

"Thanks, Sam. I'm looking forward to a nice quiet life as a PI." Smiling, she added, "Until I get the next call from DC."

EPILOGUE

The team was extracted by helicopter to the secret airbase and then a military flight to Phoenix.

The Chicago mobsters were released, but before they left, Jean had a conversation with them. "You go and tell your boss it's over, and if I have to come to Chicago to convince him, just let me know, and he'll become the hunted."

Jean also called Chester and made a complete report. She thanked him sincerely for his support.

"You're welcome, Jean," he said. "And remember—the door is still open ... anytime."

Next, Bob called Jack Williams and made his report, including telling him about SS Colonel Karl Heller and how the Nazi hunters want this so badly.

With everybody safely back home, Mildred decided it was time for a party. She invited the entire team—Sam Bailey, Sarah Bailey, Pat Franklin, Jake Blakely, Ranger Tom, and a certain Tijuana policeman who was good at acting as a Mexican government official.